The Beginners

The Beginners

REBECCA WOLFF

RIVERHEAD BOOKS
a member of Penguin Group (USA) Inc.
New York
2011

RIVERHEAD BOOKS
Published by the Penguin Group
Penguin Group (USA) Inc., 375 Hudson Street, New York, New York 10014, USA • Penguin Group (Canada), 90 Eglinton Avenue East, Suite 700, Toronto, Ontario M4P 2Y3, Canada (a division of Pearson Penguin Canada Inc.) • Penguin Books Ltd, 80 Strand, London WC2R 0RL, England • Penguin Ireland, 25 St Stephen's Green, Dublin 2, Ireland (a division of Penguin Books Ltd) • Penguin Group (Australia), 250 Camberwell Road, Camberwell, Victoria 3124, Australia (a division of Pearson Australia Group Pty Ltd) • Penguin Books India Pvt Ltd, 11 Community Centre, Panchsheel Park, New Delhi–110 017, India • Penguin Group (NZ), 67 Apollo Drive, Rosedale, North Shore 0632, New Zealand (a division of Pearson New Zealand Ltd) • Penguin Books (South Africa) (Pty) Ltd, 24 Sturdee Avenue, Rosebank, Johannesburg 2196, South Africa

Penguin Books Ltd, Registered Offices: 80 Strand, London WC2R 0RL, England

Library of Congress Cataloging-in-Publication Data

Wolff, Rebecca, date.
The beginners / Rebecca Wolff.
p. cm.
ISBN 978-1-59448-799-6
1. Teenage girls—Fiction. 2. New England—Fiction. I. Title.
PS3623.O56B44 2011 2011002768
811'.6—dc22

Printed in the United States of America
1 3 5 7 9 10 8 6 4 2

BOOK DESIGN BY AMANDA DEWEY

For Cybele, Caitlin, Cassie, Cathy, Cate,
Katherine, Caroline, Cintra, Katy,
Christina, and Colie

and Nic, Daphne,
Theo, Valerie, Susan, Sally & Laura,
Amy & Ted & Tamara, Natasha,
and of course Giuliana

The Beginners

1.
Late May

I was standing there in my usual spot behind the counter at the Top Hat Café, looking down, thinking about evil, buttering toast. *Last night I dreamt about the Fourth of July. Perhaps that will be the day that I die—this year? If not this year then maybe the next, or maybe in forty-two years.* I gauge my reaction to the news of my impending death on a day when fireworks are the only identifiable landmark for miles around, when you picture a black night sky and small similes of stars against it, from the perspective of a craned neck and an open mouth, soundlessly *ooh*ing and *aah*ing. I can see it all so clearly. I am fifteen years old. I like to scare myself.

But I don't know that it is myself.

The worst dream I ever had involved a house and a field. I was outside the house, under a big sky. It was all in Technicolor blues and greens. I had gone to this house to help save my "best friend," a sort of grinning scarecrow figure, from persecution. He was accused of having committed a murder with an ax. The body of the dream consisted of the straw man chasing me over rutted roads and into a field, finally catching up with me where I was halted at a tall, wooden, electrified fence. All this under a wide, solidly blue sky. At the fence my friend revealed to me, through his toothy grin, a truism. "Your best friend is your worst enemy," he said, and then proceeded to outline the punishment I was to endure for my crime.

With nothing in sight except the brilliant sky at all edges of the horizon, my horribly smiling friend tells me that I am to begin eating myself alive, immediately, starting with the tips of the fingers of my right hand, and that no sooner will I finish eating myself than my innards will be all outside, and I will be turned inside out, and I must then begin all over again, and eat until I am outside-in again, and then begin again, ad infinitum, or ad nauseam.

But this, even, is not the full brunt of the punishment. This is just the flesh of the sentence. The skeleton, when revealed to me, is what terrifies me most, what causes me to wake up in a state of such white-hot horror and disgust that I can still recall it, although I dreamed this dream when I was barely more than a child.

"Your sentence," the scarecrow says to me, "is to enact, over and over, the contents of the worst nightmare I ever had: me, your best friend. Now I will stand here and watch you eat yourself, as I have seen it only in my dreams, heretofore. Forever after, you will be the subject of this nightmare, not me."

Is it evil, I wonder, as I stack the toast, cut it into halves, and arrange the halves on a small plate, to act consistently with one's wishes, even though one knows that among the consequences of these actions is pain and sorrow for those around one? Or is it evil to wish for things that will cause pain and sorrow. Or are these the same thing. Or is it evil . . . does evil contain . . . is evil *bigger* than any one person's actions, or thoughts, or wishes? Evil as a floating contingency of being, like a hat that lands on one's head. If that were so, then it would seem to exonerate one from any kind of personal responsibility.

THAT FIRST DAY, in the café, I am amazed that I did not notice their entrance, the Motherwells, Raquel and Theo, a good-looking young couple. I was ringing up a check at the register when I heard a distinctive voice, rich and low, cutting through the general hum. "Theo, this toast is as dry as a witch's tit." And then laughter that was at once nervous and uncontrolled, like that of a child awake past her bedtime, running on the energy of a new hour. I looked up in the direction of the one table in the window, which at certain times of day is too bright with sun, and saw her there with a man, or tall boy maybe. (Theo is younger than she, slender, though strong.) His feathery hair was an ashy, dirty blond, and he wore loose shorts made of a fabric woven in Guatemala, or some other far-off land, and tennis shoes and a T-shirt. He seemed at ease in our homely setting. They had a newspaper—it did not look to be the *Valley Republican*—on the table between them and some plates of eggs with bright orange yolks, as yet unbroken, and toast, and coffee. That might have been the very toast I had buttered, preoccupied as I was. Danielle, the other girl, had served them invisibly.

I had been working at the Top Hat, after school some days and on weekends, since the day I turned thirteen and my father suggested it. "Ginger, I think you're old enough now to earn some pocket money," he said, and I went right down and got myself a job, first as dishwasher, then as cashier, then to take orders and serve, and now I was entrusted with the ultimate responsibility: I could open and close the place. I was good at all of this, but especially at serving the patrons. I had known the Top Hat menu backward and forward since I was a little child, when my mother would bring me in after school for milkshakes and french fries. Often I knew what customers would order before they opened their mouths.

It was not just for the extra twenty-five dollars a week that my parents had urged me to apply to Mr. Penrose for a job. I believe they were already concerned that, even at my tender age, I was not sufficiently engaged in the life of our small community, its comings and goings. I never knew, for example, who was whose best friend in school, who was having a birthday party that weekend. I simply didn't care, as long as I had Cherry. Cherry did all the caring for both of us.

But my parents were always prodding me to put down my book and go find the other kids. Why didn't I walk over to the village green, where they often gathered after school. Any hijinks I might engage in, my parents seemed to think, must be an improvement—healthier, more productive, more life-affirming—on sprawling endlessly on my belly in a patch of sun on the short-haired carpet in the living room with a stack of library books, shelling and chewing pistachio nuts. I think they thought I was lonely.

I was an indiscriminate reader, and regularly plundered

the stacks of the Agnes Grey Library (erected with monies donated by said dowager lady) for obsolete Hollywood biographies, racy novels of early women's liberation whose heroines neglected their children and "screwed" their gynecologists, whole series of masculinity-charged spy novels featuring recurring protagonists with names like "Jim Prodder," men who concentrated as much energy on their sexual technique (he could peel a grape using only his teeth and tongue!) as on espionage, *anything* by Jane Austen, whose sharp eye for the materiality of romantic longing I found instructive as well as entertaining; anything, for that matter, that said "novel" on the cover and promised to feature a family, or a doomed love affair, or a failed life, or a dark secret, or a sexual awakening, or a path to crisis littered with coincidence.

And the Top Hat offered another diversion for my wide-ranging tastes: its owner, my boss, Mr. Penrose, kept a constantly updated collection of pornographic magazines in a stack in the cupboard under the employee-bathroom sink. I often sat quietly with one of these in my lap, sometimes during my break, sometimes for an hour or so after closing time. These clandestine studies left me feverish, with knots in my loins, and they also gave me a heady introduction to a power that might someday be mine, one not like the more circumscribed, esoteric powers I honed in my solitude. This was a power that could only be exercised in the presence of another.

THE TALL WOMAN at the table in the window squinted as a shaft of sunlight found her in her seat, as I had known it would eventually. She scooted her chair to evade illumination, and in moving caught my eye in its fixed gaze, which she held as she stood up and came toward the counter, carrying her plate of toast. Her friend watched her as though he watched a slow-moving missile. I inserted two fresh slices in the toaster before she could speak. She leaned against the counter and, with nothing of consequence left to be said, asked my name.

"Ginger?" she repeated after me. "Well, that's fitting. I always admired Ginger on *Gilligan's Island*, who was so glamorous even after being shipwrecked for years. I hope I haven't embarrassed you, I know how redheads hate to have attention called . . ." She trailed off and turned sharply to look back at the man I assumed was her husband.

I studied her closely. After all, it's not every day you see someone new. She looked rich, somehow, I thought, despite the nonchalance of her attire; perhaps it was her total confidence in her worthiness of my attention. I figured they must be travelers. Every so often in summer and fall we get runoff from one of the more accessible towns: families, mostly, looking in vain for a motel. I felt emboldened and I asked her, directly, to name their destination.

"Actually," she replied, glancing again around to where Theo sat, now leafing through the paper, "we're not going anywhere. We've just bought a house. We're your new neighbors, the Motherwells, Raquel and Theo." She said her surname as though it felt funny coming out of her mouth, the way a king might come and tell you his name was Commoner. Commoner the King. "It's next to the high school, out on Route Seven. You could come by, after school, if you'd like.

I'll draw you a map. We've been here for two weeks already, without a single visitor."

I was surprised both at the invitation—*what had I done to deserve it?*—and at their so-far unremarked presence, but more sharply I was disappointed that she'd guessed, or, even worse, *assumed*, that I attended the high school. I liked to think of myself as ageless.

AT FIFTEEN I still possessed a child's native capacity for belief—some call it naïveté but I prefer to think of it as a positive attribute, a capability—and enjoyed a commensurate appetite for phenomena in which to believe. Another appetite that diminishes as we mature. Already, now, telling this story—though I have not yet achieved majority—the weight of adult accountability descends, and I assent to the banality of truth, to the scale's discernible tipping on the side of whatever is the simplest explanation. The simplest explanation for any phenomenon is usually the correct one. The correct explanation is the simplest one. A ghost is a draft of cold air on the skin, a neuron-fueled shape in the dark hour of sleep. A mind reader is, at best, someone who pays closer attention to detail than most, who is wide open to suggestion. At worst, she is a con artist. A witch is a woman with an enemy or two. Is this simple enough to sustain us? I ask you.

RAQUEL TOLD ME, one day, when almost everything had already happened, when I had looked at her face so often I could hardly even see it anymore, that someone had once told her that she had a muddy, brown aura. A chance encounter with a psychic healer from Copenhagen in a bar in Lisbon. The woman clasped Raquel's becalmed face in her smooth hands, then gently released it as though to send her away, to push her off like a little boat from the shore. And when Raquel told me this she laughed, but I could see the brown webbing falling over her, restricting the motion of her jaw, her mouth filling with the dusty stuff.

I LEFT THE CAFÉ that day at six-thirty, as usual, after giving the counter and tables a final wipe-down and separating the bills in the register into rubber-banded denominations, then stashing them in the little safe in the stockroom, switching off the lights, and locking first the front door, from inside, then the back door, behind me. I could indeed be trusted.

My bike was where I'd left it, where I always left it, propped against the fence by the trash cans, lids ajar, fat orphans wanting gruel. As I rode home I thought about the newcomers. As far as I could remember, no one had *ever* moved to Wick. But was that possible? I supposed some had moved away and then scurried back—my own father, for example, before Jack's birth—but that didn't really count. That was like a trick question on a first-grader's math quiz: What's two plus two minus two.

Did this mean that I had never before met anybody I hadn't known my whole life? I guessed so, unless you counted newborn natives, who came bawling to the town and were duly presented in their swaddling clothes.

These were my first adults.

. . .

RAQUEL WAS TWENTY-SEVEN, but she could have been nineteen, or thirty-five. No even number. Her face was long, her eyes green and narrowed like canoes. No one ever knows what you mean when you say that eyes are green. We tend to picture emeralds, stoplights saying "go," or grass the green of meadows and clearings (two of her favorite words). In this instance understand green like moss, like lichen, like the forest floor at the deep end of summer, about to turn brown. An enviable green, rather than the green of envy. Now you can picture her clearly, gazing into the mirror as one might at the sky, unaware of the identity of her observer but always appreciative of a compliment. Yet never equipped to respond appropriately.

Her hair was brown. She was tall, as tall as Theo almost. I remember once we were passing in front of the mirror upstairs in her back bedroom when she caught sight of our reflection. "Look at how scrawny you are, Ginger," she said, and her arm slid around my waist and held me. I examined instead the wallpaper, which looked very old and was patterned with small bouquets of cornflowers, realistically represented, against an unrealistic ivory ground.

"It's possible you haven't hit the full flush of puberty yet, but more likely this is just the way you are. Stringbean, willowy, all those words that mean you'll never have to go through the anguish us more 'womanly' women do." She held her fingers up and wriggled them, to indicate quotation marks. I caught myself staring at the rounds of her breasts beneath her T-shirt.

We stood still before the mirror and I watched her grow uncomfortable in a split second of silence. She was trying to think of something to say, already. For Raquel there was no continuity, from utterance to utterance, story to history. The currency in which we traded, in Wick. So she filled in the blank with awkward chatter. "When you stand before a mirror with someone you must see yourself together, and decide how it feels. You must acknowledge that you stand in some relation to each other: tailor to customer, sister to brother, mother to the bride, or two naked people who have fornicated and now must look again, harder this time, at their partner, in the upright position. It is meant to be an emotional moment, usually: tearful mother smooths bride's hair; lovers' eyes fuse with renewed desire and they return to bed." She laughed at herself, and we turned away from the image of our own fusion.

At home that night I went up to my room and sat down to begin my homework and to wait for my mother to call us to the table, my father from his chair in front of the television, where he watched the nightly news and dozed. I never found that I had much to say to my father, but I knew the things he would like for me to say. He seemed perfect to me, or at least complete, unassailable. I knew he loved me. I could feel it emanating at short range from his armchair, from his place at the dinner table or the kitchen counter, and even sometimes from his cluttered work space at the print shop, where he laid out a flyer for a sale at the shoe store.

I heard my mother's call from downstairs. We had lamb chops that night, and so I know we also had small green peas and mashed potatoes and mint jelly. Frozen peas, reconstituted potatoes from a box, jelly from a vacuum-sealed jar; these are the ends by which we come by our means. What more can we ask? My mother hated to cook—"didn't care about food"; "would just as soon have gone without"—though she never said this out loud, only muttered it under her breath as she stripped the yellow fat from raw chicken breasts, or sliced a bitter cucumber expertly against her pink thumb into the salad bowl. I am grateful that she saw the necessity of feeding her growing daughter as long as she did.

AFTER DINNER I had difficulty concentrating on my homework. There was a French exam to study for, a short essay to finish for my English class, and a final project for History, but none of it coalesced in my mind in the way that it must if I were to attend to it. I thought about calling Cherry, which I did most nights, and sometimes simply to distract myself from more tedious tasks, but I had a strange feeling, an unusually wordless, spatial feeling, that what I really wanted to do was to stay even more alone than usual, not to extend myself at all. Not to write a word or to say a word, not to move even, not to disturb the silence of my little room, with the desk lamp throwing a small bright circle on notebooks and assignment sheets, and all else dim in the dusky blue shadow finding its way through my curtained windows. Spring was dying a winsome death outside. Crickets rubbed their legs together in the yard, and someone's dog barked down the road. It all felt static, and I felt suspended within that stasis, but then strangely at the same time I was restless. It seemed as though I ought to go outside and disrupt the stillness, change something. Should I run into the yard and holler, and wriggle my arms and legs "like spaghetti," as we had been instructed in gym class, as an antidote to sedentary habits? Or should I ride my bike down to the video store and rent a movie, something my mother would like, a big bowl of popcorn between us on the couch? This was one of the ways that I endured her. But it was too late already for that. Even in the time that I had taken to think this, darkness had fallen completely and I found that I had locked my door, and was lying on my back on my bed, and had pushed down my pants and spread my legs and with my middle finger was gently seeking something I had previously only read about.

2.

It is an early morning, a few days later. I am alone, walking through Wick, starting from one end and heading to the other. It is so early that birds have only just begun to sing, and the day's weather has not yet taken hold. We start out always with this same pale mist, the same cool yet humid air. It could be mid-October, it could be early July. But it is May.

I am on my way from the Endicotts' house, Cherry's house, to my own, where I will slide as quietly as possible in through the kitchen door and then down the hall past Jack's room, silent, into mine, where there is a book I need for school, for my English class. We have been reading *Frankenstein*, and today is the day we will be quizzed on our comprehension of Chapter Twelve, in which the monster relates his covert observations of an "amiable," if poverty-stricken, family of cottagers. *My thoughts now became more active, and I longed to discover the motives and feelings of these lovely creatures; I was inquisitive to know why Felix appeared so miserable and Agatha so sad. I thought (foolish wretch!) that it might be in my power to restore happiness to these deserving people.* My classmates are wretches, who have neither the time nor the place for books. A test is administered to them toward the end of the dumb agony of their high school careers, which determines that they are qualified for going into sales, or the service industries, civil or private sector. Or certainly the military will have them.

My friend Cherry and I are different. We are not exactly studious, but we have the raw materials for brilliance and we know it. We see it mostly in the course of our endless conversations, in which we dissect our days, which augur an indescribable richness of days to come; a *richesse*, as Cherry's mom would say. Her name before she married was Bouchette. She has helped us immensely with our French.

It's also in the way we reflect each other's perfection. We can sit together in front of a mirror, or a television set, or a window, for hours on end, and everything that passes between us seems to be recorded—giggles, silences, commentary—in the annals of righteousness.

Raquel will later tell me that this is called "an inflated sense of self." She says that it is "better to be mediocre, because then you won't run into trouble."

But we have so much fun. We mock everybody in school, especially other girls, and we complain about our teachers. We do our homework together, sometimes: the exercises at the end of the chapter, book reports, even take-home tests, which, of course, you're supposed to do alone. When Cherry insists, we put on eye makeup together, and then take it off and put on another color.

Cherry is two years older. I skipped second grade, and she

stayed back one year, the year she had mono. Still, she often says that I am the more mature of the two of us. She means intellectually, for clearly in the physical realm she is ahead by leaps and bounds ("as she should be," my mother says, in a rare effort at shoring up my self-esteem). She's had a couple of boyfriends, the last of which broke up with her because she wouldn't do more than kiss, and then instantly started going out with this other girl Barbara, who is called Barbie by everyone. We make bitter fun of Barbara for this. Cherry stopped eating for three weeks when this happened, which made her a very delicate creature indeed, on top of her usual condition, which is diabetes, and for which she must inject herself, and take unusually good care of herself, and monitor her blood sugar by pricking her finger three times a day. For weeks she had to be physically restrained—and she counted on me to restrain her—from placing herself in the traitor's path like a forlorn doe in the sightline of a hunter whose gun is pointed at bigger game, or like one of those political activists you read about who tie themselves to a beloved tree and wait for the chain saws. Now she seems to have transcended her anguish, although she walks the other way when she sees them, and there is this older guy, my brother's age, Randy Thibodeau (Tib-a-doe), who works at the auto-body shop and who has stopped her on the street several times just to talk to her about the weather or something. And he showed up one time at a school dance, with one of his younger brothers, and lurked around in the bleachers, while a lot of the boys gathered around him, listening to stories about the girls who dance at the Lamplighter. Jack used to hang around with Randy in the woods behind the high school sometimes, listening to music and laughing about escape. He always planned to escape.

THERE IS NOT MUCH TRADE, and no industry at all, in my small town in the middle of Massachusetts. A few working farms are hanging on in the hilly, rocky, but rich country around us, mostly dairy farms. Otherwise we just service the town. Electricians, plumbers, roofers, morticians, teachers, nurses, shopkeepers. We have no hospital but there's a clinic where you can get your blood pressure checked or a prescription for antibiotics.

Wick is a drive-through town. From a car, it is picturesque. It is the kind of town that makes you gawk a little. *Who in the world lives here.* Heading south on Route 7, a sharp bend in the old two-lane blacktop gives you the feeling that you might tilt, as the road slopes downhill at the same time. There, on your right, you'll see the Wick Social Club. This is a place for men—an unwritten law, but the men of the town do gather there, including the selectmen of the Town Hall and a lot of the business owners, and then some of the men who are just fathers and mechanics or work in the post office. My own father was, still is, one of the few who does not spend a fair bit of his free time, after work, before supper, after supper, Saturday afternoon, even Sunday, at the Club. It used to be closed on Sundays, in deference to some stern, longstanding bylaws, but that policy long ago shifted to one of compromise: on Sundays the Social Club serves as a sort of informal Town Hall, a place where men can meet and do their business, or discuss important matters, such as zoning laws or budgeting for the new fiscal year, with a beer in one hand and a pen in the other. My father liked to keep to himself, as he put it, meaning he did not meddle in town politics, nor did he rely on drunken pledges to keep his business afloat on the waters of Wick's small economy. Instead, he and my mother chose to provide an indispensable service.

Now you're on the outskirts and you pass an old barn on the left that advertises a Polish bakery in three-dimensional lettering on its side. The sign gets repainted every few years. We have a lot of Polish families in our town, and Ukrainians. They came in the middle of the century, fleeing persecution of some sort, settled right down with their families and began doing business. My father's parents were some of these. The dry cleaner is Perchik's, the Shell station is owned by Mr. Kosowski, and the Qwik-Go franchise was purchased by the enterprising Lasky family. We've got the bakery, and a small deli where you can get kielbasa and knishes, not to mention pickles and pig's knuckles in brine. All my life I would go in after school with Cherry to ogle these in giggling disgust.

The Polish influx was our last. Before them had come French Canadians, in the twenties and thirties, who labored in the creation of the Ramapack Reservoir, never dreaming that they were sealing the coffin of their new hometown. They built their houses along Route 7, Pelletiers and Robichauds, Greniers and Roucoulets. Now their houses are old, too. The pastel paint job is more than a little dingy, the porch pushes away from the house, the window cracks and goes unrepaired, the screen in the door is ripped, dysfunctional. On the far end of town, out by the school, is an Orthodox Catholic church, attended by both the Poles and the

French-Canadian families. Next door to that is the "new" graveyard, the Catholic graveyard, too well-tended for my taste.

Our town, seen from way up above, might look like a diagram: a vertical line running north and south along Route 7, and then a line perpendicular to that. This is the Old Road, which divides and surrounds the village green with its white houses, and then runs quickly into the hilly country to the east. Here are our few farms, a few very old farmhouses, with ceilings so low you practically can't stand up straight, and a lot of good places to walk and go unseen. At the top of the green, where the roads converge, are the Town Hall and the Wick Calvinistic Congregational Church, with its mossy old graveyard. These whitewashed edifices sit and face us as if in the hope of setting a good example, an elderly couple keeping their hands from idleness with hobbies and charity work.

There used to be more to diagram. The Old Road runs down to the west, down into what once was a valley, home to three prosperous communities, and is now nothing but a watery grave. On county maps the Old Road is traced faintly, fainter even underwater as it runs beneath the Ramapack Reservoir.

MY TOWN IS SMALL, dreary; yet somehow elegant, concise. We have everything a town needs, and a few things a town doesn't, like Janine's Frosty (schoolchildren, screaming with laughter: "Janine's Frosty *what*?") and the Qwik-Go, open twenty-four hours, right there on the side of the road as you leave town, heading east toward the city. On your way out we have the Lamplighter, a windowless concrete cube crowned by a satellite dish, where girls we never see in daylight park their cars, take off their clothes, and dance on the pool table for dollar bills. We are in between the city and the rest of the country. We are more than ninety minutes away from a large university, far enough to be unthinkable for commuting. Or no one does it, anyway, because with the kind of winters we have here, as harsh as any the settlers might have dreaded, a commuter would be greatly disadvantaged. And therefore the property values have never gone up. You can still buy a house for a song.

ON MY WALK through town I am not thinking about any of this. I am concentrating solely on my immediate and most familiar surroundings. The air, the ground, the trees, houses and storefronts that have been the same and will be the same for the duration. I pass Gumulka's Market, the Congregational church, the Agnes Grey Library, Claire's Fashion Shoppe, Breslak's Shoe Store, the Movie Magic video store, Cluett's Appliance ("Sales–Service–Parts"), and the Acme Pizza Parlor, upon which daily descends a horde of schoolchildren. Across the street is the Top Hat, where I don't have to work today, and above my head is my parents' shop, with the painted window that says PRITT'S PRINTING.

ALTHOUGH I HAVE NEVER yet left my town to go anyplace else, I am working on developing a sense of distance from it, the distance that is necessary in order to make this keen emotion out of nothing other than available beauty and will. So that I could walk down the street in the early morning toward my home and focus my attention briefly but conspicuously on a blue house with a leftover plastic pumpkin on the front porch, or on a view between houses into someone's backyard where a kiddie pool is decomposing, cartoons of kiddie pools decorating its circumference, and instantly be satisfied, as a great well is uncovered in my heart, and when I drink from the well the liquid is sweet but briny, like tears in the back of your throat or like the sea, which I have never tasted, and the feeling lasts just as long as I want it to. Sometimes it is the whole walk, and sometimes it is only until I feel the beginning of a smothering, a twinge of suffocation. This is unpleasant, and I grow uneasy, but just as quickly I can drop the whole endeavor. I walk on, or I get where I'm going, and the day proceeds like a diamond, bright and efficient.

In this case I reach my house and enter through the kitchen door quietly, then slip into my room and grab my book. I have already groomed myself (face, neck, ears, teeth, hair) in the Endicotts' dim bathroom, whose eggshell-blue walls promote a calm demeanor in the mirror. It is time to be on my way. I hear my parents stirring in their bedroom, opening drawers and murmuring. Nobody comes to look for me, to question me. They already grow accustomed to my absence from their home.

3.

Late May

Cherry's mom gives us sandwiches and milk at the big kitchen table. She asks me about summer plans and I tell her the usual: longer hours at the café. "When are you going to start helping your folks out at the print shop?" she asks, turning around from where she stands, scrubbing potatoes at the sink, and Cherry says that she thinks I should find a boyfriend soon, and maybe *he* could help my parents out at the print shop. "Like going into the family business, y'know?" Neither mentions Jack. Increasingly, Cherry's thoughts turn to boys, and boyfriends. She even goes so far as to talk about husbands, and babies.

I cannot think like this. I use my allotted visions of the future to puzzle out smaller states of being. More internal movements . . . shifts in understanding. Will I always be this person that I am? Will my powers expand, or contract? Are the fleeting, unbidden visions that I have of myself in the future—striding on a street somewhere, tall buildings shadowing me; crouching, blind, in a damp basement, imprisoned;

burdened with odorous goods in an outdoor market—are these premonitions, or inventions? What is the difference?

CHERRY AND I GO outside after lunch and meander around the green. Kids from school are parked on the grass near the general store, smoking and waiting for nothing to happen. "Why don't we see what they're doing?" Cherry wonders, hesitantly. I suggest that instead we go over to the mill, and begin our summer properly. And this is what we do.

We walk past the church, heading down toward Main Street, and Cherry tells me—I can't believe what I'm hearing—that she is thinking of quitting her job at the library and getting one at the drugstore. Maybe, she says, she'll go to the community college in Springfield after she graduates and learn to be a pharmacist. She's been talking to Mandy Ensler, who works at Cobb Drug (we are passing it now, and stop briefly to look in the window at a towering display of toilet paper and foot powder) and who says that it's a good job, and decent pay. You get a big discount on cosmetics and any other thing you might need to buy at the drugstore. Cherry says that the library is dull, and musty, and that she's always being corrected in her shelving by one of the old ladies who have worked there for a hundred years. We follow the curve of Main Street as the business district ends and we are on our way out of the town center, toward the mill.

This is absurd, this idea, and I tell her so. She is destined for better things than doling out tablets and capsules and directions on how to take them, with food or on an empty stomach or at bedtime. This is just the sort of employment, the sort of *existence*, no less, that we have always scorned. Can you imagine, we say to each other, and I say to myself, when I am alone, what that would be like, to be that person, to suffer that circumscription, to see the limits of your life in every direction at all times? At least at the library she is surrounded by books, which are limitless, if not unquantifiable, and I have heard that there is a science to shelving called "library science"; I will ask Mr. Penrose about this.

THE MILL IS INACTIVE. Its many small windows have been dark for three-quarters of a century. Cherry and I have had the luxury, all our lives, of whiling away hour upon hour just watching the play of the day's changing light, filtered through surrounding foliage, upon the old blasted red brick, and playing our own game as we watch.

Now it comes into view, and I have the same syrupy feeling of warm anticipation tingling in my arms and legs, in the pit of my stomach, as I often do when I sit down on the shag-carpeted lid of the employee-bathroom toilet to look at a magazine. The promise of our game is that rich. We don't speak as we climb over the reflective guardrail, warm to the touch in the spring sunlight, and down the slope of the dry riverbank to our usual spot. Clean, sedimentary smells rise up from the riverbed.

But this day turned out to contain an ending, rather than the beginning I had anticipated.

The mill cast its two o'clock shadow, and we lay just out of its reach. Cherry had an idea: "Let's talk about boys," she said, "instead of playing castle." The cool rooms of the castle filled with dust at her careless words; its two-foot-thick stone walls trembled. I lay looking up at the imperturbable blue of the sky.

"All right," she said, rising on one elbow, "if you won't talk about boys, let's talk about Randy Thibodeau. He's really more like a man. Did you notice that he kept looking at me when Terry was sitting right there? Now Terry hates me, and I haven't done anything."

So this is how it's going to be, I thought. There is a way to grow up, I'm sure of it, that does not require of us this abject absorption . . . in what? In the hypothetical thought processes of a boy—or man—we know only by family name, by house, by car? In charting his actions and pondering his motives and interpreting his every glance? But I did the best I could, under the circumstances. I met Cherry halfway, offering up the young couple I had seen at the Top Hat. I told Cherry she would undoubtedly find the man handsome, the woman pretty. Immediately I was pressed to make a full description: hair, height, coloring, build. My best proved good enough. By the time I had finished elaborating on Theo's sandy hair, his long arms, his dirty feet in their leather sandals, Raquel's statuesque figure and strangely inert, catlike, dolorous expression, Cherry was suitably thrilled at the prospect of the visit that we—really I—had been invited to make.

WHEN CHERRY AND I were small we used to brew potions from cigarette butts we picked up in the playing field, under the bleachers where the high school kids dropped them. Butts and pine needles and hydrogen peroxide, with a toadstool thrown in if we came across one in our travels. We would never have called ourselves witches but it was certainly witches' spells we hoped to cast: we lifted them from an old book with a green marbleized cover I had found at the library, entitled simply *Spells*. I have never been able to find it again. They probably took it out of circulation. It was very professional, though. The ingredients it called for were an intriguing mixture of commonplaces—things we might have on hand, like water from a hundred-year-old well, or a twig with a fork at the end, even leaves from a hemlock tree—and things that we could only just bring ourselves to timidly covet: mandrake root; the fatty layer of a stillborn babe; a frog with two heads. Often we made substitutions of other noxious substances. The spell we wished most would work was entitled "To Make Oneself Invisible, and Walk Amongst the People." Our dealings with the book tapered off substantially after my mother noticed that I was growing what she called "superstitious." My brother Jack had leaked to her a secret I stupidly shared with him: I had been followed home from the mill, where we were practicing our spells, by something shy yet persistent—a lonely ghost, I thought, that transformed itself into a particularly large green leaf, its pale, veiny underside pressed against my bedroom window, when I turned to confront it. I would have offered it some solace, if I could.

But the mill was the closest we had ever come to true magic. That we had never seen its real interior was certainly part of the spell it cast over us, or we over it.

For to us it had been a castle, and we two queens abandoned long ago by our royal families when the kingdom was captured by neighboring armies and all the people fled. Only Cherry and I remained, in the vast, dark, desolate castle, but within its walls, its dank, serpentine hallways, its tiny rooms into which light filtered only through meager, slitted windows punched in the thick stone, we thrived like glowing white mushrooms. We prospered, even, foraging crows' eggs from the nests in the turret, relishing the crunchiness of mice roasted in the huge, man-sized fireplace that heated whole rooms in the bitter winter.

But it was always summer in the castle, and we could be comfortable draped only in a few scarves, spending the days just brushing each others' hair into glorious coronets, or whispering reassurances that, although surely the royal family would never return, eventually we would find our way out into the surrounding countryside and locate other survivors of the scourge. Maybe some of the more lowly townsfolk, those whose company we tended to favor anyway, such as Tim-Tom the Tailor, or Merrykin the Midwife, or Jangler the Jewelry Maker. For though we had been born with royal blood, we did not relish the high station, the isolation thrust upon us by our noble birthright. . . . I startled. Cherry had flipped over and sat up with an abrupt, almost violent force. I sat erect, too, and the spell was broken. Her knees up, elbows propped, clasping her face between her palms, she cast her eyes down at the grass and spoke with a deliberation that made time stop.

"Ginger, I said I don't want to play castle anymore. It just seems kind of stupid to me now." This was painful for both of us. She was not accustomed to having to point anything out to me. "I mean, I feel like we're too old for it. I think some of the kids from school heard us the other day, and I just felt like such a baby. I was really embarrassed! I can see how maybe since you're only fifteen . . ." Cherry's lovely, open face had a dull cast to it, a mirror over which a veil had been thrown.

This should not have come as a surprise to me, and if it did it was by means of my own absorptions, which kept me from allowing certain perfectly obvious phenomena to affect me, or afflict me—to penetrate. Though we'd been playing our game since we were little, and it had never seemed stupid to me, not once, Cherry was increasingly engaged in games I did find stupid. Makeup kits with ugly colors, and bra catalogs, and cheaply printed teen magazines promoting false idols. "Stupid" was for this world, not any other we might create.

Playing castle, however, was just one of many means I had for removing myself from the tedium of our earthly kingdom as it had been constructed for us by our parents, our schooling, and the routes we must take between the two. If Cherry didn't want to play anymore, that was all right by me, really, and I told her so. I was ready for something new as well.

The relief on her face was more painful to me than her admission had been, as I could see from its depth that the game had been over for her for quite a while. "It's time to go home anyway," she said, and I could not argue with her.

SLEEP SETTLED ON ME thickly that night, and I woke from what felt like only its middle to see dawn creeping up on my coverlet. I had been dreaming a crowded dream full of unfamiliar characters—people I hadn't had time, or whom it hadn't seemed necessary, to name or even make distinct from one another. It was a mob, practically, but its intent was unclear. For what purpose had they congregated? Awake I wished I could remember some of the individual members, as in my dream they had interested me finely, exquisitely, acutely.

But it was the quite familiar, rhythmic sounds coming from my parents' room that had awakened me, slower sounds but as shrill in their way as that of an alarm clock stuffed under a pillow: my mother's weeping—atonal, abandoned—and my father's rhythmic, automatic shushing. *Sh sh sh sh sh sh sh sh sh sh sh sh*, the way I had seen new mothers soothe their infants, rocking from one foot to the other, patting, jiggling. Both my parents were asleep, but my mother was weeping and my father was sh-sh-sh-ing. I turned on my side, my back to the bedroom door, to better vicariously receive the soothing, closed my eyes, and drifted back into the populous dark.

4.

As the last day of school approached, I found myself thinking often of the Motherwells, wondering what had brought them here and what it would be like when I saw them again. I wanted to see them again. Would they really want to see me? Maybe Raquel was just being polite.

I told my parents about the new people I had met. I could see from my mother's suddenly straight spine that she was terribly interested as well. Her clean, freckled face sharpened to a point, and she wondered aloud if she should ask them over for iced tea, with some crackers and cheese, or if that might seem nosy. Perhaps they had come here to get away from it all and she shouldn't disturb them until they'd had a chance to settle in . . . ? I interrupted her with the news that I'd been invited to visit their home, and was going to go soon, with Cherry, possibly after school tomorrow, the last day of school before summer vacation. It is often an unexpected force that drives our most significant decision.

"Oh," said my mother, and nothing else. She turned back to the newspaper she had been scanning, standing at the kitchen counter, jabbing her thumb at her tongue before turning each new page. It pained me to see that she was envious, that she felt excluded, that she resented my being singled out. That she was lonely, having made few close friends among the lifelong residents of Wick, and wanted to live through me. I hated to be party to the complications I was so eager to read of in novels.

AND NOW it had arrived, the last day of school, always anticlimactic. I stood looking at the playing field out the back entrance, watching the graduating seniors rushing from gaggle to gaggle, getting their yearbooks signed. They would see each other later that night, and the next day, and the next. There was no promise, with the end of school, of anything particularly new, just the hazy heat that settled over Wick like a blanket and the relinquishing of one's in-school identity (the weird skinny girl who reads all the time, the pretty girl who hangs out with the weird girl) and the stepping up of one's workaday identity (the girl who works at the café, the girl who works at the library)—this latter identity, in most cases, having more to do with what the rest of life would look like than did our halting, remedial discussions of *Macbeth*, or *I Know Why the Caged Bird Sings*, or the Pythagorean theorem for that matter.

But if it did not offer climax, still there was a kind of warm-bath quality to the summer that I looked forward to very much. Cherry and I would slide in together, clutching hands, and every day after would be essentially the same: waking up without a single purpose; the lack of decision as to where to go and what to do; the inattention paid to time-pieces, which would keep us out all day, away from chores, away from mothers' instructive voices. Our only obligations were to arrive at work at the proper hour, go to sleep, wake up. We didn't even have to eat, though Cherry must take her kit with her everywhere we went.

BUT HERE WAS something extra, something new. In the pocket of my jeans was a crumpled paper napkin, and on it a crude, ridiculous diagram of our town, in Raquel's hand, a big X marking the site of their house.

I had looked for Cherry in our usual after-school meeting place, in the last row of the auditorium, but did not find her. Now I was surprised to pick her out among the rushing throng of seniors all crying and hugging and inscribing deeply felt platitudes. Oh yes, I thought. She would have been a senior this year, but for the glamorous illness that kept her in bed for months and months of what should have been her freshman year, months during which I was at her bedside every day. So, this is, in a sense, *her* throng. Her crowd. Still, I couldn't help but feel that she was over-doing it a little, as I watched her throw her arms around Terry Sheeler, the very girl with whom she was nakedly competing for the attentions of Randy Thibodeau. With her head over Terry's shoulder Cherry finally caught sight of me, and waved a little wave. I thought she looked a bit like a caged bird herself.

. . .

WE LAUGHED AT THE MAP, derisive but excited, as we left school for what felt like good, book bags loaded with the contents of our lockers: swim goggles, tampons, sweaters, music, mirrors, books, notebooks, the hideous self-portrait in acrylics from art class. The idea that we would need directions to anything in Wick was ludicrous, but then on inspection there was something thrilling about seeing our town laid out in these proportions, these distinctions—the vision of a stranger. This was Wick as we had never before seen it, and as I have never been able *not* to see it since; as I have described it: lines intersecting, lines proliferating, lines decomposing underwater. The X marked a spot just over the hill from the high school, headed out of town. We walked that way, and there was the house, regular and old, dilapidated and forlorn-looking. No car in the driveway, but I thought I saw a pale oval, a face, floating in the upstairs window above the porch.

"She just invited us over, without knowing anything about us?" Cherry asked, as we stood by the roadside looking down at the unremarkable house, and I thought that the pedestrian skepticism in her tone masked a fear, or at least a hesitation, that did not become my bosom friend. She invited *me*, I thought, but didn't say, and then still more silently wondered at my silent bid for sole possession. With another glance at the window above the porch, now empty, I told her I didn't think it looked like anybody was there, and that my bag was getting heavy, and we turned and walked away, toward home.

. . .

HERE WAS RANDY THIBODEAU NOW, parked in his pickup truck in front of the movie theater, just slithering out of the driver's seat onto the sidewalk, directly into our path as we walked down Main Street. Really into Cherry's path: I might as well have not been there at all, with the negligible nod he gave me. I thought of a day long before when he had sat at my kitchen table with Jack, after school, eating frozen pizza, their long legs stretching under the table, and my brother had reached out and grabbed my earlobe as I walked by, causing me to stop short and to screech in pain and surprise. He was showing off for Randy, and my pain included that at an unexpected cruelty from one who had been known to be kind. Jack wanted, that month, that year, to be like Randy; he wanted a motorcycle like Randy's; a jacket like Randy's; he wished to try on Randy's skin. But Jack was lighthearted and light-featured; courteous and freckly and kind of smart, like me. Randy is dark, with snarly brown hair and a pointed face like that on the otters you see on nature programs. His skin is smooth, nut-brown even in winter, and particularly smooth on his hardworking arms, which are often on display in a cut-off T-shirt. Randy laughed with Jack at my little-sister antics, my futile, pinwheeling attempts to free myself, but Jack only let me go after Randy punched him fast and hard on the offending bicep, diverting him and then dancing away backward like a boxer. "Your sister's cute, leave her alone," he said.

"Hey, Cherry," he said now, by way of greeting. "Where ya going?"

"Oh, nowhere. What are you up to, Randy?" was Cherry's coy, encouraging reply, and she turned around and walked backward to smile at him, and it was abruptly that I told Cherry I would call her later, and didn't wait for an answer, and continued quickly on my way, alone. I had to be at work in an hour anyway.

5.

Most of Mr. Penrose's porn was of the soft-core variety, and featured articles on subjects of interest, presumably, to men, but sometimes to me ("How to Reach Her G-Spot: With Your Finger!"), and a profile of the naked girl in question, whose sloping hips and globular breasts looked to have been caramelized, candied, like sugar burnt in a pan. Some of it was hard, though, and practically wordless, and looked more like paper traps in which images were kept against their will: isolated parts of the body, male and female, frozen in conditions of helpless engorgement, in situations of impersonal lubrication. Sometimes a woman's naked breasts were spattered with what looked like a cupful of glue, and she smiled as though she'd been given a polite compliment; sometimes the dry head of a penis was introduced to the tip of a wet tongue with great formality. These images were accompanied by captions, surprisingly concise, accurate representations of what they set out to describe. If you didn't have the pictures, I thought, this language might do just as well.

amateur babe fucks dildo
two big-breasted chicks having hard threesome
bound brunette roughly fucked and dominated
teen spreading legs for super cock
mom with massive juggs gets rammed hard
two babes reaming their butt holes
brother tricks sis into wild fucking
redhead and brunette in horny lesbian foreplay
    on bed
pretty blond teen cached in bathroom for action
military man gets lucky with mom and daughter

I noted as well the pedestrian quality of these narrations, their everydayness, their accessibility. For the most part, despite their astonishing variety, these were materials to be found on hand in any home, any bedroom, any imagination.

Often I wondered, as I felt the heat rise between my legs, my own engorgement, if it would be possible to get as much titillation from actually engaging in these activities as it was from looking at still photographs of the same, with their shorthanded captions. Most things, I had already learned, tended to happen too fast, when they happened—to rise to the occasion, to return a kind word, to demonstrate a flush of affection, to seize on the material of an inspiration—and I supposed that sex acts did also. How could one get enough distance from the proceedings to find the point of origin, one's perspective on it, the angle of observation at which the image becomes optimally arousing? I supposed you'd have to have a mirror, as the pair of lovers on whom I was now spying did, an oval mirror in an ornate gilt frame reflecting the face and neck and large, white, tremulous breasts of a very pale young woman wearing the penny loafers, kneesocks, and short skirt of a schoolgirl, bent over the back of a chair in front of the mirror, her eyes and mouth all stretched into the pointed O of orgasm, while behind her was a tall, naked man with short dark hair whose long back was arched and rocky buttocks clenched in such a way as to imply the apex of a thrust.

I could feel his thrust, and simultaneously feel her O, as though they occurred in tandem somewhere down in the lower part of my stomach, instead of in a magazine in my hands. I don't know if this is a sympathetic reaction, an involuntary somatic function, or if it is simply a case of extreme aesthetic appreciation, but I know that I reveled in that sensation every time it occurred. It said to me that I was in preparation, that I was going to be tested, that I was equipped to meet the coming challenge. I was sitting on the toilet's lid in the bathroom at the Top Hat, after closing time. The magazine I held up to my face was called *The Beginner*, and featured pictorial essays, some more elaborate than others, on deflowerings, male and female. My favorite part was the Letters to the Editor, to which readers wrote in with their own narratives of "beginning," as it was referred to, rather poetically, I thought. Each issue offered a "Very Special Beginning," a real virgin whose introduction to sexual knowledge, or at least to penetration, was simultaneous with his or her introduction to the camera's quick-blinking eye. The boys and girls, all just over the age of consent—their birth certificates reproduced on a facing page—were taken by practiced hands to a sweetly lit room, and laid down in silky coverlets, and propped on fluffy pillows, and gently aroused, with fingers, tongues, feathers, restraints, and other tools, to the point at which they could no longer refrain from begging to be entered, or to enter. The language they used for this begging was strikingly consistent. The transcripts printed in full.

From deep in my heated concentration I heard the unmistakable sound of the clicking of the cylinders in the deadbolt at the café's back door: Mr. Penrose, coming in to collect the day's monies. I must have stayed longer in the bathroom than I realized, as he usually came by after his evening beers at the Social Club, when all the men disbanded and went home to their families or girlfriends or empty houses. I quickly flushed the closed toilet, stashed the magazine under the sink, and turned on the tap, washing my hands as loudly as I could. I opened the bathroom door just as Mr. Penrose was passing by in the narrow hallway connecting the back rooms of the café to the front. I had to shut the door again to keep from jamming it into his surprised face.

"Ginger, you're still here?" He opened the door and peered in. The genuine puzzlement on his face disappeared just as quickly as it had come, to be replaced by the dawning of an embarrassed certainty. He averted his eyes quickly from mine and down to the cabinet under the sink, then just as quickly back. I froze, my hands wrapped in paper towels. He said nothing more, but his strong arm, with its brown leather watchband, its blue broadcloth sleeve rolled tightly to the elbow, went up to rest his hand on the doorframe, his chest seemed to fill the doorway, and then my heart, that physical organ, began to try to escape my chest, jumping, like one of the organs I'd seen trapped on the page, in involuntary arousal.

For what was I but a schoolgirl, and he a gentle adult of great experience? The implied relationship made my just-washed hands grow clammy. I wore cut-off corduroys, not a skirt, but this was hardly an insurmountable obstacle. And here we were, alone in a room with a mirror, albeit a small one. I might need to get the stepstool from the stockroom, but at least I would be able to watch my own face, caught not so much in ecstasy as in a frieze of determination, Mr. Penrose's once-familiar face now rising and falling over my shoulder like a hypermasculine moon, an expression of simultaneous aggression—the force that must be necessary to mount from behind a girl one has known since her birth—and humiliation. *Oh, how he must hate to be so powerless before the temptation of my young flank, my interior, my offering. . . .* How he must hate himself. I thought then that the one in power in this position, the one closest to the mirror, the one who is entered, must be sure not to betray her innocence, her uncertainty, her obscure longings, or she would run the risk of sharing that humiliation, that powerlessness. She must be as impenetrable above as she is yielding below. Sex was not a shared experience, it seemed to me. Sex must always carry with it, clearly, the threat of degrading one's power, rather than enhancing it.

"Well," said Mr. Penrose, removing himself from the doorway and coughing into his hand, "come on out of there and let's sit down and have a soda. It's been a while since we've even talked. We used to chat all the time, didn't we, Ginger. Now that you work for me there's hardly ever a moment for a little friendly conversation." He laughed a short but hearty laugh, halfway down the hallway already.

It was true. We used to talk all the time, Mr. Penrose and I, when I was a little girl. My mother would sometimes leave me perched on a stool at the counter with my strawberry shake while she went around to the shops and did errands, and I would sit and tell Mr. Penrose, as he leaned his elbows on the counter and seemed truly interested, all about what I had been reading. In return he would relate to me a story from the newspaper, or sometimes the plot of a novel he'd picked up at the drugstore.

As we sat at a small table with our sodas we rolled setups for the morning: a paper napkin tucked around a knife, fork, and spoon. We did not talk about books. Instead, Mr. Penrose asked me what I was going to do with myself after graduation next year. His daughter Daisy, who disdained a job at the café, was in my grade at school; she, he said proudly, was planning on the military. She hadn't settled on army, navy, air force, or marines just yet. An image of Daisy rose before my eyes, on her back, fat legs in the air, camouflage pants around her ankles like a bulky yoke, getting plowed by a slim, dark, disproportionately well-endowed man naked but for a turban. But Mr. Penrose seemed to have something he wanted to say.

"Ginger, I'd like you to know you have a spot here at the café as long as you want one. You're one of the best employees I've ever had, and it's handy to have someone like you around, someone I can rely on to manage things for me. For such a young kid you're sure steady." I tried to detect in his tone any hint of double entendre, prurient interest, or even of plain salaciousness. Did he envision an ongoing narrative, rather than a simple "beginning"—me waiting for him night after night in the bathroom, naked but for a cook's apron tied around my slim waist?

But the truth was more startling. It seemed, from the plain question in his tired brown eyes, that he actually thought that I might be persuaded to stick around Wick and work at the Top Hat for the rest of my life.

WHEN I GOT HOME I called Cherry and told her to meet me in the morning at the mill. No, I assured her, we would not stay there long. We had somewhere new to go.

6.

Saturday

The long walk gave Cherry ample opportunity to tell me all about her afternoon with Randy. It seems that they had hung out for a while in his truck, just parked there on Main Street, and then had gone for a drive out to the reservoir where, to no one's surprise, least of all mine, he had kissed her. Cherry's narration was prosaic. It was up to me to imagine that it was shady under the new green leaves, that their quickened breath sounded loudly in the cab of the pickup, that they had kept the windows shut against gnats. That the radio was broken. That she was surprised when he did not press her to take her shirt off, or at least to let his hand wander beneath it, to her white, teardrop breasts, their pink, untried nipples.

Cherry was more voluble on the subject of Randy's recent initiation into the ranks of real manhood. He had been invited, after several visits under the supervision of his own father, Teddy Thibodeau, who ran the town dump, to become a member of the Wick Social Club, and was thereby privileged to take his after-work beers on those hallowed stools, rather than in the darkened office of the auto-body shop, or at an even less distinguished establishment. Rumor had it, Cherry said, that he and a few of his buddies had been hanging out at the Lamplighter. I wondered what they'd seen there. "Live girls"—girls from some other town? Maybe girls from another country. Cherry was relieved that Randy would have no need for the Lamplighter now. Her proprietary pleasure made me anxious; it implied a connection I could not see, an invisible tether being woven between them. Magic.

IT SEEMED EERIE and wrong to walk by the high school just one day after its evacuation. It was a husk. But to get to where we wanted to go we must pass it. And now there were two cars in the strangers' driveway, one dark red, shiny, recent, and one a scuffed powder blue, a little hatchback from some other era entirely. Up close, in the early-afternoon sun, the house looked positively unclean.

It was small, and had stood empty for a long while. It had been the site of after-school mayhem in the form of silver graffiti on the eastern side—"Sox in '86"—and then, in black, a pentacle had been described, with the word "Sabbath" inside it, a reference to an antique but deathless heavy-metal band. The siding under its coat of grime was sea-foam green, a color peculiar to objects of a certain era. Dishes, in thrift shops. The shallow front porch was a shabby white, nothing on it but an empty plant hanger and an aluminum beach chair with a shredded seat, folded up and leaning against the wall.

Something about this house would always put me in mind of a stage set, or even a sketch for a stage set. Each room had in it only exactly what was sufficient to lend it the characteristics of whatever sort of room it was. The dining room featured a rickety, square wooden table, painted black, around which sat four mismatched straight-back chairs and upon which stood a brass candelabra, with holders for three candles, all covered in wax drippings. And that was all.

In the living room, a fireplace, a couch, a big stuffed chair, a braided rug, and a lamp. In the kitchen, a round brown table with three chairs and a stool. Later we would discover the rooms' more intimate contents: a Scrabble set, with letters missing; a complete service for four in the cupboard; a Chinese wok and a few pots and pans; one big knife, exclusively Theo's, which he wiped clean immediately after use. They had a coffeepot unlike any I had ever seen before, a glass and chrome device they referred to as the Plunger, because you pressed the grounds down to the bottom of the beaker, leaving, invariably, some very strong coffee that was lukewarm and had grounds in it. I was accustomed to the coffee at the Top Hat, grown muddy as it burned off throughout the day. The Plunger came from Europe.

WE STOOD on the porch for a second, Cherry and I, and then I knocked on the frame of the screen door, and the woman from the café appeared behind it *immediately*, as though I had summoned her from out of thin air, or as though the door was a television we had turned on by knocking, and she the show that filled the screen.

Again I was struck by the warmth of her address. "Hello, Ginger!" she cried, with obvious pleasure—it almost seemed like relief—and then became abruptly self-conscious. "It's just I haven't seen anyone for days and days—I'm like a little mole in a warren, or whatever you call the holes underground that moles live in. But here's Theo . . ." And the tall man appeared behind her.

"Come on in," he said, and Raquel swung the door wide. We stepped into a miniature hallway. The house looked much bigger from outside.

I introduced Cherry and then there was a slightly awkward pause. What were we doing here? What did we have to offer this handsome couple? They reminded me of models I'd seen in a mail-order catalog, representative of people with extensive wardrobes, people fluent in other tongues, people who evidently didn't live in the small town in which they had been born.

"What can I offer you?" Raquel simultaneously echoed and preempted my unspoken question as she led us into the little kitchen, its diamond-patterned wallpaper and dark-painted cabinets in uneasy relationship. We accepted glasses of iced tea from a pitcher—not scooped in individual portions from a can of powder, as my mother made it—and then we were seated at the table. *All right*, I thought. *What can you offer us.*

"What an extraordinary town we live in, don't you think?" Raquel began. "I just feel like my life is starting all over again, fresh, here." Cherry and I looked at each other. This was a promising beginning.

Theo came in and took a beer from the refrigerator—at

only one o'clock—and leaned against the counter, twisting the top off. His cotton shirt was unbuttoned and I could see a thin slice of thorax, abdomen, the little hairs on his lower belly. This could be discussed with Cherry later. "So these are the daughters of Wick?" he said, and smiled, and slugged. Cherry, across from me at the table, sipped nervously from her iced tea, looking up over its rim. Like me, she couldn't tell whether he expected an answer.

"And what fine daughters they are," Raquel sang out. "This is the proof we were seeking. Look at you! Wick is just the sort of wholesome environment we would want for our own little hatchling." Raquel smiled sweetly at Theo.

"Oh, are you expecting?" Cherry found her footing in this familiar subject. Lots of girls in Wick got pregnant by senior year and were married shortly afterward. I scrutinized Raquel's flat belly in her white T-shirt, one that looked like it belonged to Theo.

"Not yet, but with any luck by the new year . . ."

"Raquel," interrupted Theo, gently. "I'm not sure that Ginger and—Cherry?—need to learn everything about us all at once, huh?"

"Theo, these are growing girls. The more information they can gather the better, don't you think? Why be coy? And I'm sure we have a lot to learn from them, as well. The wisdom of youth, country wisdom . . . you know, the simple things in life being so difficult to grasp and all that. Why, when I was a young girl I would have given anything for someone to just be honest with me, you know? I grew up thinking babies came from a man and a woman sitting too close together on a park bench. I mean, I wish someone had talked to me about birth control"—at this Theo groaned, and left the room, while Cherry giggled in apprehensive delight—"and orgasms, and different positions . . ." That was it. We were hooked, small silver fish with our jaws open wide.

We had received concise instruction in birth control in a special unit of gym class, somewhere between volleyball and basketball, but no adult had ever spoken to us about the activity that made it necessary. We knew very well that it went on, and Cherry had spent more than a few thrilling evenings rolling around, fully clothed, on the couch in her parents' den with this sweaty boyfriend or that, but to hear it—sexual intercourse—spoken of in the context of actual living adults, free to pass their time as they liked . . .

The afternoon flew as we three sat around the kitchen table, drinking iced tea and later eating popcorn (Raquel swore it was the only thing she knew how to cook), and Raquel told us all about how she had tried the Pill but it caused her to fall asleep wherever she was, at odd hours of the day; how condoms made her queasy just to look at (especially *used ones*); how the diaphragm was just right as the insertion of it gave Theo time to *calm down*, as she said, matter-of-factly, so he could *hold off longer*. And about how she, Raquel, required all sorts of manual stimulation, simultaneous with penetration, to reach orgasm, and how this was best accomplished by Theo's approaching her from behind; and about how she would like to have a child sooner rather than later. How (and she leaned closer and said this in a very low voice) she had a plan to prick her diaphragm with a pin: Theo would never know.

So now, already, we had a secret, the three of us, and when

Theo eventually came back in Raquel sat straight up and fabricated. ". . . so that's really the whole story of how we settled on Wick as the right place for us. It's wonderful to be in this town that has so much history. It means such a lot to me to feel a sense of continuity, of connection, to think that I may actually belong somewhere, after all." She concluded her partial speech triumphantly, and gave Theo another, sweeter smile. "I have to go to the bathroom. Will you entertain the girls for a moment, Theo?" She left the room and made her way noisily up the stairs.

Her empty chair faced us. Theo slung himself into it. He looked at us steadily and for a moment we looked at him; then at each other—I registered Cherry's flush; then down. His gray, reflective gaze put me in mind of a body of water. One could not make an impression upon it; only be washed over by it, dashed by it, drowned in it.

He leaned forward suddenly. The table squeaked. His voice was round, articulated. "Don't you girls have something more wholesome to do with your time?" He was stern, even severe, though what he said was, I had to assume, meant as a joke. We had been invited. Or at least I had. "Why aren't you out milking cows, or braiding one another's hair in a field, or slaving over your college-application essays?"

We tittered like mice. "That's next year!" Cherry exclaimed, literal as ever. I was embarrassed for her and was about to make an interjection that I hoped would impress him with its sophistication, when Theo sat back and spoke so quietly that we had to cease all motion and lean in slightly to hear him.

"I remember when I was your age . . ." Cherry rolled her eyes. "I thought the sun rose and set in my own asshole." We laughed again, in surprise, looking to each other for reinforcement, and I saw Cherry grip the arm of her chair as though to push up out of it. "I thought there was nothing I couldn't have, or do, if I wanted it badly enough." He regarded us for a moment, his flat gaze flicking from Cherry's face to mine, and back again, like the forked tongue of a snake, while the single pointed tip of his own pink tongue slipped out of the corner of his mouth and rested there for a moment, as though he wished to have a taste of his own skin.

"I've been waiting to be disabused of this notion for a long time. Do you think you could help me, girls?"

It was impossible to tell what he meant. I could read neither his tone nor his face nor his actual utterance. It was all I could do to laugh again.

But Cherry took him too seriously. Or not seriously enough. "It's true! No one can do whatever they want to," she chided him.

But he didn't seem to have heard her.

"Giggling is fine," he said, and though he looked at both of us, his eyes still darting, I felt as though he spoke only to me. "I encourage you to giggle all you want, all you can. . . . But I also encourage you to take care of yourself. Stand up for yourself. Guard yourself carefully . . ." He spoke to me as though I was a single representative unit of *you*, as though Cherry and I could not be divided. But I thought that what he ought to have said was that we must take care of *each other*;

stand up for *each other*. "You won't be able to tell when . . ." and then he raised his eyes and we looked around to where Raquel stood in the doorway.

"Are you conspiring? You're not planning a surprise party, are you?" She looked from one to the other of us, around the table. She joked lightly, but the uncertainty in her eyes was genuine. I felt as though I had somehow betrayed her, though I had done nothing but attempt to understand. We wouldn't be able to tell when *what*? When we had heard enough? I didn't think I could ever hear enough. It was difficult to say whom he might be trying to protect. Perhaps he had been about to issue one of those bland proclamations about how these years were the best in our lives and we had better enjoy them while we could. Though it seemed obvious to me—something in the way he held himself, loose-limbed, coiled—that he took great pleasure in his present time of life.

Then he uncoiled, and all levity, and duplicity, resumed. "I know you don't like surprises, sweetheart. No, Ginger was just telling us a ghost story. The one about the girl whose head falls off when she unties the ribbon from around her neck." I knew that story. It was one of my favorites, though I could never remember its premise, only the denouement.

"Ginger and Cherry have to get home soon, Theo. We must bid them farewell." Raquel gave us a wink and flattened herself against the doorframe, indicating that we should rise and pass by her. We did, Cherry with more willingness than I felt.

"Come back soon! I'll be lonely here." Raquel stood waving on the shabby porch, watching us walk up the hill.

As we wended our way, Cherry couldn't stop exclaiming about Raquel's bold, instructive lecture—"Who does she think she is, a gym teacher?"—and Theo's titillating aside. "Do you think he was flirting with us?" she wondered, incredulously, and I nodded vacantly, reeling my thoughts away from this banal interpretation.

7.

Sunday

Cherry's house is a big white beauty on the village green. Mr. Endicott is from one of the first families of the town. They own a farm up in the hills, still a working farm, and he is our town lawyer, as was his father before, handling divorces and custody disputes, deeds and wills and lawsuits. He is also a great storyteller, drinking-buddy, and bowler. My parents have always been friendly with the Endicotts, and Cherry and I were habitually together as small girls. We had in common that we were only children, or at least the seven years between Jack and me made it feel that way, even before it was that way.

Only children are rare in a town full of Catholics. Cherry's parents worship common sense. Scraps of paper are collected for leaving phone messages, the time between taking off your socks and getting into bed is to be used for turning your socks right-side-out and putting them in the hamper. I had been sleeping over at Cherry's for so long her parents had consigned to me a little daybed built into the bay window in Cherry's room. They called it "Ginger's bay."

I loved the Endicott house. It was drafty, and had a spare, straight-up-and-down look to its walls and steep staircases. When they built houses back then the idea of "space" had not yet been consumed by the people who lived in it; every inch of this commodity in the Endicott house was parsed out into little rooms with low ceilings, almost every room with its own fireplace. The Endicott family had, of course, installed central heating, but still, often Cherry and I huddled upstairs under layers and layers of quilts and comforters. On Saturday mornings, even in high school, we would bring all our blankets and pillows downstairs to sit on the floor in front of an old black-and-white movie.

TODAY WAS SUNDAY, and it seemed we just could not stay away. Or it was I who could not, and Cherry had not yet found the strength to resist the force of my temptation. Late morning found us walking aimlessly, then, with an unspoken but unerring sense of direction, toward the Motherwells'. First we went and sat in the rain under the dripping overhang of the high school's auditorium, a separate structure from the school itself, round and windowless like a grain silo. Then we stood for a few minutes on the hill, looking toward their house. I could see a light on in the upper bedroom, a cozy yellow glow in the dark gray. A car drove by packed with a bunch of kids from school, speeding on the wet road. "They should be more careful," Cherry said, turning her face away as we approached the Motherwells' house, but I perceived a measure of wistfulness in her disapproval. I think she might have liked to be in that car.

"Gosh, you know, girls, it's really lucky that you decided to come over again today, because if you hadn't I would have gone completely insane, sitting here all alone in this downpour."

This was believable. Up in the bedroom, under the roof, we might have been under a taut black umbrella. Theo was out somewhere. Raquel didn't volunteer any details. I had to be at the café at three. It had been raining since early that morning; outside the grass glowed in the mud and I had a delicious, sleepy, encapsulated feeling in the warm chamber.

"I drive myself crazy, when I'm alone. Of course, being with others can be just as intolerable . . . but I may have found a happy medium. I was just writing in my diary." Raquel held up a small, leather-bound, gilt-edged book with a clasp, about the size of a box of animal crackers. "Isn't it priceless? Did you ever have one like this, with the little lock and key? You could contain an entire girlhood between these pages. I keep it here"—she pointed to the top drawer of her dresser—"with my underwear, and I keep the key separately, hidden, as any proper girl would, in this little dish." She seemed to be inviting us, erstwhile intruders, into her privacy. The white dish sat on top of the dresser and appeared to contain, besides the key, a jumble of earrings, none of which I would ever see her wear. Her lobes were always bare.

I had kept a diary a long time before, when I was eleven. It was given to me by my parents, on the advice of a grief counselor. The diary was pre-dated, and on every page I wrote something pristinely impersonal. The day's weather, homework assignments, entries in the long list of every book I had ever finished, including author, title, and date begun. I did include a note the day my first period arrived, the bloody "guest," as my mother called it, on the last day of summer vacation when I was twelve. And that was where it ended, the journal of my mourning.

Cherry, I knew, made a habit of slavishly recording in a little notebook each interaction that occurred (in the halls at school, at the riverbank, on Main Street) between her and whichever boy she was obsessed with at that particular moment. She had five completed volumes in a shoebox under her bed, and was at work on her sixth. But she didn't seem interested in the subject of diaries.

"Tell us about how you and Theo first met?" This was something Cherry could get enthusiastic about.

"What? And further darken the mood of this dreary day with a sordid tale?"

I looked at Cherry and thought we must be thinking the same thought: this was the *perfect* day to be told such a story. There could be nothing more delightful than to be filled to the brim with an account of a foreign experience when outside the day was damp and chilly and packed to its brim with familiarity. A good story is second only to a poignant reverie.

"Well, I suppose it's really kind of charming. We met fairly recently, you know, so I haven't had a chance to tell it much." She shifted her weight on the bed and crossed her legs, settling in. I thought she looked beautiful, there in the yellow light of the little bedside lamp, her long dark hair around her shoulders and her arms and legs bare, a bleached-red cotton sundress covering the remainder of her. The soles of her feet were dusty. I thought she must be a little chilly, and tugged the sleeves of my sweatshirt down over my hands as though it might warm her.

"Theo and I were both students in the History Department at our university. Getting our PhDs, we were. Don't worry, girls, I'm not a doctor. We stopped short of that. His area was the history of religion; mine just plain old American history, with a concentration in certain unpleasant episodes.

"We didn't know each other well, though we'd been in the same department for several years. He always scared me a little, when I ran into him on campus, or around town. He seemed so indifferent. At department parties he might sit and read a book; in the university library I once came around a corner and found him pressed up against a student—a girl I'd taught in a seminar—his tongue firmly rooted in her mouth. They were practically humping. This was clearly illegal, by all laws of the university, as well as the tacit laws of good behavior, but something in his manner granted him an imperviousness, a candy coating that made him slip easily down the throat of any situation. Maybe it is not so mysterious. He is, after all, a handsome devil." She appeared, for a moment, to be caught in a reverie of flesh.

"He always seemed to have lots of friends, unlike me—but like me he had difficulty keeping them. I'd see him all the time with one woman, or a group of fellow students, and then the connection would appear to have been severed. They would walk past him in the department halls without a word—with a wide berth, even.

"And then last spring—only last spring!—we found ourselves in competition for a fellowship, one that allowed the winner to spend a year researching a proposed project.

"I remember the day we both waited outside the office of the chair of the department to find out who had been awarded the fellowship. We exchanged some pleasantries, and then fell silent, but soon I found myself distracted from my contemplation of the projected year of intensive research, not to mention the honor of the award itself, by Theo's graceful concentration—his cheek, the tendons of his neck—as he sat across from me in the waiting area." Raquel uncrossed her legs, and crossed them in a new configuration. She looked closely at us and smiled.

"Do you know, yet, girls, the rare pleasure of a mutual attraction?" The question was rhetorical. "There is a sensation of illumination, of being held, with the other, inside a bubble of light. It is almost as though you cannot see each others' eyes because they are so lit up. The glare is infinitely reflective. It casts you back upon yourself if you look too long, and that is the very last thing you want. You want to see the other, for as long as you can.

"But while this experience provides the ultimate thrill of mutuality, it is also a platform for the ultimate doubt: an insecurity that thrusts every certainty into relief. *Is it really true. Is it really so. Can I trust what I'm feeling. Is this a feeling? How is it different from delusion. Can I base my actions upon anything contained within this feeling, which is quite possibly a delusion. How will I know if I don't ask.*

"And so I asked. 'What will you do if you don't get the fellowship,' was my entrée, a bold one, implying confidence in my own chances of winning. His reply was decisive. 'Live with you and spend your money,' he said quietly, not missing a beat, his eyes on mine longer than I could stand. 'Oh, really,' was the response I mustered, and just then the sheepish chairman opened his door and beckoned us into his office, where he made it painfully clear that Theo had won, with his proposal that he drive across the country, intruding upon a different house of worship each day, recording the congregation's responses to his presence and asking them a set of probing questions he had developed toward an eventual dissertation. He jokes that when he finally writes his book it will be called 'The Devil Came to My Church Today.'

"Theo held the door for me as we left the chair's office, my failed ambition tight around me like a shroud. Just outside the building he stopped. The day was bright, windy, all the clouds blown out of the blue sky. 'It's enough for two, if we live frugally,' he said. He smiled at me, and it looked as though he was unused to smiling in any casual way. I realized then that he was serious. He was proposing. That we spend the year together, the two of us; that *we* should be the project: an experiment in bliss, conjugal or otherwise. When you get to know Theo better you'll see this side of him. He is definite about his desires, and how to achieve them. If he took infinitely more care with the effects of these desires on others, he might be a world leader. In this case, with his clarity, he would save me, no matter if it were incidentally. If I hadn't recognized this radical vision of his for what it was, I probably would have thanked him for his gallantry and gone on my way. But I could see that what he was offering me was something potentially far more gratifying than the chance to concentrate on my field of study. He offered me nothing less than a shared reality. A life inside the bubble, with him." Raquel's forested eyes were bright with the deep memory of this life-changing event. I had never heard of anything so providential, not even in one of the countless cheap romance novels I had devoured in a particularly gluttonous phase at the library. But listening to Raquel, watching her serious, finely drawn face describe acmes and zeniths of humor and discernment, I could easily understand how Theo had been so inspired. She made me think of *la belle dame sans merci*, the eponymous antiheroine of a poem we'd read in class, an imaginary woman who left her real-life swains spellbound, on a hillside, the blood drained out of them, "alone and palely loitering." They could never find her again. But he had found her, whoever she was. I wondered if it mattered to him who she was, or if he had perhaps taken an even greater leap than Raquel realized, shooting himself at her randomly like a proton, a spark from a fireplace, like a freewheeling ember of meaninglessness.

"It didn't seem enough just to leave the office together and stay that way. We decided to quit the program together, though we wouldn't tell the department till after we'd spent our year's worth of funding. We still haven't told them. We would take the money and drive across country, like any other red-blooded American couple with a functional hatch-backed automobile, but we would not stop at any churches. We gave ourselves the whole summer to make the trip, and left our small university town a week later. We drove all day and all night, heading northwest, through Ohio, Illinois, and North Dakota in a blur of navigation and convenience-store coffee.

All the way I was pointing out perfect sites for our new life, little towns in the middle of nowhere, and Theo was saying, 'No, it's too soon.' Because, you see, we didn't realize that this would be a round-trip voyage. We thought we were gone for good."

Gone for good, what a strange expression. I looked at Cherry, a question dawning on my lips, but her face wore the look of politely suppressed boredom she wore when she was being chatted at by some friend of her mother's at the library. This was not what she'd expected. I, on the other hand, was suffused with borrowed bliss: I was in a little car, passing through dozens and dozens of towns even smaller than Wick, and never stopping. I was alone in the car.

"Now, looking back on the trip, it seems obvious to me what we thought we were doing. We were forging ever westward. We were pioneers, luring each other on with the nugget of that last frontier. We wanted something new, and what could be newer than the huge landscape in front of us, so unsettled to our crowded New England eyes? We passed through farm towns, dairy towns, mountain towns, cowboy towns, ranch towns, tourist towns, and in all of them I could see a place for us. I had no trouble visualizing our niche and just how we might come to occupy it. I would have babies, Theo could read. We both could have jobs at the local toothbrush factory, or teaching at the high school. God knows young minds always need forming." Raquel smiled, comfortable as she was in her monopoly on our attentions.

"By the time we got to Glacier National Park, in Montana, we were completely fatigued, not to mention malnourished from subsisting on peanut butter and soft white bread. So we decided to stay there for a while. We rented a spot in a campsite. It was late May and still quite cold. You could see snow up on the peaks. Even down where we were at night it might drop to thirty-five degrees, and in the morning we would wake up in the back of the car all cramped and stiff from sleeping clenched together.

"I can't remember a more idyllic time. Every morning we got up and had instant coffee and bread and apples, then we'd go hiking. The park is infested with bison. You find their huge spiral droppings all over the place, on every trail, in every meadow. They look just exactly like a massive cinnamon roll made of shit." At this we giggled, ceremoniously.

"But I was reluctant to go on any of the more difficult trails. *Reluctance* characterizes my attitude toward this brief sojourn in the wild. I know exactly what relationship I am supposed to be enjoying with the environment—it's meant to be one of sublime, transcendent communion. An understanding, if you will, is meant to spring up between me and the leaves on the trees, me and the meadows and the wildflowers growing wildly on those meadows, between me and the warm rain that fell on our heads and shoulders one day when we were caught in an early summer storm." Cherry coughed lightly, and when I glanced her way she caught my eyes purposefully, but I did not want to be distracted. I returned to Raquel my full attention.

"But no acorn can be my friend, when I know what sort of growth will come out of the bond. The wet grass drives me mad with discomfort. The wood elves shun my tread. My gosh, girls, look at the time! Am I boring you?"

I did look at the clock on the bedside table; it was two-thirty. Cherry stretched beside me, and yawned a little. "I guess we do have to get going soon," she said, her voice thick from long silence. But I figured I could stay for another twenty minutes and still make it to the Top Hat on time for my shift.

"Well, where was I . . . oh, yes. So. We left the park finally, and set off again, on little back roads, and made our way through town after town, all rife with possibility, until we reached the Pacific coast, in the state of Washington. We stayed in a motel in a logging town, took showers and stretched out between stiff, bleach-saturated sheets for several days. That was where Theo was struck with the desire to call home—'just to let them know that we're all right,' he said." Raquel paused here, sighed. I regarded her solemnly, aware that some great plot-twist was approaching.

"We never made it to the promised land. Sadly, it turned out that everything was not all right at home. Theo's mother had found a new lump in her remaining breast, after years in remission. They had started her on chemotherapy immediately, and she was very ill, throwing up all the time, weak, dizzy. Ted Senior said that he needed Theo's help. Could we please come home?

"We got hitched at a stop on our speedy, no-frills return journey, at Details National Park. A justice of the peace performed the ceremony at our campsite. I have snapshots—do you want to see them?"

I was about to say that I *would* like to see them, very much—not that I needed proof of the veracity of her tale—but then Raquel spun to look at the clock by the bedside.

"Ginger, don't you have to be at work?" She was cajoling me. I had an unpleasant awareness suddenly that I might be a third wheel. Did Raquel like Cherry better than she liked me? That would be no surprise. Certainly Cherry was the gregarious one, the entertaining one. She had more winning ways. She was, on the whole, more representative of the norm of teenaged girlhood, and I understood already that Raquel greatly admired whatever was normative. "I don't want you to be late on my account. All that's left of this story, anyway, is the sad part, the boring old adult part, where we settle down together and try to make each other happy." I had risen off the bed, was about to make my parting address, when Cherry answered for me.

"Oh, please, that's not boring. What was it like? Did you call your parents right away after you got married? Were they *so* excited?" I noted Cherry's new expression. Greedy. Lustful. It was as though Raquel had opened a thick vein for a freshly minted vampire, one burdened, burning, with the hunger of a lifetime.

I felt stifled in the damp coziness of Raquel's bedroom, the rising smell of drying textiles. The patter of the now-light rain on the windows promised some relief outside and so I made my exit. Raquel waved a little wave and made warm promises of future days just like this one. Cherry said to call her after work. I left them comfortably established, and as I went down the stairs I heard Cherry say, in her soft, slightly toneless voice, "But were you in love?"

8.
Sunday Night

Later that night, as promised, I spoke with Cherry on the phone, as I did almost every night, even when we had just spent the whole day in each other's company.

"I *have* to *tell* you," she said. "Something about the Motherwells. You're not going to believe this."

On the contrary, I thought that I would probably believe anything anyone told me about the Motherwells. I had just spent the afternoon and early evening leaning against the counter at the Top Hat, musing over all the fantastic truths I had yet to absorb, all the credulity that was still mine to be exercised. Another form of power.

"I'm sorry," she said, "but those people are so bizarre. Raquel told me the weirdest things about her and Theo. Maybe I shouldn't even tell you. It'll just freak you out . . . I know how squeamish you are about boys, and sex, and that stuff."

She was only waiting to be convinced of the impossibility of the idea that she would withhold *anything* from me. I suppose this is one of the bonuses of such a friendship: until something unspeakable comes to pass that truly cannot be repeated, *even to your best friend*, there can be no doubt that you are like books open to each other's eager eyes. This is probably the lesson of such a friendship, in fact: if there is one person whom you tell *everything* to, there must be some people you only tell some things, and some whom you tell nothing. Parents usually serve well in this last capacity.

"After you left . . ." she began, and I shifted my weight from my right hip to my left, where I knelt lopsided in front of the desk on the thin gray carpet in the telephone nook. "Raquel started to tell me things. I'm sure she would have told you, too, if you'd stayed. How was work?" Typically, her narration was scattershot.

I assured her that work had been, as always, uneventful. I suppressed a problematic visit from Randy: he had lingered outside the café with his coffee-to-go, smoking a cigarette, and more than once thrown his wiry glance in the direction of where I sat—although perhaps he was just checking the clock on the wall above the counter, or perhaps the glass was impermeable at that moment, glazed as it was by the low late-afternoon sun skimming down over the row of opposing brick rooftops, and he glanced luminously in the direction of his own reflected self. Cherry resumed.

"Wouldn't you think that everything was perfect between them? They seem like such a good couple. But here's what happened. This is so weird." Cherry proceeded to tell me a tale of a dream Raquel had had—or was it a dream? This was as unclear to me as it had been, probably, to Cherry. Apparently Raquel was a heavy sleeper, but since sharing her bed with Theo she had been visited by strange visions and sensations. In her bed she was smothered by a limb over her nose and mouth, dumb and immovable; in her bed the skin of her buttocks was pricked, over and over, by needle-like protrusions, as though she were a pincushion, or a voodoo doll. "She loves him," Cherry asserted, reassuringly, "but sometimes she feels a little bit scared of him, she said."

My own mouth was stopped with a heavy burden of dumb flesh. I woke unbreathing, in an incredulous panic; my friend's arm, my friend whose body I slept next to each night, had come to smother me, maybe involuntarily, as some kind of fatal by-product of our mutual unconsciousness. Or, even more frightening, of the subconscious. The closer to conscious desire the implied impulse rose, the more unthinkable it became. I felt the words frothing like distemper in my mouth: *What just happened?* I would say, inquiry arising out of a silent state that knows no hesitation, no calculation, only pure utterance.

I was spacing out, while Cherry vivaciously spilled more of the details of an increasingly troubling tale. My own dreams usually have something to do with the insides of houses.

". . . And he's like 'What? Why would I be sticking pins into your ass?' And this time, she said, it was like the roles were reversed, because he was the one who sounded hurt and betrayed—it was like he couldn't believe that she would think he would do such a thing."

OF COURSE that's the question: What part of her was it that believed him to be capable of doing such a thing? And how could she allow him to see this part of her, even in half-sleep? It seemed an atrocious intimacy, a violation in itself.

"So, what do you think?" Cherry asked me again, all charged and full of appetite. "I don't believe a word she says. She seems kind of nuts to me. She kind of creeps me out." But I was still caught up, the casing of my body actually punctured, like the skin of a sausage, by a fork.

"I think they're both really weird," Cherry prompted, hopefully, but when I did not feed her the line she required she gave up, said that she was going to go catch something on TV, and that she would see me tomorrow. "Sweet dreams!" she cooed, and laughed, and hung up.

But of course I could not sleep, and of course I decided to ride my bike for a little while. I say *of course* because it was dark out; *of course* because I was already afraid, even before I thrust myself out the sliding glass door into the backyard and around to the side of the garage. My back as I rode away from the house felt larger than my whole body, like a target, with the raw, unprotected feeling of full exposure, total vulnerability to whatever forces might alight. It was really like an invitation to these forces, to be out in the night alone with my thoughts, which grew increasingly loud as I pumped along toward the Motherwells', fighting off visions of what might be behind me. I said *of course* to myself, out loud, because there are some things we know not to do if we wish to stay safe, to avoid danger. Watching a scream-fest we know the young girl must not, if she wishes to keep herself out of the plot, allow herself to be separated from the group. She must not go skinny-dipping in the lake. Certainly she must not display any willingness to be touched. Activity of a playfully flirtatious nature will get her a nonspeaking role, but if she were to offer herself to the dark, the dark would certainly take her. And here I was: I could not tell to whom I wanted to expose myself more.

A LIGHT WAS ON in the kitchen. I went around to the back and stood at the door for a minute. At the bottom of the dingy lace curtains I could see elbows on the round table and the remains of dinner. Wineglasses and a candle. I knocked, and, after half a minute, knocked again. I thought I heard a faint call to come in—the wind, or my ears playing a trick, fulfilling a wish. I opened the screen door, then the inside door, and I was in the hallway. As soon as I heard her voice, so clear, so definite, I knew that the invitation I had heard had not been spoken out loud.

"For example, when I hear a phrase like 'dewy pussy.' It gets me completely wet." Raquel. I froze.

"Oh, and do you hear 'dewy pussy' often?" Theo's voice, gently quizzical.

"If you only knew how many of my waking moments are spent rehearsing new word combinations. Or sex. Rehearsing sex. Or rather, thinking about sex."

"There is nothing conceptual about sex. Sex is not in the abstract."

"It depends on what you define as sex. I can come in a split second if I think of certain words, certain phrases. When I'm all alone. Dewy pussy." Dryly; sotto voce.

"Oh, really?" Theo sly, teasing. "Why aren't you thinking about me, when you're alone?"

She laughed, sighed. "It's all about separation from reality."

"Isn't everything, for you." This was not a question.

"Oh, but this especially! If I were to try to conjure up a vision, a fantasy, of actual physical contact with you . . . it just wouldn't do the trick at all."

She sipped some liquid. The glass came down on the table with a resonant *ping*. "Because when I think of a phrase like 'dewy pussy,' it is actually my own . . . that is referred to, and what is exciting to me is the idea that my pussy could be, and probably will be, referred to by someone in the future—near or far—as 'dewy.' And this excitement in turn actually produces in my body the phenomenon, or state, if you will, of 'dewy pussy.' "

This time she allowed the two words to issue silkily from between her lips, to be drawn out like a shining ribbon.

Theo's voice was a little lowered. I had to strain to hear him. "Keep talking—"

"Hang on to your hat. I'll let you in on a deeper secret."

"It's about time," Theo said, and I jerked backward toward the door, in the dim hallway, in thrill and panic. But if I made a noise now, or knocked on the doorjamb, or cleared my throat, it would become instantly obvious to the two of them, in the kitchen, that I had been standing motionless in the hallway, eavesdropping, up until that moment. On the other hand, they *must* have heard me come in: the door was heavy, and the screen door had slammed against it and bounced and then slammed again, before coming to rest. If I just stood and listened, the dilemma would only be aggravated. My deceit grew more heinous, my culpability increased with every word that I heard.

But there was nothing I could do. The noise then of another chair scraping back. "Let me just clear this off a bit . . . now, come here." Steps, and then, in rapid succession, the *zzzzip* of a zipper, the crush of clothes moving, pushed off of limbs. "I don't think we'll break it, do you?"

What I heard now was all flesh. Nothing I had names for except "suck," and a smacking like a candy bar; sometimes a brushing noise, just pure friction. The table squeaked a little, but not much. Then:

". . . and just 'fuck.' 'Fuck me hard,' or 'fuck me now,' . . . ah, you're fucking me. . . ." Her voice had deepened, seemed to be coming from a more complicated place in her throat, a strangled place. There was a flapping, a slapping of flesh on flesh, and the table's joints squeaked.

When Theo spoke his voice was hoarse, almost a whisper, but a stage whisper.

"She is beautiful, you know. I for one would fuck her."

"Well." Long pause, of speech but not of action. "I'd fuck her, too." Her breath seemed to be caught in her throat.

"So, why don't you?" Theo said, rather coolly. The table protested loudly.

"Careful, angel. Because I'm fucking you, you bastard. God. Also, you know, because fantasy isn't . . . reality. As far as I can tell, darling, *you* are my reality."

The table creaked and creaked. The sound of their breathing got louder, speech concluded by mutual agreement. I gauged my distance from the door, then commenced creeping backward.

"Mmm . . . just pull out . . . when you're gonna . . ."

I closed the door behind me with as much caution as I had left in me.

9.

One evening later that week found me dreamy, standing at the sink back at the Endicotts' with my hands in soapy water. Outside, the night sky showed an awareness of the blue it had recently been. Cherry dried the dishes as I washed them. We did not speak, had not spoken much all day. I felt we were at an impasse, though she could not be privy to it. The novelty of this private experience, of knowing something she didn't, and wouldn't, was both a pain and a pleasure, as in fact I also knew it had to be Cherry the Motherwells referred to—"she" of the black hair and flushed cheeks, the overripe lips and white skin.

On the other hand, Cherry had told me, teasingly, that she had seen Theo watching me. And she thought that they took more of an interest in me. They were both so intellectual, she said. I had been intent on my book, one day, on the porch, she said, when she saw Theo watching me. I was indulging myself in some decidedly unintellectual but deeply rewarding fare: the first volume in the Dragonriders of Pern series, *Dragonflight*, in which, on a distant planet, infant dragons hatch from giant eggs and seek to make an "Impression"—to bond telepathically with a human "rider," who will be their eternal companion and guide. Cherry also said, lightly, though with a sidelong glance as though to gauge the aftershock, that she thought I was getting obsessed with Raquel and Theo. It felt strange to be so observed.

Now I was going back over that first encounter, in the café, thinking how it held in its virgin arms a discreet premonition of all that was to come. Every moment does, though, I thought. In every instant lies a pattern, a code, from which every antecedent moment can be predicted. Much like the way we live out our family's story, the way I look, and Jack looked, just like my mother, and just like my father, equally, according to the bias and predilection of the observer. Our whole bodies represented perfectly by fine lines: limbs, lips, eyelashes, hair, extremities. Freckles excepted.

ON THAT FIRST DAY I had been shy, and therefore quiet. Raquel made her showy advances while Theo looked on, amused, perhaps wary, certainly appreciative. The outcome was pleasing to us all. They looked like adults to me, and unfailingly glamorous, though that glamour would acquire somewhat of a patina of familiarity as the summer passed and I spent night after night in their company, more often than not going to sleep on their couch long past midnight, having called my parents to say I was at Cherry's and I'd come right home after breakfast tomorrow to do the chores I had neglected, plus some extra.

I had brought Cherry to their house with me because I was scared to go alone. Scared just in the way you're scared to do anything for the first time. There was hardly anyone in Wick whose home I hadn't been inside on one occasion or another, at a wake, or a birthday party, or delivering a box of paper goods from my parents' shop. That is supposed to be the beauty of it, isn't it? I'd even been inside the churches, although my parents didn't belong to the Catholic or the Congregational.

"What are you? Jewish?" a boy once asked me, in front of a knot of kids at recess, with a look on his face, equal parts boldness and apprehension. What if I was, I remember wondering at the time. What would he say to that. There has never been a Jew in our town, and consequently any stereotype he could have had prepared would have been wildly trite and dated. Couldn't he have come up with something more menacing, more profoundly foreign? What about "heathen," or for that matter "devil worshipper"? I suspect the fact that everyone knows my mother isn't from around here had paved the way for this more pedestrian suspicion. I used to press my mother for stories about where she came from, the world outside Wick, every night when she was putting me to bed, but she would never comply. She was concerned for my night's sleep. She needn't have worried.

I WOKE UP in the middle of the night in my little bay window at the Endicotts'.

Cherry had switched on her bedside lamp. I sat up, squinting, and asked her what was wrong, in a whisper. She didn't answer immediately. She sat, hugging her bent knees, her face resting on her crossed forearms. Her hair was all in disarray, as though she'd been tossing her head on the pillow.

"I don't know exactly. I've just been having strange dreams."

Cherry and I often told our dreams to each other in the morning after a sleepover, over cereal. Sometimes hers bored me; sometimes they were fantastic. Her diabetes affected her sleep. If her insulin levels were off, high or low, her dreams went wild. She remembered them in great detail, while my own enjoy widely varying degrees of lucidity, ranging from the completely muddled—those that linger only as a vague cobweb of a mood in the morning light—to the absurdly willful, in which my waking brain conducts its business with the figments of the dream in complete lucidity, and every movement of the unconscious mind is conversant with the conscious.

But, oddly, Cherry could not remember what had been so terrible as to wake her up that night, only that it gave her the greatest relief to come awake and realize, after a moment, that the consequences, or the realities, or the conclusions reached in the dream were null and void. She went to the bathroom and did a blood-sugar test, something I always loved to watch, as she pricked her index finger and squeezed out a big vermilion drop. She was fine. We settled down in our beds again.

10.

The maroon car slowed, crept along beside us, tires crunching. We were on our bikes in the breakdown lane, riding to the mill for a quick sandwich in its shade before I had to be at the café.

"Hey, where do people go to get wet around here? I just drove all the way from the city and I sure could use a swim."

It was a hot June, the sun high in the sky at one o'clock, bleaching everything but the blackest contours. Theo leaned over the steering wheel in the shady interior of the car and rested his lean cheek on his knuckles.

"Oh, I know, me too," Cherry said, pushing her sweaty bangs out of her eyes. So easy, for her, to make an offer of herself. "The reservoir is good for swimming—do you know how to get there? But you have to find the special place."

The reservoir had several different entry points, most of them quite wooded, and cordoned off except to those with hunting and fishing permits, but swimming was forbidden at all of them. This was, of course, the source of drinking water for hundreds of thousands, probably millions, of city dwellers. There was, however, one entry in particular that was generally recognized by kids in town as the proper spot for gentle recreation, primarily because it was hidden from view inside a small inlet, all the way across the reservoir from Wick. You needed a car to get there, and so we didn't often go, now that the necessity of being driven everywhere by our parents was so unappealing.

"I know all about *some* special places, my girl"—Cherry laughed, and blushed—"but I'm a babe in the woods in this town. I don't know anything. I need your guidance. What do you say, young ladies? We can pick Raquel up on our way. She'll be pleasantly surprised." I wondered if Cherry was thinking about pillows, and pincushions, or if the heat had pushed all thought away. Or the immediate thrill of this interloper, his easy elocution, his interlocutions, his lanky body slung over the wheel, was enough to silence all but the helpful native in her.

"Ginger has to go to work," Cherry began, and I felt a dreadful sensation of heaviness. I was ballast, a spoiler. They would cut me loose. It was happening even as I sank. For a moment I considered alternatives: Could I be late for work? Could I call in sick, or pretend my bike had a flat tire and I was far away and couldn't get back? Unused to deception as I was, I couldn't think that fast.

"Oh"—Theo shaded his eyes and squinted out at me, smiled a rueful smile—"what a drag. Ginger, could you spare Cherry a little while so she can aide me in my quest?" I felt, strangely, as though it were, actually, my decision whether Cherry could go with him. What should I tell her? But she was already acting in her own best interest, moving to lock her bike to the stop sign.

"Ginger, I'll just see you later. Let me have my sandwich. I'll call you tonight, okay?"

Theo stretched his long arm across the empty seat and shoved the door open; she climbed in and waved and I watched the car grow smaller and turn the corner. I was alone. I rode my bike to the mill and ate my peanut butter and jelly, quieting my mind as I chewed, in preparation for the long afternoon of servitude ahead.

AT THE CAFÉ, Mr. Penrose greeted me with incomprehension in his eyes. "Ginger, did you miss us? Can't get enough of this place, can you?" Danielle stood behind the counter in my customary spot; this was a Wednesday, the slowest day of the week, and there was only ever one waitress on the schedule for the after-lunch crowd. I retraced my steps, looking for the flaw in the fabric of this particular reality. I distinctly remembered double-checking to make sure I had the shift this week. Sometimes Mr. Penrose changed things at the last minute to accommodate a special request.

"Thursdays are too slow for two girls, sweetie. Sorry! But since you've come all this way, how about a milk shake at the counter, like old times?" Mr. Penrose picked up the tall metal shaker, the wet ice cream scoop, but I shook my head. *Thursdays.*

It occurred to me that I actually had no idea what day of the week it was. Summertime held me in its loose embrace, and now the Top Hat had released me; I was free to pursue the day, whatever day, to its rightful end. I laughed at myself, at my errors, and made an excuse about needing to get home for some chores. I backed out the door, jumped on my bike, and rode as fast as I could, pumping wildly up the hill toward the Motherwells'.

But only one car was in the drive, Raquel's old blue car. I had missed them. My first impulse was to keep my momentum going, to get myself as fast as I could to the reservoir—quite a long ride—and join them there, but then it occurred to me that I might have rather managed to arrive before them. If they had, for example, stopped at Cherry's to pick up her suit. Her big empty house—no one home at this time of day. That would mean that I might have a moment alone with Raquel. What would I do with it? I couldn't think of anything to say to her. I just might prompt her to speak. I advanced on the house, but as I climbed the porch steps I became filled with the conviction that Raquel was not inside. No one was home here, either. My certainty was the same kind of one-way-mirrored certainty with which one knows when one has just hurt another's feelings. Nothing has changed, nothing has been said; it is a petite alteration of chemical composition, of electrostatic energy. Feelings have been hurt. A house is unoccupied.

PRIVATE PROPERTY IS INTIMIDATING. But when one has grown up in a town as small as Wick, one has a certain proprietary claim on every inch. An inalienable right. This was earth that I had turned with the force of my will, my imagination. I could take a minute or two to explore their impositions.

I pretended to myself that I didn't know no one was home. I didn't, really. I sent a long, psychic *halloooo* through the screen door at the front, and waited for the silence and deadness of the house to confirm itself before I went around the back and in through the door by the kitchen, pausing to sweep my fingertips across the top of the table, upon which we had drunk our iced tea, upon which love had been made within the range of my hearing. For my benefit the windows were wide open. A small breeze shared the run of the hallway with me. No one sat at the round table. No one was in the living room, and its drawn shades made me feel sleepy. I thought that I might just have a quick look around the house. I felt that I had only seen the surfaces of the rooms, only what they wanted me to see, what I had been shown.

I went up the stairs. I poked my nose into Theo's study, where I had spotted an enticing bookshelf full of unfamiliar titles, but found myself propelled instead toward the bedroom. There was a mirror, a tall, oval mirror on a kind of wooden stand, on the floor, almost full-length. I stood before it and watched myself grow, and shrink, and grow again, as it pivoted gently on its dowels. I put out a hand and stilled it, then my hands moved to the buttons of my shirt and I unveiled myself to the mirror: the sweat of my exertions, my hidden stem, my bones upright and incandescent.

I thought I was beautiful—then I thought maybe it was just the deep, bluish light of Raquel's cool bedroom at the back of the house, carving my haphazard forms and lines into a relief of symmetry, regularity. I thought maybe to touch myself.

Then there was a noise, a heat, a *shush*, a brush with flesh. My eyes, trained on the specifications of my own form, struggled to recalibrate to the negative space surrounding me.

Wha?—I jumped, and whirled around, and faced nothing. Had I felt a hand on the middle of my back, a living hand, warm and insistent? There was no one, just a lumpy, unmade bed and a little bedside table, the unlit lamp, the dresser with the big knobs. I turned back to the mirror—incrementally, deliberately, my eyes fixed on the middle distance—and was just in time to catch a white cheek, a shoulder, long dark hair slipping past the doorjamb. I froze. *Thump thump* down the hall. *Bang*, the screen door. I stayed still, waiting for the cough of the old car's engine turning over, but heard nothing, and when I buttoned my shirt and went down to look out the front door the car was still there. I flew out into the sunlight like an exorcised spirit.

A NARROW OLD PAVED road loops around the reservoir, passing access roads with yellow postings for hunters noting the official number of the entry. I don't know how they came up with these numbers, which don't seem to correspond to anything, but I suppose this is the way the official world works, as mysteriously as the unofficial.

Riding with growing purpose, I tried to imagine why Raquel might have been hiding in the house, spying. Why she had not gone with Theo and Cherry to the reservoir. What she might have been thinking when she crept up behind me. I had been so sure there was no one home: Why did she flee the scene? Did she think I would not know it was she behind me? Maybe she was dreaming, and not thinking at all, and now wandered idly in the summer-green woods behind the house, a spray of tall grass in her fist. That left Theo and Cherry swimming together in cold water sparkling in the colorless sunshine, drying together under the round white sun.

The road to the reservoir was virtually all downhill, into what had been a valley. One didn't notice this so much in a car, but on a bike it made for a speedy, thrilling ride, and for arduous work on the way home. I would have to stand on my pedals and push hard to get up the steeper inclines; I would be glad for the trees' shade. The thrills of speed and wind as I whizzed over the cracked, unkempt asphalt were complemented by my anticipation of their faces when they saw me emerge from the wooded path to the water. They would be engaged in some play and I would join them, would merge with them, sit quietly and watch them and freckle my shoulders in the sun.

But when I arrived at the banks of the reservoir, finally, dripping with sweat, I found myself alone yet again. The shore was silent and still, the sand untroubled; there were no signs of recent revelry. The sky itself had assumed a telling quietude. A whitewash of clouds obscured the sun and cast a flat, smooth, cooler light. All the heat of the day had come to nothing.

An unmistakable sensation advanced on me: I roamed around, pacing the sand in small circles. Everywhere I went and at every juncture *I had chosen badly.* I had followed the wrong leader and been left behind, left out, alone, alone, an avalanche of disappointment, unfair, unfair, a hot, childish, bitter rage of unmanageable impotence. I sat down in the sand, screwed up my hands into fists and rested my face on them. I fixed my eyes on that same middle distance and tears filled them.

But it was impossible that I should cry with no one there to see it.

After a few minutes I began to feel useless on the sand, with my unspilled tears. I rose and walked limply to my bicycle.

11.

July 4th

For several days I read, and helped my mother weed the garden, and went to the café, and allowed things to return to normal, with the exception of the absence of Cherry. I thought she must be with them, for she was not with me.

I almost enjoyed this disengaged time. I ran parallel thoughts continuously: How she must be missing me, and how elegant, to be free of all entanglements. A free agent, as my father referred to himself on those rare nights when my mother went out and he was left to fend for himself. Did I need Cherry? Did I need anyone?

And yet when she called, her familiar voice made me feel that everything was as it had always been, without exception. She asked me to come with her to the Motherwells', said they'd invited her for lunch but that she didn't really feel like going by herself. She asked me to come with her and then to go to the parade, and then later to the fireworks, for it was indeed the Fourth of July. She said she was sorry she hadn't called, that she'd been working at the drugstore a few hours a day to see if she liked it, and that she did.

I asked her, quite casually, as a means of prompting the usual flood of chat about this or that, about swimming with Theo. "Oh, we were there for hours," she said. "We stayed till practically sunset. It was really fun," she added blandly, and I swam, suddenly, in waters of disorientation. I saw the sun, setting over the empty beach, but I also saw the sun setting over a beach with three figures. I saw the sun setting over a beach with two figures and a third in the woods, watching. I saw the beach minus the sun, for I do not think the sun sets over that shore. I thought I had better say something, and Cherry said, in reply, that I must have come just when they all had swum way out, together, and stayed for an improbably long time, dog-paddling, far beyond where they could touch bottom. "Raquel knows how to do backflips," Cherry said, but I did not want to say anything about Raquel, as I was uncertain now of anything I had seen, or felt.

That afternoon, after lunch, Raquel preempted my unasked questions with a set of her own, more easily formulated ones. She was curious about my parents. I told her how Pritt had evolved from Pryputniewicz (Prih-poot-na-wits), how my father had changed his name when he went away to become an actor in New York City, and then kept the new one after his parents died, when he returned home with his disgruntled, pregnant bride to carry on the family business. He said the new name was easier for customers to remember. Pritt Printing was one room, right upstairs from the insurance agency, where he and my mother made all the business cards, wedding invitations, announcements of birth and death, letterheads, etc., for the whole town. They had contracts with the school and municipal offices, and now that all the technology was advancing so swiftly, they'd bought a computer and a fax machine and with these devices they serviced all the printing needs anybody could come up with.

"Well, that just sounds wonderful," Raquel said to me, and, to look at her, you'd never believe otherwise. Her eyes were shining, her hands folded in her lap like a small girl at charm school. "I just love hearing about families. It's like walking around town after dark, looking in at all the lit-up dining rooms, all the people settling down for dinner, or, after dinner, to watch TV all together. Something middlebrow, like *60 Minutes*. A sweet melancholy comes over me."

She got up from the armchair in the living room, where we had eaten tuna fish sandwiches, and bent to pick up our crumb-strewn plates off the floor. Cherry fidgeted on the couch next to me and I could hear a little sigh of what I thought might be impatience. It must irk her that Raquel did not express interest in her family.

"Doesn't everybody love that? What I hate is when I'm out walking around at night looking at lit-up windows and that sweet melancholy *doesn't* settle in. It's just a walk."

She was gone in the kitchen for a minute, during which Cherry gave me a little look that meant "Can we leave now?" When Raquel came back she caught the tail end of the look and it made her laugh.

"What do you think you're doing?" Raquel sat down on the couch next to Cherry and reached across her lap to take her hand. She applied pressure. Then she gave Cherry a look—raised eyebrows, a tipped smile—which seemed to say *How's that, for wordlessness?*

"Hey, are we gonna go to the parade?" Cherry broke Raquel's small spell with a query that smacked slightly of desperation. She whipped her head around toward me and I shrugged. I'd already forgotten, to tell the truth, about the parade, the fireworks. I would have given anything, I thought, to be sitting where Cherry was now, my hand in the palm of Raquel's hand.

"Don't you want to go and see the fireworks? They'll be starting as soon as it gets a little bit dark."

"That's called 'dusk,'" Raquel interjected, with a small, inward-turning smile.

"We could bring a blanket," Cherry rambled on, "and just sit on the green. It'd be so much fun! I bet some of the other kids would like to meet you and Theo, Raquel. They've been asking me about you. I never know what to say." Cherry's hand still lay in Raquel's. I watched Raquel stroke its palm gently with one finger. Did Cherry shiver? She giggled nervously. "Well, if you don't want to go I think I'll head home now and see if my parents are going. You know"—she turned to face Raquel again, and delicately withdrew her hand at the same time—"that's what we all do, every year. We always do that, don't we, Ginger?"

It was true that that was what we always did, but I would rather do what we didn't always do. I would rather stay here and just *listen* to the fireworks, listen to the distant sound of hands clapping after each modest crack and flash, the humble show our town could afford.

Cherry stood to go and gave me another wordless look. This one said: *Do you really want me to leave you here?* In reply I stretched out on the couch, taking up the space she had recently occupied. I rested my bare feet tentatively on the coffee table, and was not rebuked.

Now I was finally alone with Raquel, and though I had been afraid that she might be disappointed in my companionship, that I might be the one she could have spared, if this was the case she was a good actress, and within minutes had woven a kind of web around the two of us, a cocoon of questions and answers and frilled, generous, engrossing chatter. She wanted to know how I liked my job at the Top Hat, and my coworkers; she wanted to know about all the teachers at the high school—which ones were beloved and which were batty, which gave out A's to the athletes by default. I told her all about our reading of *Frankenstein*, and the day we had been required to act out scenes from the life of the Monster and his maker.

Involved as I was in describing for her the hilarity of hirsute Petey Kosowski's passionate rendition of the Monster's even more impassioned demand that Dr. Frankenstein provide him with a mate, it wasn't until Theo stood behind me and placed his hand on the top of my head that I heard, retroactively, his approaching footsteps. "Stay right where you are," he said, and I jumped slightly at the light, synchronous pressure of hand and voice. "I'm going to pour myself a glass of wine. Would either of you like one?"

"Oh yes, darling, I would," Raquel replied, and I nodded

my head tentatively in concord. Only then did he remove his hand. I thought that later I would dig in my drawers at home to find my diary and start a new chapter. I might title it "He Touched Me."

For I needed a new place in which to put this sensation, to let it sit and accumulate motive. Did he mean it? Did he intend to place his hand on me in such a way that I could still feel its warmth, with him in the other room? With these inquisitive thoughts I felt myself slipping into a foreign mind—Theo's mind—with a new kind of force, one I'd never exerted before. I understood for the first time Cherry's various absorptions, her efforts at interpretation of the actions of the boy-of-the-moment, which at times approached the level of telepathy. Maybe Theo had wanted to touch me for a long time and only now found this casual means, a perfectly reasonable, unnoticeable spot of time in which to lay hands on me. I felt a thrill stronger even than his touch as I entered his mind, and found it to be so like mine—cold, strong, hopeful—a sympathy so bright and potent between us that I could not determine a point of origin for it. It extended forcefully in our two directions, a ray of light with no discernible source, only vectors of equal and opposite momentum. A mutuality.

I looked at Raquel to see if she might have registered his touch—sympathetically?—but she only smiled at me. "I always love it when Theo comes back from the city. I feel as though absolute truth has been reasserted. He's been to see his parents. His mother really. She's still not quite herself." I remembered that his mother was ill, and had a brief vision of a light-strewn bedroom, gauze curtains diffusing the rays,

Theo sitting beside her plump bed, she a finer, paler, frailer version of her tall, dun-colored, monochromatic son. He held her hand in his and read to her from a book of sonnets until she fell asleep.

I had thought to find an appropriate moment in our tête-à-tête to ask Raquel how she did it, her appearance and disappearance in the house, her presence and absence at the reservoir, but now Theo was here, holding three round, full glasses of deep red wine in his two hands like a bouquet of gigantic, mutant roses. He stood in front of Raquel, who relieved him of one, and then he did a little dip and handed me mine. I held it in my two hands as I saw Raquel doing, as though I warmed myself at a fire inside a crystal ball. It was my first glass of wine. I'd taken sips of my parents' but had found it metallic and bloody. Now whatever distaste I might feel was negated by my sense that we three were sharing a potion, one that would make it possible for us to finally become invisible, or to see in the dark, or to read minds, or to understand the language of animals.

12.
Mid-July

One day soon after it seemed as if the sun beat down in its noontime position all day, too hot even to make the usual movements across the sky. I thought of the reservoir, the relief it offered us, and of what I had missed out on already. I wanted to catch up.

Raquel loved the idea. "Let's go right now, without further delay. We've just been lying here like snakes on a rock."

"We're so suggestible," Theo concurred. Raquel rose swiftly, considering the heat, from her ragged lawn chair on the porch, where she had been reading a faded paperback. Theo lay stretched out somewhat awkwardly on the swing, squinting at an old Sears catalog that I'd noticed in the hallway on our very first visit, what felt like years ago. They both had an air of such languor I could hardly believe they would summon the energy necessary to open the doors of the car, much less drive it. But Theo rose with a grunt, as though he were performing a single, purposeful sit-up.

"Oh, good!" Cherry clapped her hands in unchecked

enthusiasm. She looked particularly summery that day, I thought, a little proudly, in her pink tank top and faded red gym shorts, cheeks flushed with heat and black hair in a ponytail. Tendrils escaped at her temples and the nape of her neck, curling in the humid air. I didn't know if she was more pleased at the thought of some relief from the heat or relieved to break the surface tension of our sanguine foursome, in which I was, increasingly, immersed. I could see her dilemma, but couldn't name it.

She had wanted to tell me something the night before, on the phone. Her father wasn't pleased, he had told her, a little more sternly than she was accustomed to, that she was spending so much time with these new people, these people nobody knew. Cherry had taken this to heart. She'd promised him that she would ask before the next time, even if she were with me. She had asked today, and been granted permission. I thought it was lucky that my own parents didn't seem to speak to hers as often as they used to, now that we were a little older. They would not be likely to ask the same thing of me.

WE TOOK THE OLD ROAD out of town, the one that heads straight to the heart of the water, then veered off onto the loop, heading north, to go over the top and down the other side. Theo drove recklessly, in the middle of the road, even coming around corners. Lots of town kids drive like this, to the very same destination but usually at night, with a trunk full of beer and a backseat full of squealing underage girls.

Now we were going on our own brand of outing, one with a delicate balance of adult and youthful participants, and I felt happy, absorbed, pinioned in this tenuous equilibrium, as though we were some new kind of four-headed or four-hearted beast. Some of these were things I had always wanted to feel.

The road itself was shaded all along by thick summer leaves overhead, but just on the other side of the trees you could see the promise of sunlight on blue water and open sky above.

The swimming area opens out just at the spot where a church once stood, and you can still see the lines of its foundation in the shady soil. A dark blue pickup I recognized as Randy Thibodeau's was parked by the side of the road. I glanced at Cherry as she slipped out of the backseat, holding on to the seat in front for leverage, glazed from the heat like a child. She rolled her eyes at me, looked at the truck, looked back at me, raised her eyebrows and rolled her eyes again, twisting her lips—a pantomime of "who cares." I knew she did. She certainly cared enough about Randy to be "totally pissed off" that he hadn't called her after their recent, to her quite earthshaking, dalliance. Theo and Raquel were already down the narrow path to the slip of sandy beach, towels slung around their necks. We followed after, pulling our clothes off, swimsuits on, in the shadow of Randy's truck.

Randy, on his ratty beach towel, appeared to be engrossed in the chatter of Brianna Pickering, who worked at the video store. "I bet she gives him free rentals," Cherry whispered in my ear, with gratuitous spite, I thought. What had the hapless girl ever done to us? Cherry should be grateful to her for diverting the attentions of the prodigal Randy.

Just then my own were diverted by the sight of Raquel and Theo stepping out of their shorts, holding on to each other's shoulders for balance. They stripped off their shirts and stood completely naked in the sand.

I heard Cherry gasp and whisper, "Oh my God." My own shock and embarrassment was complicated by the fascination of my gaze. I had never seen anything so beautiful as the two of them together on the shore of the reservoir. Each body was so different from the other. Hers was fluted and scrolled where his was spare and elastic, proportioned for maximum ease of entry, like a knife into sugar as he dove. She waded serenely, round and rounded parts moving like a soft machine, into his wake, and stood, patting her abdomen, underarms, breasts with cool water—a trick of acclimation. Then she glided forward into a smooth breaststroke.

They seemed to me to work the way a cliché does: it gets used over and over because it is useful. It is difficult to imagine the source of the usage, or an end to it. Yet I also have difficulty finding the proper cliché to describe their union: "birds of a feather," no; "peas in a pod," definitely not. Perhaps "oil and water"; the words themselves stick together although separation is what they illustrate, form denying content for once.

Cherry and I flattened facedown on our towels and tried not to die of shame, or to explode with laughter. We were not responsible, and yet we were. Randy and Brianna took this opportunity to light up a joint and pass it back and forth. I smelled the mulchy, nutritious odor of pot. Theo and Raquel had swum far out and looked to be dog-paddling, facing each other, talking, oblivious.

Stoned Randy lurched from his towel with a grunt and swung over to where we lay, smoking joint in hand. He walked right past me and squatted down next to Cherry: "Hey, want any?" I pinched her thigh, touching mine, hard, and propped myself on my elbows.

Cherry sat up on her towel and for a minute I thought she was going to accept. But she had sat up only to make her enthusiasm for him more obvious. "Oh, thanks, Randy, no, I've got some stuff to do later, I have to drive us back, anyway, but thanks." I listened to her lying with interest. I wasn't sure I'd ever heard her do it before. "But how's your summer going?" Why was she keeping him here? Raquel and Theo were swimming back now, heads bobbing in unison. Any minute they would emerge, dripping, dangling, and glistening.

"Oh, you know, same old shit. Now that I'm out of school summer's just like every other time of year—only hotter." Cherry giggled like an idiot at this banal observation. "So, what's up with the circus freaks? Store run out of bathing suits? Or don't city people think they have to follow the same rules as anybody else?" I refrained from pointing out to Randy that we were all breaking the rules, simply by swimming in this water. His own lower half was modestly encased in a pair of old cutoffs, which had molded themselves to his wiry legs, the hair dried in snaky rivulets.

Cherry laughed and fluttered her hand in the air in front of her face, as though to dismiss the Motherwells from Randy's view. "Yeah, I dunno, I think they just forgot their suits at home," she lamely explained.

"Forgot their brains at home more like it," Randy retorted. "Well, we've gotta get going. I have to be at the garage at three. Grease monkeys never rest. See you later. Hope to, anyways." Cherry's face lit up like a lamp rubbed by a genie. "Stay out of trouble, Ginger," Randy added with a smirk as he pushed off with one hand, sinewy forearm, joint held aloft, and I relaxed my tightly held muscles—jaw, shoulders, abdomen—into the hot towel. I did not like for Randy to address me directly. I listened as he and Brianna gathered their things and left, my cheek down on my arms, my eyes closed, the perfume of wet sand in my nose.

WHEN I WOKE the sky was a deeper blue, and insects had begun to hum in the brush. Cherry's towel, beside me, was vacant. Theo and Raquel lay a few feet away, on their backs, eyes closed, arms splayed. Raquel's breasts had fallen to either side of her ribs, leaving a smooth expanse of breastbone.

I sat up. My mouth was dry. Cherry was down the beach a short way, wading in the shallow water where reeds and lily pads grew. Her hair was wet.

I tiptoed past them, noticing Raquel's burnished pallor, Theo's dusky blond skin, the sandy color of his pubic hair, the darker blond skin of his penis, darker still where the skin was wrinkled and on his testicles, where black blood showed purple beneath the skin. I stood thigh deep in the water and looked down to see what might be living in there.

"Sssst," Cherry hissed and, when I looked, waved me over to where she stood. I looked back once more at the sleeping couple. I thought I saw Raquel open one eye.

Cherry was pushing lily pads around with her toe. They swayed gently all about her ankles. I stood outside the circle of their swaying and looked under the surface of the water to the muck beneath, a dense weave of brown root systems infiltrated with slimy vegetation of unknown origin. The whole mess floated like a cloud of smog over the already slimy bottom—the soil was dense with clay. Beneath the roots and above the bottom was a half-foot of invisibility; it was impossible to be sure of what one stood in.

"Hey, are you jealous of me?" Cherry asked, looking up at me but down again quickly. I could not think what she might mean by that. My mind blanched. "I mean, I feel like you never want me to talk to anyone, and it's like, I know we're best friends, but, I wonder sometimes if you feel annoyed because I'm more popular than you, and they never invite you to do anything, or something like that. And maybe that's why you want to hang out so much with these . . . I mean, I don't really get why we're here."

Her mildness, even in this confrontational stance, was as sweet as the breeze that had begun to pick up over the water as the day grew later. Her sweetness and my blankness canceled each other out. I could not tell her that she was wrong. I could not tell her anything at all. And now Raquel splashed over to us, sleeveless T-shirt restored, white cotton underwear damply covering the dark triangle at her crotch.

She leaned in to our silence and spoke conspiratorially. "This reservoir has an interesting history to it, doesn't it? When we signed the contract on the house the realtor said something about some other towns that used to be here, but they weren't here anymore."

"Oh yes, it's true!" Cherry abandoned her demure reserve, all excited at the prospect of gossip, even antique gossip. Or maybe she was simply glad for this diversion. I felt a strong impulse to restrain her from telling too much, or in fact anything at all. This was our town's open secret, and I didn't know what Raquel would do with it. But Cherry continued unimpeded: "You can see the foundation of an old church, in the grass, right back behind where we were lying. Some people say, but they're just being ridiculous, that when the water gets really low, when there hasn't been much rain, you can see chimneys, even the tops of houses, rising above the waterline. But that's really not true. They totally leveled all the towns. There were three of them. It took years and years, the whole thing. They knocked down everything and evacuated every last person before they let the river fill it up." Here she spoke as though from a script; I'd heard her mother telling it just this way to Cherry years ago, when we were little and very eager to go down and scout out steeples and rooftops peeking from the dark water.

"Well, how do you know that's true, Cherry?" Raquel voiced my thoughts exactly. "Have you ever dived down deep and looked? Or were you there when they were doing the leveling?"

"Oh, of course not." Cherry was all sincere assertion. "It happened when my parents weren't even born yet, or at least they were little babies. It happened when my grandparents were young. They remember it perfectly, believe me. My great-uncle was one of the overseers of the gravediggers."

"Oh, my word," Raquel breathed. "They dug the bodies up? What did they do with them?"

"Why, they buried them again, of course! There's a huge cemetery out on Route Seven for all the people who were dug up from the towns. They brought the stones and everything! Some of my family is buried there."

Raquel looked up at us, from where she had been gently digging in the mucky bottom with her toes. The heat of the day had turned the tops of her shoulders, the tops of her cheeks, her nose, all a peachy color. Her eyes radiated a silty green, the color of the mud. I felt as if a trap had snapped shut somewhere behind them. "I believe," she said softly, "that some of my family is buried there, too."

WE LEFT THE RESERVOIR with our heads full of new information. Now, it all made sense, these visitors, these *rootless cosmopolites*—a phrase that had seeped out of my history textbook and into my consciousness. Raquel was doing research. Raquel was writing a book! This was a book that had begun, she told us, as we stood in our hushed circle around the swaying lily pads, as her doctoral study on the history of the New England witch trials—her proposed fellowship project—but which had evolved into much more than that, when she and Theo found Wick. Now the book had taken up a more personal, singular set of concerns. It seemed that Raquel could trace her ancestry along a dramatic timeline of tragic conclusions: first, to the scene of the famous atrocities in Salem, where at least one of the innocent women hung as witches was her direct ancestor; and then to our own flooded valley, where long ago yet another of her unfortunate ancestors, with the unlikely surname of Goode, had been persecuted in the name of righteousness. And then later, those that remained were forced out of their homes and displaced, dispossessed—a final debasement. So the book had grown from a simple, potentially dry, potentially superfluous historical treatment of a much-documented set of mistakes to a memoir of a family curse, which would not incidentally include revolutions both cultural and industrial.

This was the coda to the story she had told us that day in the rain, in her cozy bedroom, and to the lie she had blithely told that first day of conversation, in her kitchen. Now it all made sense, the presence of Raquel and Theo in Wick—*what they were doing here*—and this, to me, I can confess now, was something of a relief. I had longed for mystery, and excitement, and even confusion, if it came naturally along with these, but now that I'd tasted of them, in the form of this strange pair. . . . Once it became clear that they needed to come back east, to give up their pioneering dream for the sake of Theo's family obligation, Theo, she said, had been all too happy to support her in this year of research and writing with the fellowship money from the university. They would stay in Wick and here together be both responsible and productive at the same time: Theo a good son; Raquel a good scholar. And they might even be so productive as to produce a child, a child of Wick.

IT HAD GROWN COOLER, and I turned toward the shore. Theo sat up as if on cue and reached for his T-shirt. Ominous silver clouds rolled above the tips of the tall pines that ringed the reservoir, and Cherry shivered a little and said, "I've got to get back soon." I noticed that she hadn't offered any comment on Raquel's surprising admission, and later that night on the phone she querulously observed that Raquel had made her feel like an idiot, duping her into an enthusiastic recounting of something about which Raquel obviously knew much more than she did.

Our ride home was silent.

I HAVE NOT YET mentioned that I never swim. It's the kind of prohibition that stands in the way of group activities, but if one is steadfast and consistent, after a while it comes to seem natural enough. *I never swim:* not in daylight, but especially not at night, when there is no hope of seeing the bottom, of moving away from whatever dead body or body part or soft, rotted remnant one might be about to bump into with a bare foot or hand. There, in the dark, exposure is complete: one's skin to the black water; whatever is in the water to one's skin.

13.

It was out of habit that I asked her, and I felt something quite close to relief when Cherry made an excuse. Rather than coming over to see the Motherwells with me the next day, she would go back down to "the res," as she put it, with Randy and some of the other kids from school. "I'm just going to go swimming at the res with Randy and a few kids from school" is exactly what she said, and I noted that she used the slang that we never would have used before.

But though I was relieved to be free of the encumbrance of Cherry—my rival, it now seems necessary to say—I didn't feel ready to go alone. Knocking at the door, calling into the cool, shady interior, the subsequent immersion. Almost, but not quite. I needed an intermediary, a buffer. I thought I'd go to the mill and spend an hour or two alone with my thoughts.

I lay on my back and stared at the sky, the sun graciously veiling itself behind a white-hot cloud whose edges showed purple with a coming storm. The kids at the reservoir would be doubly wet, extra-wet with rain.

The kids in my town were louts. Winter or summer, they liked nothing better than to take their parents' cars up into the hills, park, get so drunk they'd fall asleep in the back, then wake up gagging on their own vomit. Or some of them died, not having woken up in time; about once every ten years one of them did this. Jack did this, late one October night when I was eleven. He was eighteen, and never any older.

THINK OF WAKING UP to the stoppage of your own breath, waking up not breathing, having breathed your last with your unconscious mind churning in cooperation with the involuntary actions of the body, which function so smoothly unless blocked or offended by some unforeseen obstacle, such as regurgitated food and alcohol. Think of the unspeakable grief of your surviving family members.

Raquel spoke, all the time, in language calculated to impress. It was huge, and smelled of the future. She told me, every day, in so many little ways, that someday my dealings with the world would include making choices, on a scale I had never previously conceived of. "It's all a matter of what you conceive of." She said that to me on many different occasions. Often just out of the blue, the way someone else might sigh without explanation, leaving you wondering if it was something you had done.

Did I understand even half of all that came into my ears in this time? Like I have said, I was fifteen, one year ahead of myself at the high school, and of an introspective nature, but I had not yet developed a vocabulary with which to discuss myself with myself. I recorded my impressions not in a diary but as notes taken internally, permanently. (Raquel later said, on the subject of diaries, that they were lonely. "There's no one to talk to in there." Occasionally she could be pithy and lighthearted about something she felt deeply. "Felt deeply?!" she would exclaim, if she had heard me say that. "Why, I never felt anything deeply in my whole life.")

Raquel was a foreign language and I, her student, fully immersed. I did not understand so much as absorb, like meat in a marinade. It got so they would forget I was there sometimes—or at least Theo did, to my chagrin, as his notice had risen to a place of paramount importance; I'm not sure Raquel could ever be accused of ignoring her audience—and the conversation might follow an intimate path, or even, on rare occasion, fall into the comfort of silence. Or what I perceived as comfort: Raquel never failed to squirm, and look around, and smile painfully in both our directions, as if apologizing repeatedly, silently, for her share of the abyss we had fallen into. "Apologize silently?" I can hear her incredulous tone. "I don't speak unless I speak out loud. You can be sure that when I am silent, I am silent throughout. If I had an interior monologue, or dialogue, for that matter, it would indicate that there was some content preexisting the moment at which I open my mouth."

Then Theo asks her, "Well, who are you? Who are you now? And now? And now? Now?" He prods her side with his index finger, none too gently.

She slaps his hand away, shuts him up entirely. "An intellectual exercise, like everything else."

As the rehearsal of this conversation was for me. This

was one piece of business they would not conduct in my presence. Perhaps they never conducted it at all, in front of me or each other or Yahweh. I had, it seems clear, only imagined it. High above the mill's turret, the cloud released its cargo, fat drops heralding a downpour, and I made my way home in the rain.

14.

More July

It went on for days. Wick was sodden, air cooling with the expression of moisture. One late afternoon I tied a sweatshirt around my waist and left my room, where I had been ensconced for hours with something called, beguilingly, *The Uses of Enchantment*, which I'd pounced on at the library for its title but been disappointed to find was a book about, of all things, fairy tales, how they prepare one, psychologically speaking, for the witches and curses, amputations and stuntings, of adult life.

"Ginger!" My father hailed me from the living room, where he sat in his chair with the newspaper, a bottle of beer sweating on a coaster on the side table. I halted, caught at the moment of liftoff. "Ginger, what's on your agenda for the evening? An important meeting to attend?" My father often liked to kid about what he perceived as my advanced maturity, my seriousness, my gravity. I stood in the doorway and gazed into the gloom; he had only one light on to read by. "Your mother's in Jack's room doing some bookkeeping . . .

go say goodbye at least, honey." She had set up her home office on Jack's desk. I think she just wanted a reason to sit in there and look at his belongings: posters and books and records, his trumpet, his prizewinning senior history project—a scale model of the Shift River valley, pre-flood. Toys he had not had time to shed from his teenaged self. I bet she was glad to have all of that.

"Hi, sweetie. Where are you off to?" She sat peering at the monitor, bills spread out before her. I told her Cherry's house, and her frame relaxed; it did not seem to occur to her that I might be lying.

"You know, before you go, I've been wanting to talk to you about something, Ginger. It'll just take a minute. Sit down, honey." She smoothed her hand over Jack's bedspread. "It's something . . . I've always known this would come up, because you and Cherry are so close and she's older, and I think now's the time. Sit down." An order. I sat on Jack's bed.

"Now, I know Cherry's starting to really date boys, and get involved with all that, and I thought I should find out whether you need any protection. Birth control—you know what I mean, right?" Bang. My mother coolly cast herself in the role of my protector without any sense of irony, though I felt keenly the distinction between the provision of a latex condom and any true parental supervision. With an equal measure of coolness I told her that no, I did not need any protection. *No, Mom, I'm okay.* I think I blushed, or flushed, and thus indicated to her my persistent innocence and the native delicacy that made any further conversation on the subject undesirable. I kissed her quickly on her cool cheek and slipped away, down the dark hall and out the door into a day that held a premature hint of fall.

DOES IT SEEM OBVIOUS to you, too, that I required protection? How embarrassing. I have mentioned before that I felt myself at this time to be ageless, and I would posit that feeling for all children. A child does not perceive herself as such—not in the way that adults grow ever more concerned with their status, their chronos, as it shows itself ever more clearly on their bodies and in the shortening days ahead. A child has no perspective on age, and consequently cannot abide or bear the presuppositions of others, of observers, about how this or that is supposed to make them feel, because they are "just a child." Violations, intimations, reprobations, invasions. These are labels adults place on experience. This places you in a difficult, almost impossible situation. For it really is your job—you who are grown—to protect the children. For they know not how they feel. They know not how they ought to feel about anything. You must feel it for me.

JACK HAD PLAYED TRUMPET, in martial lockstep in the marching band, at school, but at home he liked to close the door to his room, put on one of my dad's old jazz records, plug in his headphones, and follow along with the soloist. His sound alternated: strong and smooth; short blasts of stridency; occasional fluttering arpeggios, flights of fluty articulation. I was not allowed in, usually, but once or twice I sat on his bed and watched, and was amazed at his mirthful frown, his plugged-up mouth, by how he seemed to be talking through the instrument, not just blowing air into it. It was an instrument of expression, just like a mouth, a tongue, a palate, its language one of feeling, purely wordless. It made me feel proud.

I had been proud on his graduation day, when Cherry and I pressed together, seated on the bleacher between my parents in our sundresses, a fine June day. Jack marched around the playing field with the band; then a short while later bounded up onstage to accept a special prize for his project on Wick's early days as "A Town of Steep Vicissitudes." *A pre–Revolutionary War site of great prosperity, Wick was in 1762 host to the nation's first market fair!* (A much-reduced version persists in the parking lot of the grocery store every third Sunday, weather permitting.) *Wick and its several neighboring towns, Hammerstead, Shadleigh, and Morrow, used the bountiful force of their many streams to power early milling and manufacturing: wood, fabric, cannonballs when cannonballs were required. The invention of the steam engine carried our products far and wide, and the mills labored overtime to fill orders, putting the area's first wave of immigrants to work doing so. Many decades of contentment ensued. But by the 1930s competition and diversification in these markets had reduced our perceived efficiency, and jobs began to drain out of the valley. Meanwhile, water began to drain in, as a diabolical plan that had been afoot in the Massachusetts legislature for many years was set into final, cataclysmic motion, in a huge and bitterly opposed landgrab. The case went as far as the Supreme Court, but just as the land had originally been grabbed from the Ramapaquet Nation, by white settlers, now the land was grabbed, cleared, deforested, manipulated; rivers and tributaries diverted, redirected, then finally, over a number of years*—inhuman, literally detached from any one human decision or approval or appraisal, the unstopped trickle of man-made disaster—*blocked with tons of granite, a dam built, the valley irreversibly flooded. Wick alone, on high ground above the insensitively named Ramapack Reservoir, remained, and remains to this day, and we its rueful citizens.*

Jack's project was multimedia, multidimensional. He'd taken photographs, written text to accompany them, and constructed with great pains the balsa-wood-and-cardboard-and-papier-mâché model resting now, collecting authentic local dust, atop the low bookcase in his room, complete with tiny little houses and automobiles, even tractors, even minuscule citizens making their way from point to point, on dusty roads. Even dust. A teensy but legible signpost pointing the way up out of the valley, to higher ground, to Wick. Cherry and I had crouched in front of the model and regarded the little towns, the lost towns, with the native disinterest of the native. But Jack was "a real history buff," his teacher said that day, shaking my father's hand, watching as Jack ascended the platform to have his own hand shaken, degree conferred with honors. I glanced into the face of my mother, leaning across Cherry to get a good look. She smiled into my eyes, even beamed, a motherly light, but I thought I could detect across her own eyes a shadow of dissatisfaction—that which colored her world, and was part of every story she ever told—the part she couldn't tell, the part left out: that which she really wanted. She was shortchanged; she had not chosen exactly this life, this town, she had certainly hoped for more; and now her firstborn son, so bright, so full of the same promise that yet brimmed in her, had neglected to apply to colleges, had chosen instead to "stick around for a while." Another mother might have welcomed this. I for one was thrilled. I could not imagine our house without Jack.

Later we walked around the commencement grounds, my parents greeting other happy parents, Jack signing yearbooks and others signing his, high fives and exclamations of joy all around. My mother kept her arm around my shoulders as we strolled and I remember thinking, with wonder, that one day I would be in Jack's place, and would have a choice to make. I couldn't imagine, then, how anyone could choose to leave the warmth of that embrace, so palpable in the sunny afternoon. There was a lot I couldn't imagine. In certain areas I perhaps overcompensated.

15.

No one answered my knock at the Motherwells', so I just went in. The living room was empty. I went to the kitchen, expecting to find Raquel, but found no one. A plate of crumbs—Raquel knew how to make toast—sat on the round table, aside from which there was no sign that anyone had been there in the last decade.

I went down the hall and put my foot cautiously on the first step of the staircase; I couldn't decide if I ought to be very, very quiet, as was my wont, or instead do the unexpected—announce myself. Aside from in conversation, and the occasional meal, Raquel and Theo seemed to spend most of their time catching up on sleep. When had they missed all these hours? And sure enough, as I ascended to the landing I saw that they lay curled up together on the pallet in Theo's study, a book splayed, cracked wide open, its spine broken, on the floor next to them. They did not move at all as I continued up the stairs and then stood in the doorway for a moment, and this seemed odd. I focused my attention minutely on the movements of their chests, on their breath. I did not believe that they were really asleep. Did I spy the shallow rhythm of a feigned unconsciousness? Had they set me a trap of some sort?

Nevertheless, after standing there for a few moments I found, to my surprise, that I felt quite drowsy: a paralyzed, lids-propped-open, already-asleep kind of drowsy. The door to their bedroom was half open, and a cozy glow from the bedside lamp illuminated the tangle of blankets and sheets on their bed. As I approached I saw that a small book with gilt-edged pages lay open on Raquel's pillow—where I might lay my head—and I sat down on the edge of the bed and picked it up.

As soon as I came to a total comprehension of what I saw—the scratchy handwriting, the dated entries—I put it down again, like it was a hot pan and I without a potholder.

Then I thought of them lying quietly—sleeping, or silently, though pointedly, caressing one another, or simply waiting—in the next room, and knew that it was desirable that I should read what lay on the pillow.

The diary began at the time of their arrival in Wick, and had been kept with extreme inconsistency thereafter.

May 13th

Theo has instructed me to keep this diary, a journal of our stolen year here together, and so I will do what I can with what I have: this perfect tool, a pen; this ideal receptacle, with its little lock and key. If he were my flesh and blood he could not know me any better. Does he want to know me better?

June 7th

I'm not sure that I have the courage to go on. All these people seem to trust me: Oh, people, people; so sweet and stupid. If I had a heart to break . . .—note: possible country-song lyric.

July 28th

My question remains: Why do people bother to write legibly in their diaries. For that matter, why do they write in English? (Or Spanish, French, Polish, whatever blasted language.) Why do we not invent new languages, or at least codes that only we can decode. I suppose Michelangelo did—or was that da Vinci? (I muse, mutter, ponder to myself, getting quite into the spirit of the thing.)

AND THAT WAS TODAY'S ENTRY. I thought that I had never read anything so sad. The ink was still a little shiny; if I touched it with my finger, as I was tempted to do, I would smear it. She must have just been lying in bed, struggling to do what had been asked of her, moments before I entered the house. And then what? She had prepared the room as she wanted me to see it, and slipped into Theo's study, where he sat working, or meditating, or whatever it was he did when he was not by Raquel's side, and coaxed him down onto the small guest bed.

In their bedroom, just on the other side of the wall, I replaced the diary, open, on Raquel's pillow and lay down facing it, on my side, with my head on Theo's pillow. The pillowcase smelled faintly of hay. I reached behind me and groped for the lamp.

I WOKE to the click of the switch, the spread of light, and Raquel's softest voice saying, "Wake up, sleepyhead. I want to show you something." *Something else?* I thought dreamily, and I dragged myself out of a swamp of sleep and muscled up to sitting. There she was with what looked like an old hatbox in her hands. She placed it on the bed and sat down next to it, at my feet, then removed the cover to reveal a pile of photographs, perhaps fifty of them, some edged in crimped white borders, some with no borders and missing their corners, as though they had been torn out of old albums. Some looked antique; their surfaces were dull, and the images were watery and uniformly brownish, the brown of a horse's coat.

"Here's what I wanted to show you: this house." The photograph she held out to me was very old indeed, and featured a family, a group of about ten people in front of a large white edifice, all posed stiffly, some standing and some sitting on straight chairs, in the manner of the earliest portraits, for which the slightest gesture or error of informality would ruin an afternoon's effort. The house looked familiar. It was square, and the dark, possibly black trim around its windows gave it a distinctly unwelcoming air, seeming to suggest that a potential visitor might be better off out of doors, where the rigors of mortality held less sway.

Their starched black dresses and suits—they were all in mourning—and careful hairdressings looked to be of an era a century before. Their faces had been scratched out, and this struck me as both unfortunate and appropriate. Whatever gathering or event this group portrait was meant to memorialize might have been better left unrecorded.

"Do you see?" Raquel said excitedly, though she kept her voice low. "These are the descendants of the Goodes who came here after the trials in Salem. Here they stayed, and this is the house they lived in. And this is a picture of them the day after their youngest daughter—she was only eighteen, I believe, at the time of her death—was executed for a crime she didn't commit, or at least not intentionally. The family legend has it that she and another girl were out swimming in the Shift River and Emily Goode was fooling around, showing her friend how her ancestors had been 'tested' for the presence of witchcraft, and she was holding her under the water just for a minute, but then the girl struggled, and her head hit a rock, and the girl died. No one was sure whether she died of the blow to her head or of water in her lungs. But Emily Goode was convicted of her murder and was hung. Even though she was well along in her pregnancy. And the family never forgave the town for this unyielding punishment, and always wore black, and did not consort with the townspeople, and kept to themselves. This is Jacob Goode, her brother." She pointed out a tall, slender, faceless man with a round hat like a Quaker's. "The two were thick as thieves. Separated only in death, and some say not even then. He was in training to be a minister, but on her execution day he renounced his faith. He never entered a church again.

"But although the Goode family removed itself from the goings-on of the town, they did not remove themselves from the town itself, as they had done before when faced with an injustice of this magnitude. They would not be forced out again from the place they had called home for nearly two centuries. And even much later, a hundred years later, when the towns were to be flooded to make the reservoir, the few remaining members of the family refused to evacuate their property. The officials, of course, tried to move them, but they were immovable; they just stayed where they were, even as the waters rose, and they were drowned in their home. In this house you see here. I suppose it was a final injustice, and they were ready for it." I looked again at the photograph and seemed to see the resolve imminent in their postures, their upright bearing, the poise of their hands. They were ready at that moment to die.

"But enough of these dusty relics! Let's go down to the water and I'll show you proof." Raquel's eyes were shining with certainty and engagement and I thought, *Ah, so this is it. This is what she came here for. Proof. And I am to be her witness; her accomplice, too.* We tiptoed past the room where Theo slept, down the stairs, out the door, and down the driveway to Raquel's car. Before I knew it we were headed toward the loop road, and around it in the deep of evening to an access road I had never noticed before, one about a quarter of the way around the circumference of the reservoir, clockwise, from Wick. This was where the town called Hammerstead lay, deep under the water. The remaining two lost towns of Shadleigh and Morrow—just to form their names with the mouth of my mind made me shiver. Did they still answer to those silent names, now that their borders were erased, their topographies washed away, their skies filled with black water?

To say the names brought back all the inhabitants, the lives, and planted them there again, lost lives with eyes peering up, hopelessly, from the bottom of the darkest day anyone should ever see.

"COME OUT HERE, it's not cold. It's like bathwater, actually." Raquel stood knee-deep, her shorts rolled up high around her thighs. I did not remember getting out of the car or trekking down the little path to the water's edge, but here we were, and there she was. It must have been about ten o'clock already. The sky had turned a violent blue, and the trees around the circumference of the water wore the black outlines that would soon spread and merge to make pitch blackness. "You have to come out here to see."

I made my way slowly in. It was indeed warm, unreasonably so. I had never felt it like this before—it was almost hot. It made me want to feel it all over me, unmediated, and so I waded back to the shore and stripped down, leaving my T-shirt and shorts in a pile, and then into the water, out to where Raquel stood, arms crossed under her breasts, regarding me. "That's good, Ginger. It will be much easier to see when you are naked." I didn't question her logic; I knew only that the dark water against my skin felt like a giant mother's hand. And Raquel's hand was on my shoulder; we were chest-deep in the water now, and so she didn't have far to go to place her other hand heavily on my other shoulder, a grip, more than a placement, and use the full weight of her body, buoyant in the water, to land on me, behind me, and push me under, and hold me there.

. . .

WHAT DID I SEE, there, under the water.

I AWOKE, UNBREATHING, in the midst of an unsuccessful gasp, with my face pressed up against the little book with the gilt-edged pages. My throat was closed, my mouth was dry, my eyes were sandy. I sat up and filled my lungs, rubbed my hands over my eyes. In the Motherwells' bathroom I splashed my face and dried it on a red towel. A faint tracing of Raquel's fresh entry was printed on my damp temple. The lock had made an impression on my cheek. I moved quietly out into the hallway, then slipped past the room where they still slept, or were silent, down the stairs, and out the door. I went to go find Cherry.

16.

At the Endicotts' we woke hot and dehydrated into a newly sunny morning, and decided to make a day of it. We landed at the mill with a blanket and some cans of soda and packaged snacks grabbed from the cupboard. I don't know how the hours passed exactly, but before we knew it the mosquitoes were out in full force, the sun was getting low. It was time to seek shelter.

Although I had felt a great deal of relief at being in Cherry's aggressively familiar company, it just seemed right—or at least it did to me, and I had the force to carry us both—that we should drop in at the Motherwells', and, once there, that we should stay for dinner. Cherry didn't protest. I was quite hungry, a little weary, and sun-dazed, and from the look of her, her glazed eyelids, her plush cheeks, Cherry shared my somnambulance. We wore our minimalist summer uniforms: T-shirts, cutoffs, sneakers. I didn't even have underwear on. I don't know about Cherry.

Dinner was in the making, and while Theo stood, cooking, we three sat around the kitchen table, drinking something Raquel called "sangria" but which tasted like a lemony fruit punch, in the path of the cross-draft created by the screen door and the open window. Cicadas made noise in the bushes; pretty soon moths and beetles would beat against the screens. We got to talking about dreams: Cherry offered up, shyly, some small comment about her own recent night terrors.

"What?" Raquel pounced. "You mean the kind that wake you up, shivering and sweating? Do they go away once you're awake? Or are you still afraid, even after? I think the most interesting part is after you wake up, seeing how long it takes for that fear to recede. I once dreamed I had no face, or rather that my face was plastic, was constantly shape-shifting, cycling in no particular order through all the stages of my life, from infancy through great age. All the next day I felt unsure of my own aspect, and didn't know how to move my lips or even blink my eyes."

I could see that Cherry was uncomfortable with Raquel's attention. She made no reply, and even leaned back in her chair, as though to remove herself. She fanned herself with a drooping hand, and took a gulp of her drink.

"Rough night for a young mind," Raquel finally said, laughing a little. Always compelled to break tension, narrative or otherwise.

"Very interesting." Theo turned to us from the counter and spoke with an air of finitude, as though it was to be the last word on the subject, but then, just as quickly, he resumed speaking. "It puts me in mind of that Zen koan; the one about faces. Of course the thing about a koan is that it brooks no explanation; you must say no more after you say a koan."

"Well, then, everything is a koan, in that case. Come on, spill it." Raquel's hair was piled up on top of her head and the green shirt she wore increased her resemblance to some lizard, basking in the black sun on a black rock.

"I'm sure you've heard this one before . . ."

"No introductions, please!"

Theo smiled, came over, and placed his hands, palms up, on the table, as though holding a book open.

"What, then, is the face you wore before you were born?" His voice lilted, as though he really expected an answer.

Raquel leaned back from the table, eyes closed like someone who has just swallowed the sacrament. "You know," she said, "in every pile of horseshit there is a teaspoonful of truth. Why, just the other day Ginger said to me"—and here she turned to Theo and waved her hand in my direction—"that I look like I mean everything I say, just like other people do. That my facial expressions are remarkably open. That in fact I'm as legible as an open book!"

I was a little taken aback by this interpretation. What I had said (although, on second thought, I could not remember having actually spoken it to her, but just thinking it) was that it seemed to me like she said everything she thought, but that she thought only of what to say. It also seemed to me—though I would never have said this out loud—that she was as proud as a queen of her malaise, and that her disaffection found an equal only in her corresponding desire to be "read like a book." It occurred to me as an ultimate irony of Raquel's situation if she were, in fact, a telepath.

"Cherry." Raquel addressed my friend like a preschool teacher would a problem tot. "Why won't you tell us what is in your dreams? It's the most interesting thing there is to tell." Cherry smiled a little, weakly, I thought; said, "I'm too hungry." Indeed, I was famished. Theo took down a stack of plates from the cupboard. I stood up to help him set the table, but Raquel motioned me to sit down again. "Don't worry about it," she said. "He loves to do that sort of thing. Makes him feel humble and centered. Listen," she said, as I sat down. "If Cherry won't tell hers, as host I feel as though I should offer one of mine. But the sad truth is that I never remember my dreams. They're as mysterious to me as they are to you. You can't imagine my dreams, can you? The next best thing, then, is for me to tell you your dream." Cherry shifted a little in her chair, rested her cheek in her hand. I wondered if she had the same achy headache that had embraced my skull. Too much sun, not enough of anything else. I wondered, too, if she had noticed that, in fact, Raquel had told us one of her own dreams not ten minutes before. Or had I heard her wrong. Maybe it was a daydream.

"LET ME SEE, how to begin. You arrive at a house, an old country house, maybe it's on a farm. It's on a slight hill; the fields all around it are incredibly green, an unnatural, sort of acid green. The sky seems to be the only boundary. In all directions the horizon line is just sky meeting field. There is a dry rutted lane, with dusty grass growing up in the middle where wheels never go.

"You have arrived at this house, in the hot midday sunshine, to see your best friend. He is a tall man, all dressed in black like a brother in a religious sect. The Shakers, or the Mennonites. His beard is long and brown, untrimmed, and his eyes are the brown of muddy topsoil."

But this was *my* dream. I'm sure it was my dream. Could it be Cherry's dream, too? I didn't dare look across the table to gauge her reaction. I wanted this dream to be mine, and if I could just hold on to it, tightly, through Raquel's relentless narration . . .

"You are inside the house. There is a big butcher's block in the kitchen. You converse over it, facing each other. He has been accused of a horrible crime—an ax murder. Suddenly, you are afraid. There is something in his eyes now, something in the dark, clouded depths of his familiar eyes that is telling you to run! Run for your life! You trust what you see. He is your best friend, after all, and would not betray you.

"Out you go, out the door and across the little road, straight into the field and across it and over more hills and straight on until you come to an obstacle: your stopping point. A fence that you can't climb, tall, made of wood but with an electrified wire running all along the top. You stand, looking up at the top and past it, at the green fields that stretch beyond, past even where the eye fails.

"There is a presence at your elbow. You turn and catch the eyes of your friend, grinning into your own eyes. He does not even appear to be winded, it is as though he has materialized there next to you. His expression shifts from second to second; his features are kaleidoscopic, they make moues and grimaces, winks and blinks and tics and tears and beaming smiles. 'My friend,' he says, and the fear that is inside you begins to bloom, like a stomach cramp, like the bends of a deep-sea diver.

"'Now you must know the truth,' he intones. You are riveted to the spot. It is clear that he has caught you. You are the culprit. Positions have shifted. That which you came to address, you must now assume responsibility for.

"'Your best friend is your worst enemy.' As he utters these words, all the masks drop away and his one true face is revealed: if he is not the Devil himself, he is certainly at least a powerful demon. . . ."

I'm certain she would have gone on, if Cherry had not slumped forward in her chair, her head hitting the table with a surprisingly hollow crack.

I was up out of my seat before Theo could even say "Oh, shit," from where he stood at the stove. I pulled Cherry up by the shoulders and saw instantly from her rolling eyes and slack mouth that she was having an insulin reaction. I ran to the refrigerator and found apple cider and some marmalade. Raquel asked, "Shall we call anyone?" in a very steady voice. I shook my head, began spooning preserves into Cherry's open mouth. She tasted it on her tongue and then devoured the spoonful. I fed her the entire jar, and by the time it was gone, she was upright and herself again. She washed it all down with a glass of cider.

"That was stupid of me," she said. "To go for so long without eating. I'm diabetic," she explained, apologetic, to Raquel.

"I'll just bet you are," Raquel responded, enigmatically.

"Wow." Theo stepped forward, seeming to insert himself between where Raquel and Cherry sat at the table. He put his arm around Cherry's shoulders. "Are you going to be all right?"

"Oh yes," she said, thickly. "I'm just going to the bathroom." She got up and went out the door and down the hall, where she had left the black fanny pack in which she kept her insulin kit. I heard the bathroom door shut.

"Raquel," Theo said, "I think we should put Cherry to bed."

"Oh, she'll be fine, I'm sure this happens all the time. Ginger can walk her home. The walk will do both of them good. Besides, we haven't had dinner yet. Once she has some of your delicious concoction in her belly . . . she'll be better than ever."

Raquel's tone was eminently reasonable.

BUT THAT IS NOT what happened. We did eat huge plates of some kind of vegetable stew, with zucchini and eggplant and tomato, over pillows of rice. But then somehow, moving as though carried out to sea by a strong current, I left Cherry there, limp on the couch in the living room. She looked blankly at me—or she looked imploringly at me and I looked blankly back; the distinction is a fine one but it makes the difference of a lifetime—and said, "Wait, where are you going?" Theo came downstairs with a blanket and pillow, which he laid at her feet. Raquel said, "Theo, really?" from the top of the stairs, and then receded, dematerializing, ascending into the silence that followed. I told Cherry I would see her tomorrow, and as I closed the door behind me I thought I saw him reach out a hand to touch her hair. I caught just the beginning of the gesture, and felt a sharp, confused stab of misery and exultation. *Sometimes it hurts, growing up:* that's what my mother said to me one day when she found me weeping, consolably, over the final volume in the Anne of Green Gables series, in which Anne has grown so far away from the delightful child she was. The loss of that child could be temporarily ameliorated by beginning at the beginning of the first book again. But this stab felt more like the thrust I felt at the sight of penetration, only higher, somewhere in my chest. My heart contracted, and did not expand again.

I had been waiting patiently for him to touch me again, ever since the Fourth of July. This waiting had added a secret centrality to every day, every evening, every interaction in which the possibility hung lightly, or sometimes with the weight of a thousand breaths, a thousand glances I shot at him. It kept me on the inside of his mind, inside that dark shell, in which he and I were equal in every measure and there was no difference in age, in capacity, in authority. I dwelt in there with him and tried to read his every motion, make with him his every decision—every time he chose to pass behind my chair or reach over me for a book or a knife or a pillow.

So now it was with excruciating clarity that I read his adult motive, his kinetic desire, and because I was so close to him I could not disagree with him. She was more beautiful. She was exquisite, and would exquisitely resist, exquisitely succumb. She would provide him with what I knew he sought from such an encounter: a freshness, a sweetness. An unconscious, living, rushing, breathing doll of life; a girl who would not think but only act, if at first defensively.

I knew I thought too much; it was cast over me like a caul, or like an aura. I did not know if mine had a color but I supposed it must.

Standing on the Motherwells' porch, my hand still on the doorknob, I brought Cherry's face up again before me—her dear face, which had taught me what beauty was. The rounds of her eyes, the slow flush of her pure thoughts, spreading concentrically like pools of water or light, or dark, making blank spots where my love had been.

I LIKE THE IDEA of auras: an organic by-product of living. A gentle, benevolent example of the baffling reserve of potentially real phenomena that we mostly cannot entertain as real, in order to live comfortably. Auras are organic, ghosts are supernatural, the mind is a combustion engine of perception, routinely creating and destroying and creating anew what matters—our hearths, our tongues. Who can dare to navigate these waters and still call herself a useful member of society? It takes all of your breath away. It cleanses your palate of its taste for that which is comfortable. Ordinary knowledge, ordinary society, ordinary love.

But if comfort is not your highest priority, then you might live as we did.

17.

The Accident

I rode my bike down toward the mill, insects whirring in the grass, the air full of sweet evening smells. I sat on the bank of the dry river, watching a pair of crows as they perched motionless, facing each other, on top of the cupola. They looked wicked, in their hunched postures of silhouetted predation. I wondered what they would eat, given the chance.

The sky began its swift evening darkening. I took a tentative stab or two at playing in the castle by myself, but found it unbearably lonely there. It had always been lonely. That was what we had once loved so much, Cherry and I: being lonely as one.

I felt a blanket of regret, of longing, of desire for her thrown over me, followed by a quick tug of relief at the thought that all I need do is to wake up in the morning and call her, as I did so often I can still remember her telephone number today. She would come to the phone and I would ask her if she was all right; wait for her to tell me *what happened*; give her my reassurances, or astonishment, or admiring collusion, or shocked disgust, as the case might be. Then we could go on as before, and we would proceed together, and I would, inevitably, grow up with her. I would be drawn into her world of petty employment, teen love, jealousy and chatter and token rebelliousness, hair-and-makeup, skill sets that turn into character traits.

IT WAS LONG PAST dark when I finally left. I rode my bike fast on the turn down the hill past the Social Club in the pitch-blackness. As I rounded the corner, I barely felt, more heard, a hot, violent nudge, a grunting cry, an engine gunning. I sat in the road. I couldn't actually feel any pain, but then I couldn't actually feel anything, so this was not a useful piece of information.

With the silence of aftermath all around me I began to put the seconds of recent experience into reverse order, working backward from final result: I had been thrown off my seat and into the road by some impact. A motorcycle had pulled out of the Social Club's gravel parking lot just as I came down the hill. It was a blind corner, and it was a miracle, my mother always said, that more accidents didn't happen there, what with all the drinking that went on inside.

Events began to move forward in time again. While I sat in the middle of the road, the motorcyclist dragged his bike back into the parking lot, where another helmeted figure stood, leg slung over his.

While the one with whom I had collided tended to his motorcycle, the other dropped his in the gravel, pushed his helmet to the back of his head, and was making toward me quickly. He knelt down in the middle of the road by my side and I saw that it was Randy Thibodeau. "Kip, man," he yelled to the other, "forget your bike and come help me get her out of the road." Kip Brossard, a boy I remembered from my brother's class in high school.

"Oh, man," Kip said, striding sheepishly into the road, "is she paralyzed?"

"Don't be an idiot, Kip." Randy's long hair was in disarray from the helmet, and he smelled of the motor oil with which he was daily anointed. "She just scraped herself up. She's okay. What kind of asshole are you, though, man, I saw you pull out without even looking. Hey"—to me—"are you all right, Ginger? You've got to be more careful. You were whipping! Lean on my shoulder. Can you move? Should I call 911? Let's get you out of the road."

This last injunction seemed like a sensible one, and so I gripped his outstretched hand, threw my other arm around his neck, and leaned heavily on his shoulder as he drew me up to my feet with incongruous tenderness. I remembered then that Randy was one of seven children, the eldest, in fact, and that he could often be seen parading one or another of his youngest siblings around on his shoulders, or squiring them to the pizza parlor for a slice. He had practice in tenderness.

Randy walked me solicitously over to a bench by the door of the Social Club, Kip dancing antically at his elbow. The outside lights winked to blackness as Randy and I sat down and I heard the back door slam, then lock. Presently a large black car emerged slowly from behind the Club. The bartender, Stan Lipski, looked out his window at the three of us curiously. “Hey, Randy, Kip, give it a rest, dudes,” he called out the window, and laughed in a suitably suggestive manner, then pulled out into the road and toward home.

“Oh, great,” Randy said. “That’s all I need is more rumors. Listen, Ginger, are you okay?” I nodded my assent, moving my head carefully up and down, then side to side, to test the stability of my vertebrae. Everything seemed to work. I predicted that I would have a large bruise on my left thigh and side, where I’d landed. My palm was skinned.

Randy left me to walk back out to the road, haul my bicycle up by the handles, and wheel it over to lean it against the wall. Kip took this opportunity to shuffle away, calling, “Hey, I’ve got to get home. You in charge, Randy?”

“Sure, whatever, man. Just next time you decide to run someone over, make sure you finish the job.” The two of them laughed, and Kip kick-started his bike and roared away.

I sat for a few minutes, my whole body beginning to throb in time with my heartbeat. “Man,” Randy said, looking me over. “My mom always used to make me wear a helmet. I would bitch her out about it every time, but now I’m like, ‘Where’s yours?’ Are you sure your head is okay?”

I nodded. He paused a minute, then sighed and sat down beside me on the bench. “Nice night,” he said, craning his neck, squinting up at the profusion of stars as though they were suns. “What were you doing down here so late?”

I didn’t want to tell him where I’d been, any of the places I’d been. I sat quietly and hoped he would take my silence for shock.

“Do you need to call your mom for a ride home? I’d totally take you on my bike but I don’t have an extra helmet.

I've got a key to the back door of the Club. You could use the phone in there."

I pictured the empty barroom, lit only by a pinball machine and the glow from the refrigerated case where they kept bottles of soda. Randy would maneuver me carefully through the door and to a chair at a table by the bar. He'd go look for the phone and come back with it in his hand, then put it gently on the table. Then he would kneel down at my feet and take my shoes off. "Let me see the point of impact," he might say, or something more directly salacious, like "Show me where it hurts." He would push my sweater up to expose my ribs, and move his mouth up to graze the delicate skin just under my breasts. I wore no bra—I didn't really need one. He might cup my breast, and kiss my throat. He would proceed from there to undress my lower half very carefully, tenderly, gently, lifting and lowering each limb to avoid injuring me further.

I didn't know that I wanted it, but it dawned on me what a perfect exchange this would make. My virginity for hers, her loss an exploitation of vulnerability, mine a gallant, courtly, supportive act. I began to rise, cautiously, but Randy stood up before I could and proffered his arm for balance. "If you're sure you're okay, I really need to ask you about something." He looked slightly past my face, into the dark trees edging the road. "I'm going nuts here. Cherry won't talk to me, hasn't talked to me in days. She's mad at me because she thinks that I'm still interested in Terry, because, now we're like, going out, me and Cherry, but she just found out that last week Terry came over to my place above the shop with some other dudes and we got really wasted and she ended up staying over. But so did, like, three other guys! And I swear they all just slept on my floor. Terry was so out of it she puked in my fish tank—killed all my goddamned fish, man." He pulled his helmet all the way off his head now in a flurry of earnestness, and wiped the sweat from his brow into his hair with a blue bandanna he retrieved from his back pocket. "You have to talk to her for me, Ginger. Just get her alone and tell her what I told you. She'll listen to you. I swear I would never do anything to hurt her. She's, like . . . I really care about her.

"When you see her, will you tell her that she's really special to me and I want her to know that?"

I have to confess I was moved by his distress and could not bring myself to tell him that it was not likely that I would soon have such an opportunity.

I gave him my word.

"And tell your mom and dad I said hi," Randy said as I started off. "It's been a long time."

I REMEMBER THE DAY Jack died. Actually, he died in the middle of the night, Halloween night, time of death approximately two-thirty a.m., dead drunk, on his back, drowning in his own vomit in the backseat of Randy's dad's car, so what I remember is the next morning, the morning that we learned of his death during the night before, when he might have been home sleeping in his bed. If anything could have kept him home. Early in the morning, around five a.m., the doorbell rang. I burrowed into my bed. I heard the doorbell but I heard it in my dream, and searched for a door to open there. Meanwhile my mother sprang to life in her and my father's room, feet hitting the floor before her eyes opened. In the graveyard, an officer on patrol had shone his flashlight on something terrible. At the door she collapsed, and Officer Collins called for my father to come and help him get her to the sofa. His voice woke me, finally. I stood at the door of my bedroom and watched my father go past in his bathrobe and bare feet; my mother wailed the news. "Jack," she cried, and the impossible made possible colored the whole day invisible: it made the day disappear into itself, a voided, emptying, vacuous processional. I could not wait till the lights went out again, but it would take a long time to get there. Someone was removed; we would never see someone again. The extraction was painful. My mother hung her head over the sink in the kitchen and wept and puked for a long time, emptying herself; my father held her hair back from her face. Then they sat on the couch, or rather my father sat and my mother lay with her head in his lap, her eyes closed. I was sitting, or standing, I don't know, in a corner of the room. My father beckoned me to them but I had the sensation that I had to keep watch over the room, that I had to keep as wide an angle of perception as possible, so that I could keep anything else from entering, unwanted.

I REMEMBER A FEW THINGS about the day before the night Jack died. It was a Saturday, the day he died, and he was going to go out that night, as he had done the night before, with his friends. No costume—he was too old for that. In the morning, his last morning, he woke up late, around eleven. I had been up for hours, eating my cereal, watching a little TV, reading my copy of *Highlights*, the kids' magazine I'd subscribed to since I was five years old. It was full of puzzles and poems and simple stories and educational games. I would cancel my subscription when I was twelve, after Cherry hinted to me that it was impossibly immature. I was lurking, hoping that when Jack woke up we'd do something fun—maybe we'd rake leaves together in the yard, and he would throw me into the piles, or maybe we would play gin rummy, one of the few games I was good at. I had hoped that later he might take Cherry and me around town, house to house, door to door, trick-or-treating, but he had made it clear that this was out of the question. My mother was probably straightening the house, as she often did on the weekend. My father might have been reading the newspaper, or working on something out in the garage. I waited, and finally Jack rolled out of his room and into the bathroom, where I could hear him lightly grunting and brushing and spitting all the way from where I lay on the living room floor, in the sun, reading my dorky magazine.

"Hey kid," he said, as he dropped down into a seat at the kitchen table and peeled a banana from the fruit bowl. "I've got to go down to the hardware store and see about a job. Enough of this freeloading off of Mom and Dad, right?" He cleared his throat. He'd been smoking, lately; I'd seen him. "Do I look presentable?" He stood up and revolved to show me the backside of his creamy corduroys, his plaid shirt, both rumpled. I loved him so much. I didn't understand why he couldn't always be as nice to me as he was right then. It was no skin off his back. He turned around to show me his front and I gave him a thumbs-up.

"Maybe when I get back we can do something, okay?" He knew how much I wanted that. My knowledge of this knowledge only slightly reduced the value of his offer. I nodded, but I knew that he would disappear into the day, off on his bike. He would bump into his friends on the green and they would drift around together all day until dinnertime, and then after dinner he would head off with Randy in his car to go loiter in the graveyard, drinking beers and laughing, leapfrogging gravestones, jumping on the backs of the dead, jeering at their misfortune, desecrating their silence, dismembering their corpses, disrespectful at the end in a way he had not been at the beginning.

18.

My collision served as a fine excuse for a retirement. I limped home, wheeling my bike, and showed my mother the purple, lake-like bruise that spilled over my outer thigh, my green ribs, my abraded palm, and her reaction was deeply satisfying: she brought out all the liniments and bandages at her disposal and went to work on me, then sent me to my bed in clean pajamas. She pursed her lips at the mention of Randy's name, and grew more silent than before. Randy, forever sleeping soundly in the passenger's seat of her sorrow while Jack dies forever in the back.

Cherry called for me several times during these days, but I would not come to the phone. I did not speak to anyone about this refusal, not even to myself. I just did not come to the phone. It was a consequence that had no action—a blank, spreading spot where the reason might have been. A growing child does not get many opportunities to regress into unreason, to retract the steps she has taken toward adult accountability. I was mute to myself like an infant. I answered my mother's quizzical looks, as she stood with her hand over the receiver of the phone, with what I imagined could be taken as a typical teenager's expression of private outrage, implying that Cherry and I had had a typical teenage falling-out. We had fallen out. My mother was glad to see me doing something typical, glad to see me at all, and I was happy to trail around after her, for a change, to go for pizza, to the library for books, to the video store to rent one of the Pink Panther movies she found so hilarious.

But then I happened to pick up the phone one morning, early, and Cherry began to sob into it immediately, like I was a slot machine, her tears, quarters. I would begin pouring out consolation when she hit the lucky combination.

"Ginger," Cherry said, hiccuping through her tears, "where have you been?" She did not wait for me to answer. "Meet me at the mill, okay, I really need to talk to you. Something terrible happened and I can't tell anyone about it besides you. I have to go now—my mom's coming up. I'll be there at two-thirty."

I PUT DOWN the phone and wondered how soon it would be proper for me to see the Motherwells again. *I should have stayed,* I thought, or felt. I could not—cannot still—tell the difference. I should have stayed.

I thought of Theo's early, incomplete warning at the kitchen table. He had enjoined us, as a unit, to *watch out,* as though we were indivisible. It had made me want to distinguish myself, I thought; to accelerate a process that had already been put in motion by Cherry's increasing preoccupations, her leaning away from me. But if "watchfulness" meant keeping one's self from harm, staying "safe," then it had been an ineffectual warning indeed.

And here I WAS, still only a child, after all, with my childhood perfectly available to me, intact as the hymen of a virgin is purported to be. I thought of Cherry, and a veil of the old love, old loyalty came down gently over my eyes. I closed my eyes and lifted the veil; beneath it I saw not my own face, but hers. I could go and meet her, sit with her, stroke her hair, listen to her version of events. I could relay to her Randy's tale of devotion. That would help her to forget any intrusions that might have been made upon her person.

But then I thought of a daring shortcut. I went to the cabinet where my parents kept the slender county phone book. Thibodeau was a common surname, and there were even several R. Thibodeaus, but after a few embarrassing attempts I hit on the one I was looking for.

ON THE THIRD DAY, still bruised but mending, I went back to work at the café. Halfway through my shift Raquel opened the door, making its little bell ring. She approached the counter, smiling, and asked me what time I got off. She suggested we go for a walk in the graveyard, the old one in the churchyard on the green. She asked me to meet her there at five-thirty. I had told my parents I would be home in time for supper, six-thirty-ish, but I supposed, opportunistically, that it was possible that I might still make it.

19.

Three towns live under that water. It is a morbidly fertile, eventually ghastly image if you give it time to settle in and materialize. Jack's scale model at life-size: dark frame houses, barns and fences and even the odd stick of furniture, all standing down at the bottom of a remarkably deep, remarkably wide well of man-made origin. Now, this is what I call supernatural: times that float in recollection but are history till we reanimate them with powerful imagination. The past is frightening. But not for any reason I can put my finger on.

Oddly enough, those had been the exact questions occupying the better part of me that day, while Raquel was coming to get me so unexpectedly at the café. "What is ghostly? What is otherworldly?"—meanwhile I was keeping my hands busy clearing plates, and filling coffee cups, and making change for customers to tip with or to plug the antiquated parking meters (nickels only) right outside our door on Main Street. I was thinking about drowned houses, their endless quiet; and graveyards, and about nightmares, musing on their respective potentials for actual fright, for real transports of terror. I was not thinking about Cherry, for I was after all a child, and a child knows how to create a new world for herself in the blink of an eye. The snap of a shutter.

A whole world of fright that the whole world knows about, the kind you get walking alone in the woods—not necessarily at night, though that helps—when you begin to allow your mind to wander toward what you know, surefire, will scare you. A face so ugly and dead, or madly gaping, or slackly grinning in idiocy, or covered in blood and abjectly weeping, that it fits the bill exactly and causes you to short-circuit and panic, and quickly enclose yourself in your own arms and then, as swiftly as possible (but without running because the last thing you want to do is attract attention to yourself, to your small, unprotected head) in your own house, and shut the door jerkily behind you. Only then can you stand to look around at what is not there behind you, but instead is inside you. It is inside you. So in the end it is only our imagination that is haunted. Or: what haunts us is imagination.

SHE WAS NOT AFRAID of the dead, she said; she was only afraid of other people. I wondered if she would talk this way if Cherry were there. I didn't think so. I had noticed a very different tenor to Raquel's conversation, or monologue, more accurately, when it was just me there, or me and Theo; anyway, when Cherry wasn't around. A less worldly, more introspective tone, as though she was talking to herself, really, though she told me once that this was quite literally the last thing she would ever do. "I'll talk to myself when I'm dead," she said. But it was as though for Cherry she had developed a patter, one suitable to the ears of a typical teenaged girl. Now she would have no need for that kind of fake talk.

"I'll tell you what really scares me," she said. Now I was listening to her with one ear, as with my other I was attentive to the possibility of unnatural rustling in the hedges, the noise of dead people's bodies risen up and watching. "What scares me is when you come face-to-face with some person or other, in a room somewhere, and you look into the other person's eyes and instead of the flash of recognition, of acknowledgment, you receive instead a transmission of void, of absence, of abyss. It's just hell, looking into another person's eyes; it's dead in there, you know. I become afraid."

When you're looking at a face, I corroborated silently, trying to talk to that face, and the harder you try not to, the more you see the impending mutation of the face, the way the eyes and the mouth threaten to slide, or gape, or hollow, to become unknown. And this is the face of a friend.

"Where *is* Cherry, by the way?" Raquel plucked her out of my thoughts like the fruit my friend was named for. "It's not like you to be without her." This was true, but I felt that Raquel was being disingenuous. She knew as well as I did—more likely, far better than I did—that things had changed.

"I AM THE DIRECT descendant of a woman who was hung for a witch." She said this the way you might say "I am the ghost of Christmas past," or "I am a fugitive from a chain gang," as though somebody else had written the words and said them out loud long before you were born, and with much more conviction. I just looked at her and waited. I was frightened. Not so much by her declaration as by the fact that we were still sitting, face-to-face, our crossed legs almost touching at the knees, in the churchyard, by a gravestone, under a tree, in the dark. There was barely any light at all from the moon, or the stars, or the houses around the green. We had stayed and stayed in the graveyard that late afternoon, and on into the evening. I was stiff with chill, with holding myself very still in the dark, and with the residual ache of my impact with the road. Every time I thought that we might leave, that we had reached the natural end of the episode, Raquel would begin to spin another tale, another train of thought, another musing preoccupation. Now I had the sense that all along, all day, she had been waiting till darkness fell to tell me this story. She had been saving it.

"This is called beginning at the beginning," she said solemnly. Her face was close to mine. I could see its outlines, almost phosphorescent as my eyes adjusted to the nearness.

"I do not entertain notions of guilt or innocence, in the telling of this story. Her name was Sarah Goode. She was the wife of Joseph Goode, and the mother of eleven children, all but seven of whom died in their infancy, and she was my great-grandmother eleven times over. Sarah was an upstanding member of her community, a small farming village up north of the city."

Everything was so quiet around us that her voice seemed to be coming from everywhere at once, from the night sky and from the headstones, the shapes of which I could just barely make out.

"She was an old woman, living peacefully with her husband on their farm, when certain townsfolk got it into their heads that she was a witch.

"You know, they did actually designate certain members of the community, usually those who had displayed an especial zeal for the task, as witch-finders, or as administrators of the tests they had devised, to identify witches more officially. My favorite of these was the infallible water test: If she floats, she's a witch. If she drowns, she wasn't.

"These small villages were rough places to try to make a go of it. The people struggled throughout the brutal winter and worked like demons—if you'll pardon the expression—in the hot, lush summer, just to put up enough food and wood to make it through another winter. It must have made some hard, hard people, this closed circle of resources. Sarah was hard. When they took this seventy-something-year-old woman to the jail, all she did was stand still with her head bowed, and pray. She said to herself, and then, later, to those who sat behind the bench and sentenced her to death, 'The will of the Lord be done, and no other.' "

At Raquel's recitation of this solemn motto, a huge shiver ran up, and then back down, my spine, which I could not help but remember was exposed to an entire churchyard full of graves, which in turn were full of the moldered bones of centuries of my townspeople. I felt as though my back was bare, as though my sweatshirt and T-shirt and skin itself had been peeled away.

"There are many theories—socioeconomic, psychoanalytic, biochemical, even—defining the factors that contributed to this sweep of spiritual executions. The Goode family, which was particularly called out on the witchcraft charge—two of Sarah's sisters were accused, too, and one hung—was well off, relative to the rest of that scrabbling community. They lived on a hill, literally *above* the rest of the town. Their farm was prosperous. They owned a lot of acreage, and even collected rent from some of the other families, a relationship always sure to incur rancor. The concept of "surplus" was unavailable to most, and this is just what the Goode family possessed. Their pantries were full, they had actual cash with which to purchase goods.

"But can you imagine such calculation? I like to think that the process was more subliminal, that the accusers (who were, you know, virtually all teenaged girls) were simply overcome with the power of their own imaginations, and with what they had succeeded in creating. Think of it: grown men sitting all day with a group of girls, eating up their every last utterance! They were possessed, I believe. By themselves. By an experience of transcendent meaning. They suddenly meant something.

"So they spun, and spun—and wouldn't you?—the most fabulous truths they could come up with. 'Goody Rich came to me in my bed and tweaked my nipple and told me I must sign the book or she would make my father's cows go dry. Then a yellow bird hung upside-down on the beam and spoke in the voice of John Rector's wife and said that she had walked beside the Black Man and drunk his spittle.' Don't you think, in a sense, that she had experienced just exactly that, the night before, lying in her bed, a fever of possibility upon her? In fact, I don't see how anyone managed to escape the ecstasy of these girls, 'the afflicted,' as they were called. Once it was seen that they would invariably be believed, that their words had a universal, indisputable meaning, for once in their grim, untranslatable lives . . ." Suddenly, unaccountably, in the darkness that was all around us like light, she was at a loss for words.

"I'm not cold. Are you? The ground is damp, though." Her voice held all the hesitant panic that moments of silence produced in her. "Shall I go on? I said I would begin at the beginning, which implies ending at the end." She scooted back on her bottom a little, uncrossed her legs and then crossed them in reverse order. "That's better," she said. "Gosh. It's getting late. It doesn't even get dark till nine o'clock . . ."

I knew my parents would be worrying about me, and I chose not to care, and indicated this with the unwavering tenor of my silence. Raquel went on, and regained her footing as the story got steeper.

"These were very religious people. Pious as all get-out. They would dig their way through four-foot-high snowdrifts to get to the frigid church where they could see their own breath, and sit and listen to the minister stamp his frozen feet and rail against the sins of fornicators and pleasure-seekers. 'Where?' they must have wondered, looking around the congregation for any telltale signs. To these folk, morality was not an issue of free will. At least they had that responsibility removed from their overburdened shoulders. If you did wrong, if you sinned, it was because you had the Devil in you, with a capital D. It was because you had actually been visited by the Black Man, and he had gained control of your soul.

"Sarah had a short trial. She was hung two days later. One gets the sense that for her it was all a matter of bad timing. Two months later, or even six weeks, the townspeople had begun to look around at one another like puppies who have pissed the carpet."

WHILE I HAD NOT always been the most attentive student, I did remember quite clearly my eighth-grade class's inquiry into this black spot of history. I remembered, for example, that one of several theories ran that the town's winter stores of grain had grown moldy in the humid coastal winds, and that the afflicted girls were high on psychedelic oats and barley and corn. Thus I could not doubt Raquel—why should I doubt her?—when she went on to tell of a concurrent history: how the Goode family, or at least what remained of it, had left their village and come inland to make a new life in this very region, in the prosperous Shift River valley.

But what I did wonder about was the seemingly universal desire to settle on every explanation for these accusations but the most obvious. What if the women and men had been burned not as a by-product of greed, or inequality, or sheer envy and mistrust, or mind-altering grain, for that matter, *but because they were witches*? Why overlook the trees that stood in the forest so sternly, so full of promise? I do not wish to take up arms against an army of skeptics, but rather to make an argument in favor of that which is, simply, more interesting. Raquel, for example, was obviously and inarguably a mind reader, for she laughed at this, laughed out loud at my silent thoughts, my thoughts which tended toward darkness, and put her arms around me, reaching across the cauldron of darkness between us. Her embrace was loose but warming, and when she let me go I felt the chill air, the damp earth, more exquisitely.

20.

"What if I told you we had seen a ghost in the graveyard." Raquel stood in the doorway of the kitchen, combing her fingers through her dripping hair. It had begun to rain as we walked back.

"Would it be the truth?" Theo spoke without turning to look at her from where he stood at the countertop, slicing mushrooms. I regarded his back, and neck, and shoulders, the long rhomboid muscle that allowed his regular motion. I suddenly saw him on top of Cherry, like a photograph from the pages of *The Beginner* brought to life, his ass between her legs, his torso obscuring hers, an irregular rhythm governed by invisible motive, an ungovernable finish. And I then saw the ghost that might have followed us home, watching them, relieved for a moment of his infinite loneliness.

"At least it's a partial truth," Raquel offered, blithely. "And you know every partial truth contains a germ of absolute truth. It's like genetic cloning, whereby you only need one dong." I was surprised by the sound, but I was not surprised when neither Raquel nor Theo made a move to answer its call.

We all sat very still and presently I heard footsteps, on the porch, down the step, moving away off through the night. The ghost of a visitor.

STATIONED BEFORE JACK'S MODEL of the lost valley, peering in the minuscule windows of the tiny houses at microscopic figures engaged in passing plates around a table, or zooming out to regard the valley as a whole, its rich soils and plentiful waterways, I have often thought of a more distant past, of the people who left the civilized but brutal coastline of Massachusetts to stake a claim on the promise of the river. They found a fertile valley and made all the motions of settling: clearing land, raising structures, forging institutions, establishing trade, begetting sons and daughters. A few generations down the line, we were flourishing. We had sturdy businesses and charming society, an outlying scenery of pretty farms and their structures. This is when the most beautiful houses in Wick were built, all gathered together like a meeting of elders: when citizens were feeling secure, stable, even flush. These houses, lining our serene village green, a monument to certainty, are truly wonderful to behold. They speak volumes about what is inside, and what is out. Inside is for the privilege of privacy and inheritance. Outside is for those who peer, and pry, and try to get inside.

Or at least this is what Raquel explained to me, one day when we wandered out to the green. "These houses," she said. "I could stare at them forever and not get enough. They satisfy every fantasy I've ever had. If I lived in one of these houses, the dream of my life would end and I would finally be living the real life. Because I could rest assured that I need never move again. These houses are not only built to last, but they were built to suit and meet the needs of their inhabitants. They held families together. No one could have ever guessed that they would be passed outside the family—much less sold to a stranger."

But Raquel expressed disapproval at the presence of the old mill in Wick, about which Theo was quite curious. He wanted to see inside, he said, someday. It simply didn't fit into her notion of what our small town should be. It was, indeed, the only remaining shred of evidence that at one time Wick had held a promise of industry and economy. It was the ghost of our utility; at one time, there was a reason to move here, and many people did. There would have been nothing odd about such a decision, back then.

21.

I told Theo and Raquel to come have breakfast that Saturday, down at the Top Hat. I thought it would be fun for all of us, to see one another back there, where we first met, but now with all that we shared between us. Like clandestine lovers greeting each other in an Elizabethan drawing room, I would serve them with teasing formality, dipping the coffeepot down over their half-empty cups like a mother bird, slinging food on their table like a discus thrower.

I hadn't given a thought, though, to our potential observers: Who would be there to see us? I had grown so used to the mobile bubble that seemed to hold us, to enclose us, and to shield us, that somehow I had envisioned the Top Hat, and us in it together, as though it were a movie set, cleared for a nude scene at the modest actress's demand.

Therefore I grew nervous as I waited for them that morning, and waited, eyes fidgeting on the door and on the street outside the window, anticipating and reanticipating their arrival. Raquel would appear first, in the corner of the window, her long bare arm swinging into view; then Theo stretching along the sidewalk in her shadow. I acquired an acute awareness of those customers who would witness their entry, to whom I had previously given no thought at all. There would certainly be other customers at the café, and they would indeed take notice of the Motherwells—after all it was a small town, and people talked. Or some people did. And I began to feel a shadowy kind of doubled consciousness growing in me, a second-guessing of my own motive. Was it possible that I had invited them here exactly in order to have a witness or two, or three? Witness to what, exactly. I might have to name it.

Even under normal circumstances I would have been unusually attuned to the presence of Todd Armstrong, who sat at the counter eating a grilled corn muffin, poring over an abandoned copy of *Newsweek*. He was a boy in my class who, like me, didn't speak much. He was tall, like me, but unlike me quite athletic. He played basketball, silently, his tunic showing off the large, fine muscles of his back and shoulders moving like levers and pulleys, chutes and pistons. Many of the boys in our class still looked generally as they had since they were small. Todd was growing manly, but doing so in a sweet way that made the result look worth the effort. His upper lip was shaded by fuzz; his pants were always a little short for him; he moved through space with a deliberation that made me think that he had suffered some dizzying growth spurts and wasn't quite sure yet where his body ended and space began. Most important, to my mind, he liked to read, and I had seen him at the library, at one of the big tables in the center of the room, making a careful selection from a large pile of thick books. I think he preferred useful texts—I looked up from Gore Vidal's witty memoir *Palimpsest* one deep winter afternoon and caught a glimpse of a tome in his large hands whose spine trumpeted *Complete Organic Gardening*. I thought it winsome that he could have been dreaming of planting on such a short, bitter day.

Now he was eating. I stood there with Agatha Christie's *And Then There Were None*—I always stowed a mystery at the café, should it prove a slow shift—and refilled his water glass every few minutes, just to watch him empty it, his rocky Adam's apple chugging like another piston in his throat, as thick around as my thigh.

He swallowed the last of the corn muffin and stood up to fish some money out of his jeans pocket. He was looking down and I almost didn't hear him. "Whatcha been doing lately, Ginger? I haven't seen you at the library in a while." The thought that he might have been looking for me in that one-room sanctuary—looking for me anywhere; that he might have actually come to the Top Hat not just for our superlative corn muffin—dawned on me electrically. He looked at me and projected something that made me look away. It was a hope, and it caused his brown eyes to look wet, and open. He shifted his gaze away, too, to the clock above my head. "What time do you get off? I could walk you home." My shift was over soon, but I couldn't leave—Raquel and Theo might be on their way right now. I mentioned that someone was coming to see me, and saw his hopes dashed. Was it the skin around his eyes that made these various expressions, or the shape of the eyeballs themselves, or the muscles supporting them? What creates these perceptible differences in the look in someone's eyes?

Todd turned to the street, as though to see who might have staked this claim on me, and nodded at a shape I hadn't noticed, leaning against the glass at the far end of the window. Half a jean-jacketed form, a scraggly ponytail, a hand pressed on the steamed-up glass, a lean hip. It was Randy. A concatenation, a roaring in my ears and a piling up of variables, too much I hadn't been able to calculate in my ambitious little plan for the morning. It was clear I was not in control of anything, and that I ought never to make a plan again. I would remain unplanned, as my conception had been, according to some hints my mother had let drop from time to time. My consciousness underwent that painful doubling, or was it splitting—a cellular type of division or like the slides of mitosis we had observed in biology class as I absorbed the situation in which I *did not know* something about myself, something that someone else did know. It was obvious he was waiting for me, Randy, and I suffered a quick revulsion—how could I have been so weak as to risk this kind of exposure? Did he know something already, or had he come to find out? I was ashamed to think that I might have dimly, self-unknowingly, like a single-celled organism, sought shelter from my friends in the gaze of this public setting. There was Randy, who owed me everything, love and death, now and forever, yet I could also plainly see, and understand, that he wanted something from me, and at the same time wanted to offer something to me. I could see it, and Todd could see it, though what he thought he saw was my fulfilled hope: my date. What he really saw in the window was a young man who wanted some answers.

. . .

THAT DAY I WALKED toward home with Todd Armstrong. He ushered me out of the café, and we nodded at Randy as we passed. Randy raised his eyebrows, combined amusement and annoyance, and tried to hold my gaze and impart something to me, but I shuffled closer to Todd and implied by this small gesture that we could not be disturbed. And so we weren't, and walked as far as the library together, where I told him I'd need to stop, by myself, to do some extra-credit work for school. I obviously didn't have any schoolwork with me, and I'm sure he found me very mysterious, and was perhaps relieved even to be rid of me, as I had been scared stiff to be walking side by side with this living, breathing human being who "liked me."

For he had decided that I was the one he "liked"—he'd told me so; announced it with the categorical definition of a schoolboy's crush. Cherry would have been atwitter with excitement if she could have shared this knowledge with me, but alone with myself I felt instead a terrible fear, stronger, more paralyzing than any I had ever felt.

Categorically, this fear felt very different from the kinds of fear with which I was familiar. I knew the fear of death, realized; I knew the fear of inexplicable adults and their hot, degenerative plans; I knew the fear that comes laced with ameliorative promise of adventure. And I knew the fear of a life that might come to nothing.

But the fear of Todd was overwhelming, immediate, crashing, for he had come unexpectedly, with a full complement of independent thought and motive, to give himself to me. It was as though I had opened my clenched fist and observed his open, wet eyes in the palm of my hand making a painful demand on me with their offering, their communication, their bald invitation to the human stuff inside, particolored if you looked carefully enough, deeply enough. I was not prepared for this communication—not up to the responsibility, the weight of it a smothering. I once responded to my English teacher's assignment that we write about "the most beautiful thing we'd ever seen"—she tried hard, Mrs. Kislak—with a short disquisition on Cherry's own brown eyes, her whole sublime personage represented axially in its variousness by wheeling spokes of gold and ochre and chestnut—but had thought better of it, crumpled up my paper and written instead on infinitely less tease-worthy subject matter: my mother's prize rosebushes, flanking our little-used front door.

I thought of the power of witchcraft. At least one citizen in my small town might have believed a spell had been successfully cast on me, in that pale green house on the hill. When we are truly under a spell we are freed from a certain natural instinct for self-preservation, and we might prick ourselves with pins over and over and over, at another's behest. We have been steeled to this, by the force of another's will and wit and craft. How else could I have withstood all that I did? How else could I have cast myself out, set myself afloat, allowed the deep waters of these days to rise? There could be no possible explanation but witchcraft, sorcery, enchantment. This is the simplest.

22.

Now it was really just the three of us, and though they had rejected, dismissed, or simply overlooked my recent attempt at an organizing gesture, I thought that I still might be of some use to Theo, in his role as Raquel's guide, or guard, or guardian. I thought I might do something to help break Raquel's torpor, regain whatever footing it was she'd lost in the world. The way was clear. Her book! I would help her to find her footing in her book. As a native of Wick, I was an ideal guide to its repositories and relics. For instance, I knew that the Agnes Grey Library would offer only the most rudimentary public documents. I had spent several weeks one hot summer absorbed in the Wick town records of births and deaths gathered there in many old leather-bound volumes, and knew that while it would be the place to determine that none of her family had settled in Wick itself, it would not tell her much beyond that.

What I had access to that Raquel, as a newcomer to the

town and a virtual recluse at that, did not, was its living, breathing historians.

WHEN I ASKED HIM for advice, Mr. Penrose recommended that I go see Hep Warren, the old man who ran the Historical Society in the little parish house next to the church.

I went by the next day, a Friday, in the morning, but the door was locked. A wooden plaque hung on a nail driven into the door, with its white paint layered thickly and full of crackles: "Be Back Soon."

I decided to wait, and walked across the green to Lawson's General Store to buy some gum. Becky Lawson was at the cash register, stamping price tags on boxes of crackers with a big price gun that went *shock-uh* as she pulled the trigger. I talked with her for a minute. She had been in my French class and we laughed facilely over the presumed senility of Mrs. Clinger, our teacher, who when she did not refer to us simply as her little cabbages called us by the names of our parents, as though she presided over a stalled classroom, an underwater classroom of permanence.

I looked out through the screen door into the haze of the summer morning, the bright grass of the green made somehow denser, more dimensional through the tiny crosshatching. I asked Becky what she knew about that whole flooding thing, over my shoulder, and she looked up and thought carefully before she said, "I dunno, whattayou know? I never thought much about it." And then we were quiet, as quiet as the giant wall of stillness that had spilled into those towns—the Lost Towns, as some of the more rancorous, or more regretful in the town called them—as quiet as the old blacktopped roads you could still walk on, but not to get anywhere. As quiet as the water's edge.

"But you know there's really nothing down there, right?" She spoke suddenly, liquidly. "A lot of times people say that there's houses and churches and stuff left down there, that you can see tops of buildings and steeples through the water when it gets low enough, if there's a drought or something, and even old roads from up in a plane, but it's not true, that's just a story people use to try to spook you. Really, they burned everything, they knocked everything down. Or sometimes people moved their houses. My grampa and gramma moved our house up from the valley on a flatbed truck. They have pictures of it over at the Historical Society."

I told her that that was my next destination.

"Why are you so interested all of a sudden?" she asked, leaning forward over the counter to peer out the screen door in the direction I was looking. "Is that what those people are doing here? Those people you and Cherry have been hanging out with?"

That's for me to know and you to find out, I thought to myself, digging up a childhood chestnut of secretiveness as I pushed out the screen door, hot cinnamon gum in hand, but all I said was something about extra-credit projects for senior history next year. Now she'd probably go tell her friends that Ginger Pritt really was a Goody Two-shoes, doing schoolwork in the middle of summer. Todd Armstrong would agree.

. . .

I CROSSED THE GREEN again and there was a favorable sign, a car parked at the Historical Society. The door was open and I blinked in the dimness of the old structure with its low ceilings, little light coming through small windows. Flies buzzed against the thick bottle-glass panes with their wavy perspectives on an age I was only partially glad to have missed.

The front room, what would have been a sitting room, served as a museum for old dresses, old plates, old chairs, old etchings. The dresses were shockingly small—child-sized. I stood next to a wedding gown on a dressmaker's dummy and my shoulders were nearly twice as broad. It must be true, what they say, I thought, about modern nutrition.

"Hello, there!" Mr. Warren stepped out of a small back room, through the doorway of which I could see dusty shrouded shapes and a desk with a round circle of light over it. I'd known Mr. Warren all my life, but seen him mostly down at the town offices, where he served as Notary Public, Town Clerk, and a few other things.

"Can I help you, Ginger?" he said, and came out into the front room, holding his glasses in one hand. I could tell that he was surprised and pleased to see me there, the way adults always are when children "take an interest" in their interests, in genealogy, in knitting, in procreation.

I told him what I was looking for, and his eyebrows flew up. "Well, Ginger, I wish I *could* help you, indeed I do. Fact is, it's awful difficult for us to track the comings and goings of folks from the lost towns back in those early days. You know the big fire in 1851 gutted the Shadleigh Town Hall and many of the records were destroyed—births, deaths, marriages, deeds, etc.—in the flames. It's a real shame. Kind of wiped out a whole lot of history. However, if you're really in the spirit of it, the Shift River Valley Historical Society up in Swansbury has whatever papers were salvaged—some of them you can still read—plus all the records after that, and it has all sorts of old photographs that people took when they were trying to document their properties before they were demolished, when the water came. The industry, the houses, the farms, the daily lives of the people of the area. Pretty much anybody you'd be looking for would be likely to show up somewhere, if you've got the time."

I thanked him and turned to go, eager to find Raquel, to tell her what I'd learned. I stopped by the door to look at the photograph Becky had mentioned; it showed a small, square house, with a pitched roof, featureless aside from its blank square windows and door, being hauled on an old flatbed truck down a dirt track though the middle of what looked like a desert, or a representation of some uninhabitable planet's arid surface, but was actually the once-thriving center of the razed village of Shadleigh.

The gentle hills of Wick rose at the perimeter of the image.

Mr. Warren saw me still standing there. "Oh," he said, picking up the thread again—and I was filled with dread that he, like so many old people do, would carry the conversation on and on, long past when I wanted to end it—"and of course there's the big Ramapack cemetery, where they moved all the graves they dug up before they flooded the valley. If you're looking for any folks in particular, you're sure to find them there. Problem is, those Canucks just laid the stones in all willy-nilly, just however they came off the truck, with no thought for which town or which family plot they belonged in. That's a real shame, too. Kind of like a second death for those people, like dying all over again." His mouth closed with some finality and his bright blue eyes clicked onto a more cordial vision. "How's your pa? Your ma?" He paused a beat over the absent Pritt, the one whose presence I seemed to feel more and more every day, an intermittent shadow at the periphery of my movement, my gaze. A spot of white, a spot of dark. I blinked to confirm its presence and he seized upon this as acquiescence. "I hear they're doing real well with the printing business? I might need to order more of these flyers soon, if we get a few visitors this summer." He held up a brochure with a line drawing of the old church on it and the hours of the Historical Society printed along with some lines of text: "Wick is no relic of bygone days. Here we preserve and cherish our modern promise and offer to the world the fruits of our everlasting labors."

Who on earth, I wondered, as I hopped on my bike, had composed that garbled message? And who would ever read it?

I thought about going by myself, right now, out to the Ramapack cemetery, to look for the Goode family, but went instead on the now familiar path past the high school and up the Motherwells' driveway. I walked my bike around back and went in through the kitchen door. Raquel was there, as always, doing a crossword puzzle at the table, a cup of black coffee in front of her.

I had thought that this would be just the beginning of a long trail of exploration, of detective work, almost. We would jump in the little powder-blue car immediately and drive the thirty miles, through the forest, along the reservoir's twisty old blacktop, to Swansbury, a little town at the top of the valley, where we would make inquiry after inquiry into the tormented history of the virtuous Goode family, the descendants of Sarah, who had departed the soiled, fouled, besmirched coastline for a new life in the verdant Shift River valley. In which of the three drowned towns had they built their homestead? And where had they gone after its submersion? Perhaps they had gone nowhere, stubborn old hardworking hands, dirt under the nails, gripping the arms of their straight-backed chairs. Might there be some record of their staunch resistance?

But she would have none of it. I trailed her outside to the porch, where she sat down on the swing with a book whose title was obscured to me by the long fingers of her left hand. "Look, Ginger, of course I'm fascinated, and I do appreciate the legwork you've done so far, but the fact is . . . that's just it. What shall I do with facts? My book will be written not out of the desire to string together a series of *facts*"—she hammered the word as though it itself was a curse—"but out of a need to illustrate a series of events that occur *out* of time, out of order, that in fact recur rather than occur. I will find an appropriately tragic means of representation for the tragic ends my family has met."

I was puzzled by her marked lack of interest in my findings. Weakly I again instructed her on the Historical Society, its records and registries. Wasn't she a historian, after all, even if she had stopped short of the official designation? Wasn't a Historical Society exactly where she belonged?

"It's quite enough for me to know that the lineage of my family took a concussive blow twice already. I don't need any further evidence of the curse of ignominy that I live under. My suspicions need only be so well-founded."

THIS WAS NOT the first time Raquel had perversely managed to draw a kind of blind down on the bright light of activity, of pursuit, of forward motion. Concussive indeed: it was as though she had struck a blow to the head of the day, and I mutely took a seat next to her on the swing and began leafing through an old sports magazine. Very old, in fact: it was dated June 1978 and appeared to have been left by previous occupants. The silence conjoining my muteness was not really quiet, was crashingly occupied, her rejection like the noise of the sea in my ears. All the approving words I had thought she would say.

But I resolved that I would nevertheless visit the Ramapack cemetery—alone or with accompaniment—and find what there was to find. I would carry on her studies.

23.

Tell me something about your friends, the Motherwells? Just who exactly are they?" My mother and I stood, facing off, nearly, in the living room. I had come in weary from my thwarted attempts, from Raquel's enervating disinterest, and now it made me desperately uncomfortable to witness my mother's attempt to appear just *casually* interested, when in fact I could see that, quite unlike Raquel, she was dying for information. "You've been spending an awful lot of time with them, considering they're complete strangers."

"Well," said my father, from where he sat in his chair, torso hidden behind the newspaper, the top of his balding head visible. "They're not exactly strangers to Ginger. Ginger practically lives at their house."

"Pete. You know what I mean. They're strangers to the town, to the area, to the Endicotts, and especially to us. Our daughters are acting like strangers to their own homes, to their own parents!"

"Now, Serena, don't get hysterical."

. . .

RAQUEL OFTEN REFERRED to my parents as "the paradigm." It was true that their arrangement was typical of all the families I knew in Wick, and for all I knew, this could be extrapolated to all families everywhere. Mom had been just a mom, staying home with me and Jack, and then just with me, until after my freshman year in high school, when she felt more comfortable with my coming home to an empty house, heating up my own can of vegetable soup. She went to work with my dad. All along, she had been doing his books at the dining room table, after dinner, after I had cleared the dishes away and Dad had washed them, but now she went to the print shop with him every morning, and did the books in Jack's room.

My parents. I felt a peculiar, uncomfortable mixture of derision and defensiveness toward them, when they came up for examination at the Motherwells'. It was exhilarating to discuss them with such detachment, as though I was not their child but instead their biographer. But what a paltry book their lives would make!

We lived in the same house they had rented when they returned to Wick, young newlyweds. Now they owned it. It was rectangular and pinkish-brown, with a flat roof and a front porch with white pillars. It was where I had lived all of my life.

My father had attended the state university and caught the theater bug. He appeared in many of the school's musical productions (*Kiss Me, Kate*; *Oh! Calcutta!*) and in a few serious roles as well. He was the lead in *Rosencrantz and Guildenstern Are Dead;* he also played, apparently to great acclaim, a fictional character in Pirandello's great tragedy. His yearbooks are testimonials to this implausible phase. In all four he appears in full makeup and costume: down on bended knee, mid-soliloquy, or in a still, staring candidly into the jaws of the photographer.

After graduation he moved to New York City, and then back almost immediately upon the unexpected and sequential deaths of the grandparents I never met (a heart attack, a broken heart)—but not before meeting and marrying my mother, who in three years of pavement pounding had scored just one Palmolive commercial and an inconclusive callback to a soap opera. She was not ready to give up yet, but she was pregnant. Jack, her own heartbreak.

I believe that Raquel was nostalgic for *my* childhood. When she was not speaking and I, therefore, was not listening to her, but instead occupied myself in some other realm—a book off Theo's shelf, or a game of solitaire—she was recording me. I say recording rather than observing because there was no quality of interaction on her part: her eyes were wide and seemed to simply register the sights they saw, more like a hidden camera than like someone behind a one-way mirror, privy to the doings of a test group. I believe she was storing the sight away for future use. She certainly saw my "growing up," as she put it, as just so much fodder. "Tell me again about your days, Ginger. How did they go?" And I would again recount the ways in which I had gone about my days ever since I was a small child: how mother would wake us up with hot cereal and milk at an early hour; how I would dress and run to meet Cherry at the point of intersection of our two lines; how we would dawdle on the way to school and sometimes be late; how the day went on and then we were free; how then the day became a paradise of freedom in which we simply *played.* I told her about the mill. How it had been the site, the locale, of all our greatest exploits. Our spells, our plots to burn it down to the ground, our plans to one day scale its heights and set up camp in the round white cupola, to live with the black birds who roosted there. I told her how violated we felt, our preteen privacy, the day Jack followed us and watched for hours as we went through our blithe routines, uttering our secret words and embodying our unscathed imaginings. I could not find words to express how much it hurt that he would do this.

And then inevitably back home again, though we would have stayed outside interminably, except that it was getting dark, or getting too cold, in winter, for even our innocent imperviousness to weather. (All children in this way are like the famous Wild Child; we have no innate need of shelter. We would be just as happy to stay outside, to stay in the bitter ocean, to sleep on grass or sand, as we are to return at close of day to the nest that has been prepared for us. Although Raquel would not have it this way. She would rather imagine a traditional homecoming. We are tired and hungry, our lips beginning to blue, a natural exhaustion reaching its apotheosis coincidentally with the dinner bell and the evening news, the lighting of the lamps and the running of baths, the scrubbing of our grubby ears and fingers.)

I must admit I have always liked to do my chores. Raquel laughed out loud when I first used this word, in excusing myself from her company. "'Chores'?!" she said. "'Chores'? Why, how delightful . . . how charming. Can I come to your house and do some 'chores'? I'm sure it would do wonders for my constitution, not to mention my disposition."

But the last thing I ever wanted was to bring the Motherwells home to my house, to ruin my newfound, twofold mystery. My mysterious parents need never meet, as far as I was concerned, my mysterious friends.

I REGALED THE MOTHERWELLS with stories that in turn my mother had regaled me with—but only if I begged, or if I couldn't sleep at the prescribed bedtime. "Regale": there is no other way to describe the thrill of newfound loquaciousness I experienced in my days—afternoons, evenings, nights—at their house, when we would sit around the fire with glasses of ruby-red wine and simply speak. I had never known anyone else to do this. Certainly not my parents, who were far too busy to take more than thirty minutes for dinner—including clean-up—and who, if they did not retire immediately to bed, might sit quietly, eyelids drooping, through some half-hour sitcom, waiting for the nine o'clock news. "Good night, Ginger. Did you finish your homework?" *Yes, Mom, yes, Dad. Good night.*

The Endicotts were too efficient to allow any gratuitous talk. "School okay? Warm enough? Full?" All their questions could be answered with just one assentive noise.

The Motherwells lived to talk. I never saw them do anything else, in fact. To me this world of constant conversation was a world of wonder, of delight. Not only did they reveal themselves to me with unprecedented honesty, but they asked me questions about myself, about my life in Wick, about growing up in this inexplicable town, and as we talked more and more intimately, albeit, at times, abstractly, I began to feel at home in their company as I had never felt at home anywhere before. Perhaps I shared some of the qualities that made the Motherwells themselves so inherently, unquestionably different. I *was* different: from the kids at school, from my parents, from the little town of Wick. Different even from Cherry. Hadn't I, after all, been chosen to be their friend, their companion, their entertainment? They seemed to prefer me as I preferred them: infinitely. They socialized with no one else in town. They did not go bowling, they did not go out for breakfast or lunch. They certainly did not attend either of the churches.

In fact, they never went anywhere. Not to the Top Hat, since that first day—since they'd found me; not to the grocery store, nor the post office, nor the gas station. I wondered if they attended to all their basic needs in the city, when they made their visits to Theo's family.

The Motherwells had come along like a pair of crows alighting, permanent and merciless, and as the summer days passed I felt an effortless environment growing up around us, the three of us—it was true! They grew close to me, and I to them. I had found another game to play, new friends to play it with.

I HAD WONDERED ABOUT all these things, silently, to myself, and with Cherry. But I found myself reluctant to respond to my parents' questions with any of my speculations. They had speculations of their own.

"They must have some family here, don't they?" My mother's tone indicated just how circumspect she thought them, if they didn't. I thought of the Goode family, but kept silent. "No one moves here just for no reason. It's not the kind of place that attracts that sort of people." I knew what "sort of people" she referred to: wealthy émigrés from the city.

"And where do they work? They must have some kind of jobs somewhere. How else do they pay their bills? Unless they're rich. But if they were rich, they'd have bought a nicer house. I don't quite understand. I never see them anywhere. I'd certainly have noticed two young, unfamiliar faces." My continued silence on the subject was, I'm certain, maddening.

I did not, for example, regale them with the story of how Raquel had sighed empathetically over my bruised side, when I revealed it to her, and planted a kiss on the fading purple pool on my thigh like a mother kissing a toddler's boo-boo. I laughed, at first, but when her lips stayed pressed to my skin for a few extra seconds I looked down and saw how there seemed to be no line between her flesh and mine, her lips the color of my bruise, their warmth equal to the heat of my tender flesh. It looked like she was eating my leg, and I closed my eyes and waited to feel the sharpness of her teeth.

24.

In the morning it was reassuring to eat my mother's frozen waffles at the little kitchen table, Doris Lessing's *The Golden Notebook* splayed open by my plate. I always wished I had some kind of device to keep the pages from flipping while I attended to my meal; now a saltshaker acted precariously as paperweight while I used both hands to cut up my waffle. The chef herself sat by my side, backlit by the bright sun streaming through the window with its yellow curtains tied in bows. I squinted at her. When had she stopped cutting up my waffles for me? She sipped her coffee and reached out to brush my hair from my forehead. "You really didn't get a lot of sun this summer, did you. So pale! It seems sad, to me, a teenage girl without a tan, but it's probably just as well. Look at my wrinkles! When I was a girl the idea was to get as brown as you could, as fast as you could. We used baby oil! We just roasted ourselves. I hope you haven't been working too hard at the café—what time do you have to be there?"

When I told her that I had the day off, her eyes widened,

then narrowed, then widened again, in internal calculation. "Well, that's great!" she concluded, rapidly. "Your father and I do, too! Why don't we spend it all together. We'll go to Janine's Frosty for a cone. I can't believe the summer's over and we haven't even gone for a cone. What is this world coming to?"

My mother's insouciance could not hide, from me, her sharp anxiety. What was she afraid of? That I would say no? That I did not want to be seen in public with them? That because I had found new friends, people she did not know, I had changed into another person, a new daughter, a pale, languid, unrecognizable creature with unknowable, inconceivable thoughts and ideas?

Really, the truth was that she had never known what I was thinking, and had never asked.

Now, though I had relished the freshness of my own bed, my clean sheets, and had found it sweet to sit reading as she moved about the kitchen, and be fed, and petted, I did not feel any particular remorse in turning her down. I had plans. It was the perfect day to go to the Ramapack cemetery. There I would find whatever trace of the Goode family remained, and this would be the starting point for Raquel's research. She would have names, dates, actual stones with deeply etched identities.

So I was surprised, and made sad, and afraid, by the vehemence of my mother's reaction to my refusal. It was like someone pulling an old leather glove out of a drawer to slap you with it. The gestures were awkward, the tool stiff with disuse. It was embarrassing.

"Do you know, Ginger, that you are not the only person

in the world? Have you given one thought, all summer, to your father and me? Your poor dad is practically speechless with worry. He hasn't wanted to say anything. But the last thing he needs is another disappearing child." These last words hit me like the intended slap. My mother had clearly been thinking. She sped on in her attack.

"The Endicotts are absolutely beside themselves. Last week your father went down to the Social Club with Jim and they were talking about these new people, and it turns out that Cherry was over at their house one night, without you, and she told her parents that she was here, and of course your father said that we hadn't seen her once all summer, since we haven't! And now Cherry won't tell them anything about it, has refused to talk about it, and spends all her time with Randy Thibodeau. I'm sure he's turned out to be a perfectly nice young man, despite everything . . . but he's certainly too old for Cherry. I mean he's got his own apartment, his truck, his job! And she's just a young girl.

"And we still don't know anything about these people! How can you expect us to let you practically move in with them, when we've never even met them! Some of the men down at the Club were joking that she's a witch, that she's put a spell on you two. Not funny! You're only fifteen years old. Just because you skipped a year in school doesn't mean that you're not fifteen. Maybe I shouldn't have let you skip that year . . . I think it really has made you a bit *too* independent. But I thought it might help you get through a rough patch. . . ." She alluded to the time after Jack's death, when we had all wanted to die.

Now that she had begun to shift the blame to herself I thought that I might insert a well-placed tidbit of information. Casually, though careful not to appear glib in the face of her arousal, I told her about Raquel's book, and that I had been helping Raquel to do research, and about the fellowship from the university, and last, about the family connection that had brought the Motherwells to Wick in the first place.

I watched the information do its work, like a tranquilizer dart in the haunch of a feral dog. I saw her relax, one part of her body at a time, and then saw the original, sharp interest in the Motherwells rekindle in her eyes, which, despite the wrinkles she had spoken of, were still clear and blue and at times painfully young. "Well, that is remarkable," she said. "I don't think anyone's taken an interest in town history since old Daniel Skagett passed. We printed all those little pamphlets for him, you know, on the lost towns, the ones you can get at Lawson's." I knew the ones she meant. They had titles like "Ghosts of the Valley" and "The Lore of Ramapack," and mostly retold old legends about eccentric townsfolk, such as the gentleman who wanted to lie in state in a glass coffin so that everyone could watch him decompose. I had never been able to get through any of them. The writing was terrible.

I thought I had better take advantage of my mother's momentary softening and so I capitulated, right there on the spot. I agreed that it would be fun to spend the day with her and my father, in whatever activities would strike the right note of reunion, of trinity. Just then my father came down the hall and into the kitchen, hair rumpled, plaid bathrobe tied over blue pajamas. He seemed pleased to see me there. Wordlessly he fumbled for coffee and then joined us at the table, where the three of us proceeded to plan our simple day.

I DID NOT ALWAYS possess such a taste for unease, such a homing instinct for the path of danger. Now, in these swift-moving days, I felt myself like an initiate craving the hazing ritual, but I remember as if it were yesterday a signal moment in which I rejected fear, literally ejected it from my body—projected it, even, across the room. I must have been six or seven, a recent initiate to that other bounded world, the book, and I sat in an armchair in the corner of the living room with one of these on my lap while my mother put finishing touches on dinner and Jack set the table in the kitchen. I could hear and see them bustling around while I sat. This particular volume had caught my notice because it was, unlike the paperbacks that dominated the bookcase, tall and old and bound in a dark, scaly kind of fabric like a red snake's skin. The book promised, in its title, not just mystery but also madness. The title alone was terrifying to me, and I had sat for more than an hour, reading silently in a state of cold anticipation, thumbing through story after story, and when, as dinner approached readiness, smells of butter and blood and vegetable matter rich in the air, I reached a page with a color plate showing, in faded yet somehow still lurid tones, a scene of such incipient horror—come to life in my hands—I screamed from deep within my brain cavity. And the book jumped, away, away, flew ten feet across the floor, where it landed open, spine up, depraved pages crushed and broken. I continued screaming, weakly, almost blind with the indelible sight, and while my mother began to scold me for the ruination of her heirloom, Poe's *Tales of Mystery and Madness*, she soon stopped, and scooped me out of the chair, and scolded Jack instead for laughing at me as she sat down and held me. I could not speak.

I TRAILED AFTER my parents into the house as dusk was settling over the yard, the street, the town. We were all exhausted from the effort of catching up with each other: just as my parents had not seen me in weeks and weeks, I, too, had not seen them, and so there was a lot of town gossip to be filled in on, a lot of news from the privileged quarters of the print shop about who was getting married, who had had a baby, who was going out of business. Ice cream had been consumed, a long drive in the country taken, and several effective reassurances had been silently offered that indeed, I was still their daughter. Now they knew all about Mr. Penrose's offer—they told me I should ask him for a raise, if he valued me so much as an employee—and about my visit to see Hep Warren, and all that he had told me about the fire at the Town Hall and the loss of the town records.

"Yes," my father mused, from the front seat, as we drove down through the hills east of Wick, "I remember hearing about that. Amazing how a disaster can just wipe out whole centuries of data. Or at least it could in the past! Now, of course, we have everything on digital files. No fire, or flood, or tornado, for that matter, can erase a digital file."

"Why, Pete," countered my mother, "of course it can! A

computer in a flood is a drowned computer, just like a horse in a flood is a drowned horse! You're never going to get a file off a computer that's been submerged in water."

"Well, Serena, I guess you have a point there," said my father, and that was the end of that particular conversation. Or at least if they continued it I did not pay attention, but instead turned my gaze to the hills and patiently waited to be returned to my life.

I excused myself right after dinner (roasted chicken, creamed spinach, white rice from a box) and went up to my room "to read," I said. But, even though I was tempted, again, by familiar comforts—my bed called out, with its smooth bedspread and the headboard whose finials I had gripped, only months ago, in the spasm of my first climax—I felt an even stronger inclination to be among my friends, to remove myself to them.

I waited until I heard the dishwasher begin its *shush*ing, the television light up with indispensable news of the world, and then I slipped quietly down the hall and out the sliding kitchen door.

THE MOTHERWELLS' HOUSE was dark. I went in through the back and heard the familiar quiet of Raquel and Theo sleeping. It was ten o'clock. They must have had a long day, too, without me. I tiptoed up the stairs so as not to wake them, paused in the darkness of the hallway, opened the door to their room without a sound, stood for a moment to make out the shapes of their bodies under the blankets, long and slim like young, fallen trees, and curled up at their feet like a dog.

25.

There is nothing like firelight, flickering on a troubled face or on the glossy jacket of a book on a shelf, to bring a room into sharp focus. I know why they say "hearth" when they mean home. When you're tending a fire and a spark jumps out after a particularly loud cracking noise and lands on your wrist you can smell, just for a second, burning flesh. Or you can think about smelling it.

It was a pivotal moment, and I will always carry this image with me: Theo, in the living-room doorway, his arms full of broken wood, and Raquel seated in the green chair by the fire, me on the big round braided rug directly in front of the fireplace. I had been looking into the fire, reaching with a poker now and then to reposition some part of the burning arrangement.

Sometimes I have wondered what it means to be "good" at something. I know that when I see a fire that's going out I am always prepared to leap forward, attention focused on the offending element, and with my hand remove whatever is an obstacle in the flame's path to more and more oxygen. The flame will happily rush in, wherever you create a space for it.

Raquel was so close to me she could have been brushing my hair, or showing me a picture from the magazine she flipped through, but she wasn't doing either: she just leafed slowly. I think it was *The New Yorker*, or maybe *Harper's*. She liked to read the index.

"These old shingles make good kindling," Theo said to the room in general as he entered with his load. I looked up and smiled. Raquel said, "Don't you sound just like a real country boy." And then she blushed, with what looked like pride.

It seemed like the perfect moment to wonder aloud, and so I did. I wondered when Raquel might be going to start working on her book, for real. Today we could make a trip together to Swansbury.

"Isn't it odd," Raquel said, seemingly by way of response, "how a fire burning in a fireplace is really just that, just itself, self-contained, burning gases merrily away, but for us, sitting here, it seems to actively *create an atmosphere*?" (And here she held up her two first fingers and crooked them, and cocked them, indicating just how suspect she found such a phrase.) When she spoke like this it reminded me of the language of dreams—not really speech at all but communicative nevertheless, in that it is hermetic. It need never leave the confines of your own system of interpretation.

"Well, yes," Theo began to answer her. "I see what you mean—"

But then she quickly said, before he could go on, "Oh do you? I'm so glad, because that's just the sort of thing I count on you for. Even as I spoke those words they seemed to lose all currency, coming out of my mouth, but then you picked them up and coined them in your own image, and suddenly, there they are, buying power restored, good for trade and the economy in general."

"Fires, small flames at the ends of candles, certain pitches in music, certain times of day . . ." Theo ticked these off on the fingers of his left hand.

"Certain slants of light," Raquel interjected, then fell pensive, with a look on her mobile face of frustrated comprehension. This was a look she often wore when she wanted to explain something, as she so often did. A look like a combination of dawn breaking and clouds rolling in.

"Yes, you see," she began again, "that's the thing. That's the thing about talking, about three people talking in a room with the firelight, with music, with air. It happens, doesn't it? The two of you can't help being there and you can't help hearing me." I noted that Raquel had figured Theo and me as *the two of us*, together, and thrilled to see us paired, thus, even if only in her perception. For though I never wished to displease her, or even to disobey her, now that she had spoken it there was the possibility of a new triangulation. "No matter what I don't or do get out of my mouth you are *all there*, your own selves, experiencing the whole thing, the event, the vibe, the atmosphere. There's nothing I can do to stop it."

"Except kill us." Theo said it softly. (If Theo seems a shadowy figure it is probably due to the quality of his attention. He looks at you when you speak to him as though you are an educational program on public television that he feels obliged to watch.)

"Yes, well," Raquel rejoined, a few beats later, "I'm afraid that Ginger's parents might object to that sort of final solution. Not to mention Ginger's own right to life . . ."

"Ginger can take care of herself. Can't you, Ginger?" He cast me a look that seemed partially to include me in the joke and partially to instruct me to keep my mouth shut. As though I needed any instruction. "I think she takes more after me than she does you, Raquel. I don't think Ginger can be stopped from getting what she wants, in the end, whatever it may be. If she wants to live, she will live."

THE THREE OF US approached the mill through the chill September twilight like thieves at the door of a bank: casually, unconcernedly, as though we had every right to be there. As though we might be customers, or the ghosts of customers, coming to buy batting to stuff a quilt, or to place an order for a length of fine cloth.

This forced entry was Theo's idea, an alternate plan to historical adventure. He proposed it, as we sat around the house that afternoon, and from the ease with which he did so I got the sense that he was no stranger to abrupt outbursts of criminal behavior. It might, in fact, be the first alternative when his usual recreations—reading, cooking, sleeping—had been exhausted.

And he proved to be good at it. He plotted a simple scheme, and when night began to fall we followed him into it like seals sliding off a rock into the ocean, one after another. We walked through town together discreetly, without hurry. No one was on the streets, it being dinnertime, and I pointed out a few landmarks quietly: the lit-up window of Pritt's Printing, where my parents still toiled; the dark library where I had spent some of my happiest hours.

THE MILL OCCUPIES a central position in my town's imagination, if not in its economy. A concrete bridge carries you safely over the dry bed of the Shift River. There, on your right, is a red brick rectangle of great structural integrity, long and massive from the side view, from across the riverbed, all the little windows in their rows.

It had been a woolen mill. It was really two separate structures: a black sign with gold lettering hung on the face of the front building, above the big red double door's archway, proclaiming "Wick Knitted Fabrics." This would have been where prospective customers entered. The small, short, rectangular building stood directly at the roadside, providing its own advertisement. Business transactions must have occurred in the offices on the second floor of this frontal lobe, offices that were graced with larger windows facing out over the road. The long rear building stood tall, with pointed roof, in back, an uncle sternly peering over the shoulder of a foolhardy nephew. On its side were wide black iron double doors, like those of a prison, which must have been where the streams of laborers would enter in the morning, and exit in the evening, dull of brain and limb, dullness the dull fruit of their dull action. On top of all this was a kind of cupola, rising high and white above the flat roof; a small, gazebo-like structure, perhaps an observation tower, though what there may have been to observe we cannot know. Approaching consumers? Mischievous children? Malicious herds of deer? Many times Cherry and I had discussed our plans to find a way inside and up into this point of highest perspective, from which we guessed we could probably see a long way in every direction. But we never did try.

The iron doors that had always looked so invulnerable to Cherry and me seemed to fairly welcome Theo in, after a few blows with an ax at the rusted mechanism that contained both the lock and the handle. The shouts of the ax against the hasp of the lock rang out in the dusk and I shrank against the brick wall, but I heard no answering cries or indications of notice. Without any hesitation Theo slipped inside, Raquel behind him, and I followed them, as had become my habit.

THIS WAS NO CASTLE. It was an oblong, dark, dirty room with a high ceiling, empty but for a few long, rough tables that appeared to be bolted to the brick walls. A staircase to the second floor crept up one wall and disappeared into a small square hole. I had always assumed that the mill would still be occupied by machinery, dusty, hulking relics of early industrial labor, but of course it must have all been sold off a hundred years ago. Theo pulled the door shut behind us and moved into the room, to stand by a window on the other side. I followed him, curious to see what the laborers had seen as they sat, or stood, or bent to their tasks.

Raquel hung back, and I felt her hesitation on the back of my head like an invasive set of eyes, a vision not my own. She spoke in a loud whisper. "What industriousness, what tireless production. What *product*, after all, could have been attempted here? If each innumerable window represents innumerable handy workers, then what an incalculable amount of work was going on inside these walls!

"Okay, this place gives me the creeps," Raquel continued, and I turned to watch her as she moved slowly backward, her hands reaching out behind her, in the general direction of the door. "I'm sorry, my darlings, but it's too real. So much history in one place, I can feel it in the air like particles I don't want to inhale. But you two knock yourselves out. I'll wait for you at home." Still facing us she bumped up, hard, against the heavy door; it budged and she backed through, pushing it firmly shut from the other side. Theo stayed silent at the window, and I stood frozen in my place between him and the door. He crossed the room, in which my eyes were becoming accustomed to the gloom even as it deepened, and stopped at another window. It seemed a cue: I went and stood beside him and together we watched Raquel recede. The air between our bodies filled with a kind of vibratory compulsion: I needed to move nearer, or farther. I struggled to stay still.

With hindsight, one sees that there were several cues, or prompts, or leads that we followed. A setup. I can still feel the heaviness that settled on me; it was odd to be on the inside, to watch her through the begrimed glass of the small window as she grew like an afternoon's long shadow away up the riverbank, slung her leg over the guardrail, and was gone. It was even odder to be now so alone with Theo. This had never happened. Still, the unexpected feeling of bereftness, and the uncomfortable sense that in some way I must now take the place of the absent woman, was familiar, reminded me of those rare dinners at home with my father when my mother had gone out to a town meeting or to visit a friend. I was so used, by now, to being three; three provided me with the proper balance. I was neither fulcrum nor lever but ballast, the one who could be unloaded, dispensed with if lightness was called for. In this new pairing I would surely be missed. I had some responsibility.

But still, even as the path lay cleared ahead of us, remember that I was quite young, and believe that I was unsure. I wondered, I really wondered, if I should follow Raquel, and leave Theo alone here inside the mill to explore. That would have been the natural choice—to remain by Raquel's side. But she hadn't seemed to want it. In fact it seemed as though she had wanted to leave Theo alone with me. Maybe she wanted us to get to know each other better, or, more likely, to have a chance to talk about her. Or maybe she had to be taken at her word: she had simply wanted to not be inside. And I did, I did want to be inside, even if what I saw there was tantamount to yet another end of my childhood. The empty mill, no castle; the mill itself strangely uninflected, devoid of atmosphere. For unlike Raquel, I found the mill's air to be altogether quiet, still, free of debris, psychic or otherwise. I found that I felt quite at ease there, in the empty room, as though all the years of my imaginings had made it ready for me, made it welcome me, much in the way it welcomed Theo.

"Come sit here," Theo said. He'd pulled his jacket off and laid it on the table next to where we stood, in the violet light coming through the window. My eyes were unaccustomed to dwelling so long on him: usually I trained them on Raquel so as not to call attention to myself. His attention. What would

I do with it if I had it? Now his form in the dimness was like a blot of light, a silvery, uninflected shape that I couldn't wholly define. I levered myself up onto the table. We would talk now; I could tell him about the castle, and he would understand, as I had not tried to make anyone else understand, not even myself, what the still fresh, still recent loss of Cherry meant to me: two becoming one, a final collapse. And then he might tell me what Raquel meant to him, so that I could know better how to place myself in relation to the two of them. Should I come nearer? Go farther? Should I leave them more to themselves or did they resent the time I spent away from them? Should I quit my job and simply stay with them, always? We could all three leave this town together, and find a new town, and I could be known there as their daughter. For some reason I felt sure that if we spoke now, in the privacy of the castle, with Raquel absent, I would be able to talk to him as I had never talked to any man before. Certainly not to my father, with whom I spoke only in well-rehearsed lines. Not to Jack, who had departed before I could learn to speak.

But Theo did not talk to me, nor did he sit next to me. Instead he placed his hands on my body, on my sides. With his hands on me I was unable to hear my thoughts, to feel myself in time. What happened seemed to happen *already*, and I ran to catch up with the apprehension of it. So I did not feel glad or afraid when he dragged me around to face him squarely and pulled my knees apart. I felt rather that I had to watch carefully, to ascertain correctly, to keep actions moving forward in time. He stood between my knees, locking his hips to the edge of the table, and I was obliged to look into his eyes, which were remorseless, though I only saw them for a moment. He showed me instead the top of his head, light brown waves in disarray. He fixed his eyes on my neck, my collarbone, and I felt his fingers at the bottom of my sweater, then up inside my shirt, and brushing over my shoulders, my breasts, pulling at my nipples.

It is confusing to be cold while being made love to. He tugged my sneakers off, then my jeans, then my underwear, and I could feel the deep, hard chill of the table against my buttocks even through the padded lining of his workman's jacket. He drew his fingers along the goose-bumped flesh at the insides of my thighs. It was as though I had fallen into water, dark water, and all perception was sharpened by the medium in which I was suspended. He knelt between my legs, and then I felt his tongue, warm on the tender parts. He stiffened it, and moved it over me like a finger. I'm not sure if I made a sound. If I did, he silenced it with his hand over my mouth, his long arm reaching up to clamp it. Then he put his hands over my breasts; then he sucked at them, his mouth slick. I could smell myself on his breath, on my skin. He arose from his knees and stood, then unbuttoned his jeans and pushed them down. His penis stood out from his body through a flap in his underwear, like the mast of a sailboat on end in the water. It seemed to pulse slightly.

I thought I knew what to do. I slid off the table and to my knees, the grit of a hundred years grinding into them. I grasped him, warm in the cold, in my fist, put my other hand on his buttock, which was cool and smooth, put my tongue to the end of it as I had seen illustrated so clearly, then didn't know what to do after that. Every description I had read simply said *suck*, but I could not fit the whole thing in my mouth and still draw enough breath to suck. I began instead to lick it, like an ice cream cone melting in my hot fist. I was surprised at how smooth it was, featureless and without flavor.

"You're sweet," he whispered, and put his hand on my chin, another on my shoulder, drawing himself from my mouth. *Sweet*, I thought, and felt like a child. And thought that would be the end of it, probably, now that he understood my inexperience. None of my reading or imagining had prepared me for the overwhelming effusion, the tactile imposition, of proximate contact with his bare skin. I will confess that it crossed my mind that I would rather be asleep. I thought I might shut my eyes for a minute and rest, away from sight.

But then I was lifted up, and my eyes flew open like a doll's, and I was put swiftly on my back on the hard table, his hands under my arms, more like a baby than a child, and then he leaned over me, pressing his torso down onto mine, holding my hands over my head in his hands. The weight of him was tremendous, and through his bulky sweater I thought I felt him shiver, or shake, a tremor passing through him that passed into me, and I tried to meet his eyes, to make another point of contact, but he bent his head to bite my shoulder through my shirt, and I spread my knees. When I felt him pushing to get inside, I spread still wider, my knees bent, as I had seen it done, and he took his hands from mine and placed them on my calves, leveraging. I put one hand on each of my knees and pulled them toward my face. Now he put his hand over my mouth, again, and pumped, short thrusts. I was aware of his calculation. Then he put his fingers into my mouth, and I kept them there, again as I had seen it done, until he pulled me off the table, turned me around, and bent me over, my cheek resting on his jacket, and came in to me again from this anterior position, and, reaching around, used his finger to touch me where anticipation was concentrated like pain. I remembered, from my first visit to the Motherwells, with Cherry, that this was the trick he used on Raquel, and to my surprise the impact of the split-second image of them together in this way, entire, from out of nowhere caused my insides to twist suddenly open and then shut and then open again, wider, like the hidden eye of a camera. "Oh," I cried, and my cry reverberated in the room, and in its wake Theo increased his speed and force until I felt him tense, his body arched away from mine and quivering like a bow. He didn't make a sound, but I could almost hear his heart thudding; then I could feel it clearly when he slumped forward again and rested his head on the back of my neck, his chest on my back. We stayed there like that for a moment, during which I became acutely aware of the chill, as the slickness at the inside of my thighs quickly cooled. After a minute I felt him flop out of me, deflated, and then more of his semen was released from me and dribbled down.

Something about the density of the evening light outside called to mind, as I bent to find my jeans, the fact that today had been the first day of school, and that I had missed it. What had I done with the hours of the day, when the scholars of Wick had been greeting one another, settling in for a new season of youth? I stood up straight, shaking off whatever small shock, a paralytic enervation, as though I had been injected with venom, had settled onto my shoulders, and felt the muscles of my inner thighs, slightly sore. Deeper inside myself a new cavity had been dug out, drilled—and had yet to be filled with any matter or substance or affect. It was the interior in which I waited to tell myself how I felt. In the absence of anyone asking me how I felt.

I knew we would go home now and see Raquel, but I didn't know what I would do when I saw her. Quickly I rehearsed a desirable outcome: Theo and I would approach the house, my hand in his, or his arm around my waist, holding me near, and we would release each other, silently, reluctantly, only as we reached the door and Theo stretched his hand out to turn the knob just as it turned from inside. The door opened, a lit rectangle with Raquel inside it, as on that first day when she had appeared in its frame like footage of a collapsing structure, a house on fire, on a TV screen. Only, then Theo had materialized beside her, and now he would appear to be beside me.

But I found that I could not invoke a precise image of Raquel against which to test my feelings. When I tried to think of her I saw instead an oblong, a sheer dull face of stone like a grave marker, without inscription. And when I thought of my own self, a self I tried to locate by shutting my eyes for a moment as I pulled my shoes on—dropping my lids and groping around inside the cavern of my own darkness for some previously undefined absolute face—a corresponding featurelessness rose up, as though the one who had just acted was this new one, an infant, practically, who could do anything. The only self I could find was one that I did not recognize.

IT IS UNDERSTOOD by every sane adult that a child is blameless, until she reaches majority. The child is not to be held ultimately responsible for her own actions, however identifiable, however intentional, however hurtful the consequences. It is the adult in the situation, if there is one, who is to blame, and it is the adult who must hold in his or her mind this contradiction, while the child is set free, free to hold fast to her side of the story, and this freedom from complexity is the stuff of childhood's fabled innocence.

When we got home we would sit down at the table, Raquel and I sipping wine while Theo "rustled something up," and eat ravenously, and Raquel would comment with searching obliquity on how you could always count on bad behavior to work up an appetite. There had been nothing I wanted to keep from her, but now there was: the sex act, once completed, was singular, unbelievable, and, contrary to the example of Mr. Penrose's magazines, unfit for reproduction or representation. If she did not know it, then she would never know it. The fact of it was another blank marker in the crepuscular landscape, and I was horrified to find that I felt sorry for her in her infinite unknowing, the way I felt sorry for my mother, sometimes, with her sharp, hopeful, finite face.

But it seemed that she felt sorry for me, too—about what, I could not be sure. What did she know?

"Little one." She placed her hand on my forehead. "You feel kind of clammy. I think a hot bath might be just the thing."

She mothered me upstairs and into the bathroom, slipping my clothes off onto the floor as the tub filled. I puffed up my shallow breast like a small bird in the winter.

26.

I had a really bad dream last night, and I wanted to tell you about it, but you were not here to tell. In the dream I had a little baby, but that was not the scary part. I wanted the baby. In a big bed, I slept with the baby curled into my side, tucked under my arm, its warm, fuzzy head against my bare skin. We were comfortable like that, and had slept many nights together in perfect rest. It was a large bed, with a light coverlet so the baby couldn't smother.

We woke up in the middle of the night. A dark night, no moon, so dark I couldn't see anything for a long time. The baby, though, the baby woke up and behaved as though possessed, like in a feature film's version of demonic possession. Hissing, writhing, jerking . . . I couldn't still the baby, I was not as strong as the baby. I shhhhhhhh*ed loudly in the baby's face, trying to shock it out of its fugue, but I couldn't see its face, I could only hear the stuttering gutturals issuing from its mouth. The baby whipped like a cord of steel.*

I needed to see the baby's face, so that I could understand better how to soothe it, but when I turned on the light I still could not see its face. A black spot, just the size of a baby's face, occluded my vision wherever the face should have been. The spot moved wherever the baby moved. I was awake in the black hours of the night in the flat, brightly lit room, with just the bed and the baby.

This blindness followed the baby wherever I looked.

27.

A confusion of ghost towns. Ghost hamlets, really: the remains of the Shift River valley. Wick, there, perched in safety above the man-made expanse of the Ramapack Reservoir and the surrounding infinity of farmland and forest. There, dotted faintly, are lines dividing up the watery grave into its former precincts, or townships. They looked so large, compared to Wick. How could all those lives have been uprooted? To where did they disseminate themselves, like so much information? Or like a flock of chickens when a bucket of water interrupts its dusty discourse.

I stood gazing at a map pushpinned to a bulletin board on the wall outside the office of Mr. Czabaj, the guidance counselor. I was waiting for him to finish his conversation with some other surly—or sheepish, or distraught—student. I had been summoned from gym class, the last period of the day. Today we were playing kickball on the field, and I was just as glad to be plucked out of range of the pummeling demands that would be placed on me in the name of sport.

I stood studying the map, and found myself oddly unconcerned about this visit to the school's conscience. Wick High had its share of troubled teens. Whether at the high or low end of the achievement scale, it was emphasized, again and again, at PTA meetings and pep rallies alike, we were all at risk for drug abuse, parenthood, and suicide. Probably in that order. Mr. Czabaj was working overtime as a one-man preventative measure. We had been lectured in our hygiene class about all the different substance-free ways to "let off steam," and talking over your issues with a concerned authority figure was at the top of the list.

The heavy wooden door opened inward, its window of opaque, beveled glass distorting and magnifying the fluorescent light of the hallway. Cherry stepped from the office, looking ruffled. Her cheeks were flushed the pink only skin of such unusual whiteness can achieve. I noticed she was wearing my black sneakers. She saw me, stopped as if to speak, then blinked and continued into the hall and down, head up, as Mr. Czabaj stepped out after her, hand on the brass doorknob, calling, "Okay, Cherry! Let's keep talking. Bye-bye!" It was the nearest I'd been to her in a month.

I followed him in and sat down in the chair he indicated: an old wooden office chair with arms. The seat was worn exceedingly smooth from the sliding of excitable bodies. I fixed my gaze first on the familiar dull green linoleum, and then on Mr. Czabaj's equally familiar snow-white crew cut and broad neck.

"Ginger. How's it going?"

I smiled, gazing across the desk at him, and he shifted his bulky weight in the big wooden chair in which he sat, identical to mine except for the addition of a cushion, and for its ability to swivel. He seemed to decide to begin anew. I had the odd feeling that I was making him uncomfortable. Something in my eyes?

"Ginger," he said, with some finality. "You're one of the finest students here at the high school. We've never had a problem with you before—and now this." Over his shoulder, through the open window, from someone's car stereo, floated strains of "Destroy the Handicapped," a song that had gained popularity among Wick's teens recently. The song consisted mainly of that refrain, or command, sung to the accompaniment of a crude syllabic drumbeat. I looked up and met the eyes of Mr. Czabaj, as he was saying something that sounded like ". . . troublemakers what-have-you?" In the ensuing protracted silence he reframed his question.

"I'd be very surprised to find out that you had. This school has a lot of tough characters lurking around. Boys and girls who don't know how to make good choices. They choose to abuse themselves with substances and get into all sorts of malicious hijinks. I know the kinds of things that go on over by the graveyard. I remember your brother, God rest his soul." Mr. Czabaj allowed for a few moments of silence, and I duly considered Jack in those moments. His reckless endangerments. His pointless, willful, selfish pursuit of pleasure, at the expense of everything. How he might regret his choices now, and wish to see me make better ones. "Now, you aren't in the habit of spending your time with any of those kids, are you? I certainly don't associate you with that kind of behavior. But I can also appreciate the temptation. I coach those boys on the field, you know, and I know that they can look pretty 'cool' when they're giving themselves lung cancer, and doing permanent damage to their eardrums with that noise. But the only thing 'cool' they should be getting from a smart young lady like yourself is the cold shoulder!" He banged his hand, palm flat, down on the desk. I had to smile again.

Again he seemed to be rethinking his strategy; after a pause in which the bell signaling the end of class rang out like an impassioned speech, and I heard doors opening and the rush of feet and bags and elbows shoving out into the hallway, he began again, more sternly this time.

"I know the period's over. I'll let you go in just a minute. Now, Ginger. You were absent from the first day of school, and without a medical excuse. You've been repeatedly late to homeroom. Several of your teachers have reported that your attention wanders when you *are* in class. You don't participate in group discussions the way you used to. Now, if you haven't been getting into trouble with drugs, or alcohol, my suspicion would be that you have got yourself a boyfriend. But if you say that that's just not so, dear, then I'll have to start looking for other explanations. And I'll certainly have to put in a call to your parents." Mr. Czabaj lifted himself out of his seat with a grunt, stood up, came around the desk, and sat on the corner of it nearest to my chair. Looking over his burly shoulder, anything to avoid the intrusion he was attempting, I noticed a sheet of loose-leaf paper on his desk, what looked like a student essay, handwritten in purple ink and with a title at the top. I maneuvered my gaze into the path of Mr. Czabaj's small, crinkly blue eyes, then, keeping my face pointed in the same direction but letting my eyes wander ever so slightly, leaned a little to the right, just enough that I could make out, in Cherry's distinct round handwriting, this topic sentence: "Evil is something you can't explain or something powerful you can't control." Above it, in blue ink, "Cherry, come see me in my office today, please. Mr. C."

"Now, Ginger. We can't help but wonder if your absence from school and your general behavior isn't an expression of some kind of inner struggle that you might be going through, like a crisis or something. Now."

I was tempted to supply Mr. Czabaj with the phrase he was searching for: "cry for help." But instead I occupied myself with marveling at his use of this all-purpose command: "Now." What did he mean by "now"? Did it serve to call his own attention back to the matter at hand? Perhaps he had difficulty keeping the past and the future straight, and needed to constantly remind himself that whatever might be going on back then, or might go on sometime soon, the problem in front of us, sitting on the desk, is always happening *now*.

"Do you want to tell me a little bit about that? I'm really here to help you, Ginger, and just because you've never needed help before, God bless you, doesn't mean you're not entitled to it now." There was that word again, and I was shocked to feel a sudden sharp closing of my throat, a pricking in my nose, the unmistakable sensation of tears rising from wherever it is in the wells of the eyes or sinus or gut they rise from, unbidden, threatening to reveal to the self and to the onlooker a depth of sorrow or disappointment or triumph or joy that one had absolutely no intention of disclosing. In fact, one is forced by tears that come from the body to remember even that one *has* a body, a body always *now*, a body incessantly performing acts voluntary and involuntary, some acts resolutely poised between the two. With the whole force of my body and mind I worked to crush those tears back down into their cave, but as I succeeded in stemming the tears another uncontrolled loosening began and to my horror I found myself beginning to stammer, a freshet of unformed thought and syllables spilling up my throat and almost to the portal of my lips, just as someone rapped on the window of the door to remind Mr. Czabaj of football practice, for which he was overdue. He spread his mouth in a grimace and his hands wide in apology while I quickly formed out of my formless leakage a small, plausible, corresponding lie, something about being late to meet my mother over at the print shop, and ran out the door. Mr. Czabaj called out to me his solicitude all the way down the hall.

Evil, by Cherry Endicott, Grade Twelve

What is evil? The dictionary may not give a real answer at all because it gives us only words, no feelings or objects to help the words sink in. When you think of evil you think of the devil, witches, dictators, etc. When you think about evil, you think about badness, anger, hurting people, etc. Evil is something you can't explain or something powerful you can't control. Some of Webster's words are morally wrong, wicked, harmful, injurious, characterized or accompanied by misfortune or suffering, unfortunate disatstrous, sin, harm, mischief bad wished upon a person, corrupt, vile, misery, sorrow. Sin and morally wrong are two that show evil well only reduced. Evil is sin to the thirteenth power.

Evil is a human characteristic for the most part, but it can be found in animals, objects and certain activities. I think evil is more easily recognized in the make believe world of myths, fairy tales, legends, and dreams. Some examples of them are; the evil stepmother in cindarella, Hades right out of Greek myths, these are just a few. They're easier to pick out because they are pure evil as opposed to people in real life which may have an evil side. There is an extensive list of things associated with evil: black magic, organized murder, black magic, the devil, etc. The question is why are they associtated with evil? My thought on this question is that they have to do with purposely causing human suffering. The devil is said to come and get murderers when they die or he kidnaps innocient people to use as servants. Or course evil is one of the things that makes life interesting. My own fears are of the evil things in this world. Organized murder is evil because it's secretive and all planned out with secret missions and messages. Cults and seances are evil in our mind because they are controling people and going against their will, or messing with destiny. Definitely not last and not least, black magic; just the colors black and red are associated with evil. All the superstitions that have to do with bad luck or losing your soul are evil. Anything that is unknown like UFOs, ghosts or life after death is considered evil. Not to mention mummies, witches or a ouiji board, and rising people from the dead which is disturbing their long sleep. The list goes on and on, but there are things they all have in common. Death, the unknown, and fear.

Some people associate power with evil; because of all the powerful things that cause disruption or powerful things they don't understand they call evil. You can't understand evil until you feel it near you: you are scared. In my mind hypnosis is a powerful and unexplained force that can and cannot be evil, it certainly can be used to go out and do evil things. With all these evil things lurking around how do we go on with our everyday lives? The answer is that evil is in our minds and comes out when we want it to, if you searched hard enough you would find the evil forces all around you but we try not to do that.

28.

October

I found Cherry down at the mill.

For so long I'd relied utterly on her constant companionship, her protection, really, her unfaltering presence in all the classrooms, playgrounds, school assemblies, hallways. Without her I found myself to be unusually difficult to see. Virtually invisible, I seemed to be, to my classmates. Walking the hallways, I understood that it had been only her physical, tactile, visceral presence at my side that had kept me material, had evinced from my schoolmates the occasional wave, or smile, or chit of conversation, all of it directed slightly to the right or left of me, depending on where Cherry stood. She had been like a magnet that collected my scattered electrons into a semblance of human form.

But now Cherry, also, did not speak to me at school. She was always looking the other way when I caught sight of her, clinging to the arms of new friends, girls we'd never given a second thought to before. It was as though I'd become invisible to her, too. I could only stand the pain of this rejection by reminding myself that I was both its cause and its object: she did not like my new friends, just as I did not like hers.

Then, a few weeks into the new school year, a few days after our sequential interviews with Mr. Czabaj, Cherry was suddenly absent. A week went by, then two, then three, and still she did not appear around any corners; she did not materialize behind her locker door as it slammed shut; most notably she did not tug on my elbow in the lunch line, as I awaited a slice of floppy pizza and carton of milk, to wistfully tell me where she was sitting. She wasn't sitting anywhere that I could see.

I THOUGHT I MIGHT learn something by observing the group of shiny twelfth-grade girls to which Cherry had lately become attached. I had watched the progression of her inclusion, her enclosure into the group, that fall; by the time Cherry disappeared from school she had already virtually disappeared into it. It was overwhelming, their collective affect, stiff and sweet as carbon monoxide. A girl might walk down the hall effulgently, and a vacuum of absolute powerlessness swallowed the watcher. I had seen Mr. Corless, the Spanish teacher, working to maintain his composure in the nearness of Cathy Dennison, a bearer of this invincible light, this unwieldy heat, this chalice of waste. And I had seen Cathy Dennison's father, Tom, struggle to fasten his eyes on his club sandwich at the Top Hat one day when a gaggle of girls came in straight from volleyball practice, all flushed and damp in their polyester warm-up suits. The true daughters of Wick.

. . .

I THOUGHT I WAS invisible, but one of them spotted me, as I sat under a tree in front of the school near the usual bench around which they congregated to light up their cigarettes after the final bell had rung. Teresa Gagnon nuzzled her face into her friend's ear; Christine Farnsworth looked at me and then back at Teresa, who repeated whatever she had said to the group at large. They all turned their glossy heads in my direction, and then Christine detached herself from the group and stood before me with the sun directly behind her blondness, a blazing halo. I had to shade my eyes to look up into her face. I squinted at her for a minute before I understood that she was not going to lower herself to join me on the ground, so I stood up, a full six inches taller than she.

"Hey, Ginger," she said, convivial. "We were wondering if you know what's going on with Cherry. You guys used to always hang out together, so we thought maybe she would have called you?" I was expecting something else: a bullying, a dressing-down, a comeuppance. *Look what you've done. You have not been a good friend. You're a slut. You freak. Weirdo.* The last thing I expected was to find myself consulted. "I went by her house, and we've all left messages, but it's like she's evaporated. It's just weird. If you talk to her, tell her we're all thinking about her and we miss her." Christine wheeled around and regained her remaining friends.

YOU COULDN'T EXACTLY SAY that I went looking for Cherry, that day, but I did think that I would find her. There were only so many places we knew how to get to. I rode my bike through town, across the little bridge and down to the mill. The oaks on the riverbank had turned a brilliant yellow-orange, and the red brick structure looked even redder against the saturated blue of the sky, that kind of deep, cornflower blue that you usually only see in decorative glass objects. I leaned my bike against the guardrail, climbed over it, and half-slid down the little hill to the riverbank, to our accustomed spot under the trees, from where I could almost discern the busted lock on the iron doors.

I SAW HER LYING THERE, facedown, under the trees. I saw her red canvas sneakers first, then her bare legs, still brown from summer. I saw her white shorts and pale yellow sweatshirt, her black hair in disarray around her shoulders. Her head lay cradled on her folded arms, as though she slept, or as though she had crumpled forward and landed gently, fortuitously.

I crouched a few feet away, and remembered the dream I'd had when sleeping with my face in Raquel's diary: the dream of the reservoir, of lost towns, of lost houses and families and drowned girls. I remembered that the last thing I saw under the water, before I woke up, was Cherry's pale body floating, her black hair wreathed around her blue face, her black lips, her empty sockets.

I DON'T KNOW what sound I made, but it was enough to make Cherry flop over and sit up abruptly. I shot to my feet and danced a few yards backward in a jig of horror. But Cherry's face was not the face of a dead girl, a girl who had been ripped away from her life prematurely, as I had imagined such a face might look: forlorn, bereft, endlessly removed, but yet infused with a gentle taste for vengeance, a need to make the living share in her despair. The look in her eyes might change swiftly from imploring to desecration. To desecrate the living. No, Cherry's face was stained with tears, pale and shiny, her cheek reddened where it had rested against her arm. Her nose was running. "Ginger," she said accusingly, and was clearly alive. "You scared me. I've been here every day, after school, but you never come to find me." A double accusation: I scared her and I didn't find her. I tried to remember where I had been yesterday, after school. Oh yes, at the Motherwells'. And the day before? I didn't seem to be able to remember that far back.

"I need to talk to you . . . I need to tell you something. I wasn't sure I could talk about it at all, but . . . now I realize it's my responsibility—" Cherry looked at me intently, wiping her face on her sweatshirt, one sleeve and then the other.

But I didn't want to hear what she had to say. It was enough to know that she was alive, and weeping. I turned to go, to leave her there. I was beginning to feel visible again, in the old way, and I didn't like it. I didn't want to let it take effect. I might have preferred it if she was dead.

"Wait!" She grabbed my arm, and yanked me roughly down to the ground. "You sit here. I'll hide your bike." I watched her clamber up the hillside, push my bike into the bushes on the other side of the bridge, and slide back down the bank. She looked thicker than I remembered her, swollen, as though she'd been left in a bowl to rise overnight like dough. She plopped herself down, facing me, and crossed her legs. The seat of her white shorts, I mused, would undoubtedly be soiled, besmirched. She was more than a little out of breath, but had an unusual air of resolution. She would say what she had to say.

"Look, I'm sorry that I've been ignoring you at school. My parents told me to stay away from you, which was really hard for me!" She looked at me, and paused, as though waiting for reciprocation. But I was waiting, too. "After that night . . . I was ashamed of myself. I tried to tell you, that day, and when Randy came instead I told him, but now he's really angry about it and I'm afraid of what he'll do. I finally talked to Mrs. Downey"—that was our hygiene teacher—"and she made me feel better about it . . . about what happened. She said it wasn't my fault—" and suddenly Cherry burst into tears again. Not just tears, but sobs, great, racking sobs that bent her over into her own lap. I sat silently, still waiting. I knew from long experience that if I offered sympathy, in the form of a pat on the back or a soothing murmur, it would only bring on a fresh torrent. I sat still, and eventually my patience was rewarded. Cherry straightened her back and wiped her red eyes again on the damp arm of her sweatshirt.

"Ginger, you're my best friend . . . you *still* are. So you have to just trust me. Mrs. Downey says I have to trust my friends to support me, and that they have to trust me to tell them the truth." Again she paused, this time, it seemed, to gather her wits, or her resolve. She plunged in.

"You have to stay away from those people." She drew herself up a little higher, placed her hands on her abdomen as though it were a crystal ball. "That night, when I got sick at their house . . . At first I couldn't believe what was happening. I kept thinking, 'Maybe he's just being nice and trying to comfort me.' But then he tried to give me a back rub, and I was like 'Mr. Motherwell, you're making me uncomfortable.' Because I remembered from what Mrs. Downey said in hygiene class that that's what you say to someone if they're touching you in a way you don't like. And they're supposed to stop. But he didn't stop—" her voice quavered, her eyes filled, and she paused a moment to regain control.

"He kind of put his face right up close to my face and just kept looking into my eyes like that would make me do whatever he wanted, like I was supposed to let him kiss me or something. And this whole time, Raquel's upstairs, and I swear to God she must have been awake, and then he . . . and then I just pushed him away from me and grabbed my shoes and ran out the door, barefoot. I didn't even stop to put them on till I was halfway back to town."

As Cherry neared the end of her story I couldn't help but hold it up for comparison against Theo's approach to me, so different, and so differently received. It occurred to me that he had never once kissed me, there in the mill. I felt slighted, a hole opening in the fabric of the memory of that night. I regarded Cherry's full lower lip: pink, tremulous, unsuspecting. I allowed myself for a moment to re-envision the scene at the mill. There I was, seated appealingly on the table, Theo's thin jacket under my bare ass. What if I had expressed some appropriate reservations. "Mr. Motherwell—Theo—I am too young. I've never done this before. What about

Raquel?" What if I had attempted to hold him at bay, to demur, to defer? Again I called up the scene, and myself murmuring entreaties, disclosing discomfort. I thought it quite possible that with the addition of only a very few protests on my part, Theo's already assured advance could have been made even more so. I could have drawn him out. He might have spoken to me, might have murmured to me, cajoling, might have kissed me; I could have tasted his mouth. I remembered now, with surprising olfactory nuance, the thick, almost burnt scent of his skin, his hair, his breath, as he had brought his face near mine on his way down between my legs. Wine, wood smoke, dried sweat, inexorability.

"And then," Cherry continued, "I didn't know where to go, because I didn't want to go home, and I didn't want to make your parents suspicious, so I went over to Randy's house and sat on his back stairs for a while, but he didn't come home. Finally I went to my house. I was completely freaked out. I felt like I must have done something to make Theo think that I wanted to . . . or maybe it was the clothes I was wearing. Do you remember, I had on my white T-shirt that says 'Juicy,' and my black shorts that are kind of high . . . but Mrs. Downey says that it's never the fault of the victim. 'That's typical victim thinking,' she says, and no matter what, it's not my fault. . . ." Again, the sharp relief she felt at being absolved from blame by this hygienic authority caused her voice to break and her eyes to fill with tears.

"And here's the other thing I wanted to tell you. . . . That day that Randy found me at the mill, when you were supposed to come meet me . . . I . . . I did it with him." She blushed and looked away from my eyes for a moment, then back, and continued somewhat apologetically. "I think I was just so upset, and he was being so sweet to me. He's been *so* sweet to me. . . . I really wanted to talk to you about it. I always thought that we'd tell each other right away when we lost our virginity"—as though we had a collective hymen—"and then it was like the opposite, it was like I lost my best friend at the same time that I lost my virginity. . . . I just felt like I couldn't tell anybody, not even you . . . or maybe especially not you. You're so good, and you never do anything with boys, and I just felt like such a slut!" Cherry burst back into tears now, her dark eyes remaining fixed on mine this time, beseechingly, and her nose pinking up. "I got home and just crawled into bed. I didn't feel that well the whole next day, and . . . I still don't feel well . . . I . . ."

This would have been the moment at which I should have offered some comfort, should have said that it sounded like she'd been through quite an ordeal, should have effected a rapprochement. I should have asked her why she had been staying home from school—*Was anything wrong?* I should at least have passed along the kind regards of Teresa and Christine and the others. But I did not. I was thinking how odd it was that I had not even considered seeking Cherry out to tell her about my own Very Special Beginning—but then these exploits, like Mr. Penrose's magazines, seemed to exist in a different realm from our friendship, which, after all, had been based in childhood, in childhood's innocence. Wasn't this what we both had been ever so swiftly paddling away from, each in her own little boat?

After a full minute of my silence it must have become clear that I was not going to offer any of the expected condolences. Cherry's face screwed up into an unbecoming ball and she sobbed. "Doesn't anything matter to you anymore?"

I WOULD NOT SAY that nothing mattered to me. I felt protective of my new life with Raquel and Theo, of its special distinction. I did not want to lose the hope it offered me, hope for a future in which nothing that I already knew would continue. In which I was already different.

It is not true that nothing mattered to me. It is more accurate to say that for me such seemingly pressing questions as the ones Cherry asked, albeit indirectly—who to trust, of whom to be afraid—had the quality of dilemmas faced in a dream, a lucid one, one from which I could wake up whenever I wished; one whose decisions I could therefore delay making indefinitely, and whose implications would only grow richer, more fascinating, the longer I delayed both decision-making and awaking.

I looked up from my lap just in time to see one large, pure, crystalline teardrop fall into Cherry's lap, onto the hand in her own lap, where it lay still and quiet. I looked up farther, to her face, where in her eyes more tears gathered, silently, waiting to follow their leader. I looked up further, above her dark hair, to the stony face of the mill, whose dark windows had once contained and reflected our shared majesty, our secret royal ancestry, our unlimited power and freedom. I looked above the mill's peaked roofline into the deep blue October sky and saw my real freedom moving, like an alternate sky, or like a veil dropped over the sky, over and above any of these realms I had known before. My real, true freedom was a mystery—was, itself, *mystery:* I didn't need to know anything more about Cherry, or about myself, or about the Motherwells, for the moment. When all was revealed to me, when the veil was dropped from my one, true face, then I would truly be a prisoner.

Cherry left me there at the mill. She did not say goodbye, just stared at me as I sat silent, and then rose up clumsily, stiffly, like a doll with no hinge at the waist, and walked away. I watched her figure moving down the road, then climbing the hill toward the big white house on the green.

29.

Mid-October

"You're never going to understand the profound sense of alienation that I experience when in nature. Are you." Raquel spoke somewhat rhetorically to Theo. I was listening, crestfallen and relieved in equal measure to find myself back in my usual role, a lucky bystander to their extended collision. My own run-in with Theo did not seem to have altered this relationship, and I do not know what I would have done with the transfer of Theo's full weight onto me—the attempt to visualize such a development left me with yet another blank spot in my cortex, a blot of unthinking—though I allowed myself to glance at him often in the simple, unpredicated hope that I might find him glancing at me.

We were out in the woods behind the high school, on a sunny late afternoon, following one of the many paths forged by kids in their desperate search for a quiet place to smoke pot at recess. This path, if followed for three-quarters of a mile, took one all the way to the muddy, overgrown edge of the reservoir. The fallen leaves on the ground seemed to hiss.

"Well, yes, I do understand it, I believe." He stopped on the path. "Probably not in the way that you would want me to. Talk and think, that's all you ever do. When you have only to act." He retreated from this typically abbreviated outburst, his back to us, hands clasped at his ass, looking at the ground, or at a stunted tree trunk growing diagonally out of the ground. He turned around quietly and we resumed our walk.

"I hate it when you say things like that. Things that ring so true. When it seems to me that you could just as easily say 'I love an orange when it's in segments' as you could say 'Niggers are filthy,' or 'Your mother sucks cocks in hell.' You are just as much of a monster as I am, Theo."

She watched his face very closely as she said that. Then she turned on her heel and ran off the path, into the forest. She ran a little clumsily but with great force, like a bear, or a stone that has turned to flesh. Soon she was out of sight.

We walked in the direction of her flight for a bit, then Theo suggested—and my heartbeat quickened at the suggestion—that we'd better wait for her at home. "That way she'll know where to find us," he said. We turned around and walked in silence.

IN THE HOUSE Theo went to make hot cocoa in the kitchen and I wandered up to his study. The bed was pushed against the wall in the corner and all the bedding folded into a narrow pallet in the middle of the floor. He'd been meditating. I wanted to look at his books.

And I wanted to ask him what had happened to Raquel to make her like this, to rip her off from the surface of the world like a decal. There must have been, I was convinced, some traumatic, some decisive occurrence: a schism of some sort. Someone must have done something to her. The fact that she never spoke of any such event almost seemed to me to be proof. There were so many things, in those days, that I took for granted. For instance, that none of the more ominous eventualities would pan out. That's how we go on living our lives, after all: hoping for, if not the best, at least not the worst.

THE BOOKS on his shelf looked as though he had made good use of them, traveled with them, slept with them under his pillow, stuck them in backpacks and pockets. I picked out one and flipped open its stained, dog-eared cover. Theo's footsteps were on the carpeted staircase and he came in with two cups steaming in his hands. I turned to him with the book like a giant clamshell I had wrestled open.

"What are you looking at?" He stepped close, setting down the mugs on top of the bookcase, and took the book from me, and it all started to feel as though it had already happened. "Ahh. The downfall of Western civilization. *Cogito ergo fuckface*. This man has destroyed more young lives than crack cocaine, broken condoms, and plastic surgery all rolled up into one secret weapon.

"Here's another one of my favorites. The tragically flawed Marquis de Sade." He pulled a thick paperback from the shelf, allowing it to fall open where the spine of the book was cracked from frequent use.

"This man had a notion, a precursor to the modern regulatory axiom about your right to smoke that cigar extending only as far as the tip of my nose. De Sade believed that his right to smoke a cigar extended as far as using the nearest eyeball for an ashtray. He sewed up a woman's vagina, once. I mean he wrote a philosophical tract in which this act exemplified his beliefs. He had great sex, with virgins and old women and young men alike. Every orifice was available to him." Theo's cool gray eyes were steadily trained on my hot face, as though he was waiting for me to signal understanding before he moved forward. I tried a smile, but it felt as though I might cry. I was waiting again, inside that space inside, which he had made for me, in which I waited for him. In which I waited in fear for him to fuck me again. In which I could not wait for him to fuck me again.

"Basically, his concept was that he could do what he wanted to when he wanted to, to whomever he wished. Not because it felt right in the moment, or because he suffered from delusions of mutuality. But because he felt free to partake in the illimitability of his actions. He loved asses. His sister's ass, for example. I don't know if he even had a sister. He just loved a nice hot asshole." Theo paused for a moment, as if in contemplation. A certain tension built up in the room.

"But the thing that makes him so lovable, in the end, is his fallibility. After all, what about the day when someone decides to hit you over the head with a frying pan? Whether your name is de Sade or Motherwell or Kissinger, your head gets opened. Your head, my frying pan; my frying pan, your head." His restive gaze sifted through my hair, fastened on my earlobe. His last words rang in the room like some kind of anti-clarion call. The silence that hung behind them was enforced as if by a curfew.

He moved past me to the bookshelf and put the book back. We sat down on the floor with our mugs, as there were no chairs. An uneventful episode. Nothing would happen, after all, between us, ever again, and I noted the voluminous relief I felt, and an equally gushing disappointment. I had just lifted my cup to drink when he put out his hand toward me and touched my breast through my T-shirt, on the top part, where it slopes positively toward the nipple. I held my cup in midair: it was the only thing I could look at in the room. I briefly considered whether we would be able to hear the door opening, closing, over whatever sounds we might make.

He said, "Are you finished with that?" I wasn't, but he took the cup out of my hand, set it down, and pulled my shirt over my head, all one motion, like a raptor plucking a field mouse. He put his hands on my bare shoulders and pushed with a constant pressure; I moved backward and down, supporting myself on my hands and then my elbows until I was flat on the folded blanket. I thought he might now kiss me—my mouth was open—but he didn't. I opened my legs. He took his hand away from my breast and rubbed the crotch of my jeans, hard, then unbuttoned them. I lifted my hips off the blanket and he pulled the jeans roughly down around my ankles, along with my underwear. I was exposed to the air.

This time was very different from the first. There was no sense in which I was attended to. I supposed that was appropriate: I was no longer a beginner. Now it was all for him. When he found his release, within five minutes, the hair on the back of my head was matted from his shoving and I felt like a piece of old wood, beaten against the shore by waves. Cold and porous.

We quickly sat up and dressed. I realized that I had shut my eyes at the start, as soon as I was laid down, and only opened them after he had stopped moving and rested his cheek on my breast. I wished that I had thought to watch his face, as it went through its motions.

We sat side by side on the floor, just as we had been, and drank our cocoa, still warm. My throat was sore from breathing with my mouth open. I combed my hair out with my fingers.

"I don't know what Raquel's been telling you, Ginger." He began in this way, the timbre of his usually light, reedy voice richer than before, as though orgasm had caused his blood to be drained from his veins, heated, then reintroduced. I simply waited.

"She can be very convincing, and so can I. But you need to be careful. We all need to be careful." Another cryptic warning, now seeming almost comically misplaced. "It is dangerous to believe one person's side of any story; there is always another. And in the end, none of it may be true.

"I want to tell you this now, because I see that you mean a lot to Raquel—" This hurt: to Raquel? Had I not met him halfway each time? Was it not important to him that I was ready for him? "And when something is important to her she will do anything she can to hold on to it." I wondered why she would think that she had to do anything special to hold on to me, when I was pinned, like a butterfly to a mounting board.

But it seemed he was intent on telling me a story. "Raquel and I have not known each other for very long," he began.

This I already knew, though it was difficult to understand how two could come to rely on one another so quickly, or at least how they could become so enmeshed, or could know each other so deeply. As I cast my mind through these configurations, I found myself rejecting each one in turn. I knew nothing, I decided, about the relationship between any two people, least of all these two.

Theo continued, and I found that I knew even less than I thought. "I met Raquel about a year ago in a treatment program at a psychiatric clinic in the city. I had just been released from jail, two years early for good behavior, on condition that I participate in an extended group therapy. She was one of eight others in the group. She'd been institutionalized for several years, and had also just been reintroduced to society. Over the course of a year, the other seven all dropped out, and that left Raquel and me and two therapists. It turned into a kind of mock couples counseling, with Raquel and I as a default couple.

"At first she couldn't even look at me when she spoke. She was incapable of meeting my eyes for more than a few seconds. The therapists worked on that a lot with her, actually keeping track of her gaze, its duration. In that room it was as though I stood for every other person in the world, to her. If she could hold my eyes as she talked to me—believe in my existence, really—then she was healing, the therapists said. And I suppose her belief in me healed me, too.

"I'll never know if it was this relationship that was set up for us, or if I simply took an opportunity to do good for once in my life"—he shook his head quickly, as though to reset his brain—"but I found, after a while, that I wanted to take care of her. I wanted to protect her, in the therapeutic environment and then later, when we started to spend time together outside of the clinic, which was of course forbidden by the rules of the treatment program. We met two or three times, before and after the group session, and then decided that we didn't need the therapists anymore."

THEY DROVE IN through the churchyard gates, under the curious gaze of the houses all around the green, over the rutty one-lane road that winds past the church itself and on into the graveyard proper. Theo parked and put the emergency brake on, as they were on a hill, and then they walked down toward the oldest part of the graveyard, where the trees were tallest and the graves showed the most wear. Only the slate stones were legible. Slate is odd: smooth as a sheet of paper; always cool to the touch, no matter how hot the day; austere yet quite contemporary in dove-gray or mauve.

They trailed amongst the stones in a light drizzle, fanning out and calling to each other funny old names like Thankful and Hepzibah. They walked around, looking at graves. This is Theo's version. They were looking for no grave in particular. They felt a common delight in burial sites: a place of unquestionable significance. There is no way to avoid addressing in some manner their connotations. When you walk in a graveyard and it is sunny and bright out you may feel illuminated in your mortal form. The soil, the ground, the grass that grows, your feet, your legs, your torso, neck, and brain. All living, and what is beneath completely dead, at the cellular level. Or you may feel the pressure of the nonlife itself, historically speaking. *All these lives, once just like mine, self-important, full-hearted. Every last one of these dead people must have had a dream of becoming famous at one time or another.*

Or you may feel, on a gray and chilly spring day like the one on which they first came to Wick, the full impact of the dead. Certain people on a certain day will get the dead inside them, filling every niche that has been prepared by all the living that they have done. First there is a heightened awareness of the potential gravity of your situation. Here you are, laughing and talking and walking on all the places where people's bodies have actually been put into the earth. It is possible, after all, that they really don't like it, that they resent this show of disrespect: your feet on their final resting place. And then you catch yourself on this train of thought and think again: "Who is 'they,' for God's sake? Do I really believe that there is a particular spirit attached to a particular dead body, actually lurking around in the near vicinity, 'haunting' as it were, waiting for some poor, live person to come around and transgress?"

And by repeating to yourself over and over these words, like "dead body," and "waiting," and "alive," as you continue to walk in and amongst the gravestones, careful not to be too careful about where you walk, you begin to see things. A white flash in the corner of your left eye: a rabbit on the path? Another on the top of that hill over there: just a particularly tall gravestone, rising above the horizon line. You can try to shake it off but you are over the threshold, now. The words used to describe the dead and their surroundings are weighty and endlessly variable: they are like the shadows of words.

Apparition, decomposition, materialization, haunt, return, still, peace, rest, eternal. And that is the truth of it. For whether the dead are at rest or returning, peaceful or haunting, that condition is eternal. The body is dead, the spirit is present. Or the spirit is dead forever; the body is always somewhere.

And now you are absolutely saturated with the language of the dead, of death. The tongue of death is in your mouth, and if you are anything like anyone, like everyone, you are spooked. It's time to go, to get out of the realm of all the significant names, the real place where bodies are kept. It's time to get back to somewhere that does not have such a specific purpose: a house.

RAQUEL AND THEO WALKED between the gravestones and Theo read out loud the ones he could make out: "Charity Putnam, beloved wife of Samuel, 1740–1762. Not very old. People died younger back then. Often in childbirth, women died. And here's Samuel. 1720–1784. He was a lot older than her. That was common, too. Look at this one; Maribelle Lawson. That's a fancy name for those plain times. She was three years old. Can't you just see her? Curls and a starchy frock.

"Wow, Lavonia Threadgill. And her husband Deodat. Those are the kinds of names that completely determine a personality. No chance that they would be the town pump and the town drunk. They must have been upstanding. Entirely beyond suspicion."

"As are we," Raquel responded airily, moving on to a tall slate stone with a long inscription. "My God, Theo. Listen to this. *Look on me as you pass by / As you are now, so once was I / As I am now, so must you be / Prepare for death, to follow me.* Keziah Snow. Seventeen-something. This man was thinking ahead. He chose to speak directly to the living, for all eternity. He sussed it out and knew that we would be open to some words of wisdom, from beyond."

Theo stood beside her, in front of the stone. It was particularly shady, where they stood, beneath a tremendous, ancient elm newly leafed out. "Or maybe he was just a bitter man, a man who had no clue what the afterlife held, nor, for that matter, what his life preceding it had held. It sounds like he thought of little besides his own demise, in his last days. When he sat and wrote, in his cramped and spidery hand, this last message to the world."

"Yes, he must have spent a lot of time presupposing his exact position in the box, underground, under the stone, under the tree, under the sky. I wouldn't mind staying here for a little while."

"Under this tree?"

"No."

"Here, in this graveyard?"

"No."

"In this town?"

"Right."

"Well, we can stay for dinner, if you like? I think I saw a little place . . ."

"Why don't we see if there's an apartment available?"

"What, for the summer?"

"For whenever. For forever. Why not here? Here seems as good as anywhere else, if not better. I bet it's cheap.

"And," Raquel continued, "this is just exactly the kind of town I've always wondered about. I drive through, on my way somewhere else, and I see a 'For Rent' sign in an apartment above a doughnut shop or a florist and I just want to stop the car and alter my path entirely, irretrievably, irreparably. The path is arbitrary anyway, why not acknowledge that truth by making truly arbitrary choices? If I lived in an apartment above a doughnut shop in a town like this, that would be the solution to the whole problem of identity, right there. In this context, who could name me? I would be void-of-course, like a moon, and like a moon I would orbit my new planet. And anyone who observed me would be changed. They would reflect a new me back at me and I would be, therefore, new."

"Only one objection, my dear. Or rather an amendment."

"What, my dear?" The endearments were spoken without irony, but knowingly.

"You won't be alone."

"You and I in an apartment in a strange, small town. Don't you see that I will be alone just the same?"

"Better yet," Theo said, with typically sudden and full enthusiasm. "How about a real house? I bet we could get one of those big old houses. I have always imagined that in a big old house I could spread myself thinly throughout, really inhabit it." His certain eyes.

"Become one with it, as it were," she said.

Theo glanced sideways at her sharply to see if she was making fun of him. It was often difficult to read her tone of voice. A single eyebrow was gently raised. When entirely in earnest, as she so often was, both eyebrows shot up.

"Why, yes. Do you have a problem with that?"

"No," she said. "My darling." These words like a sound check for another, more persuasive endearment.

One month later they drove back into town with their few belongings and moved into the house they'd purchased from Mr. Grose, the selectman, who also ran Grose Realty.

RAQUEL MATERIALIZED in the doorway, a lit cigarette in her hand. I had not heard her shut the door downstairs, nor come up the staircase, nor smelled the smoke. I was engrossed. I was remembering the bubble of light she had evoked so genuinely, on that rainy day when Cherry and I stayed upstairs in her room for hours. The bubble of mutuality that had held the two of them together, outside the office of the academic, in her story, in which at the moment of contact it had been difficult to hold his eyes, but not out of fear, or disability, or disbelief; rather it was an excess of illumination, as though the moment of being seen, a shared experience, or a shared feeling within that experience, caused something like pain, expressed as blindness. In Theo's story, he had misrepresented her pain, just as she had in her story misrepresented his desire to look at her. Everyone wants to look at someone when they are speaking. How disappointing.

"I do like to have a postcoital cigarette," Raquel remarked, deliberately casual. "Smoking is just one of the many things I can't seem to become addicted to." She crossed the room and sat down on the bare mattress. Theo held out his cup. I took it and passed it. She reached out and dropped her half-smoked cigarette in the cup, but left it in my hand. She slid off the bed and down to the floor, to our level. I sloshed the ashy dregs of cocoa around in the bottom, and the cigarette drowned in them.

"Since you're telling stories, Theo, why don't you tell Ginger all about how you ended up in prison?" She slid her eyes around to regard me. "It's probably the most interesting thing about him, in the end—though you've found out by now that he can be very entertaining, given the chance. I do hope you're all right, dear. He can be entertaining, and more than a little self-serving." I was as humiliated by the note of motherly concern in her voice as I was at the realization of her knowledge. She knew what was happening between Theo and me: nothing. Nothing was happening that did not include her.

"Again, Raquel," Theo said, speaking from out of his silence like a singer who has waited for just the right stillness to break, "just look. Once more you've provided us with what could only be described as 'atmosphere.'" He got up and walked over to the window, waving at the air in front of him, in which shafts of low-slung sunlight coming in through the panes had materialized, lent body and volume, a medium, as it were, by the curls of smoke she had blown through her nose and mouth as she spoke.

She looked to where he pointed and snorted a little, laughing, a flush in her cheeks. Still laughing: "He tried to do his own mother in."

I looked at Theo; he was watching Raquel with an almost imperceptible smile on his lips. He saw me watching him and his smile broadened, though he did not smile *at* me. Suddenly I could see just exactly what he must have been like as a small boy: confident, toothsome, amoral. I saw how his mother might have found it difficult to find fault with him for *anything* he did. He held a pillow over her face. He gently pressed it, or he brutally smashed it, or he caressed her silvery hair with one hand while he leaned on the pillow with the weight of his whole torso. Or he wielded a blunt instrument, her fine hair sticky with blood.

"That's true, but it's not what it sounds like."

"Oh, go ahead, Theo, tell her the whole story."

"There's not much to tell, is there." He turned to face me and made a little bow, then clasped his hands behind his back and thrust his chest out in a parody of recitation. "My mother was ill; her quality of life had sunk below acceptable levels. I had been asked to take care of her, and I took care of her in the way I saw fit. Which involved a bottle of painkillers, a mortar and pestle, and a cherry Coke. My father came into the kitchen just as I was preparing this merciful potion, and he reacted badly. Called the police. Pressed charges. . . . My mother was the only one who appreciated what I was trying to do. Though as it turned out she did survive the chemotherapy quite well in the end, and has since gone into full remission."

"Sometimes she'll contrive to see Theo when he goes into the city," Raquel chimed in, "and she'll slip him a few hundred dollars. Enough for groceries for a few weeks."

THE TABLES HAD TURNED, and I was like an indulgent parent, full to the brim with unconditionality. There was nothing that either of them could say, or do, nothing that anyone could tell me, that would cause me to give up on them. No inconsistency in their stories, no reversal of fact or fiction. I had moved far beyond judgment, beyond acceptance, into love. The magic spell of love. The oldest metaphor in the book. My love was for the two of them together, as indivisible a unit as Theo had once figured me with Cherry—as we had once been—that stabbing pain again. Apart from each other they were unlovable, but fused together in love they required, demanded, and owned my love. I could not go back. However, my bladder was uncomfortably, postcoitally full. I got up off the floor and moved past Raquel, my leg brushing her shoulder, out of the room, into the hall, into the bathroom. I pissed, then went to the kitchen for a glass of water.

I could hear them continuing their conversation quietly as I slipped down the stairs. I felt as though I were a ghost, and that I moved as in a dream of moving. My feet did not touch the ground, and I had only to think of where I meant to go and I was there. In the kitchen I found lemonade in a tall pitcher waiting for me on the table, and a glass filled with melting ice. As I rose up the staircase, thirst quenched, I listened for more chatter, but heard only what sounded like weeping.

I STOOD IN THE DOORWAY. Raquel and Theo sat facing each other, cross-legged, on the floor. Theo held Raquel's hand in his, palm up, like a fortune-teller.

They looked to be playing some kind of game—a word game, a guessing game? But I could see this was a game of a different sort. Raquel's eyes were closed, and her face was wet. Her nostrils and mouth had a suffused, inflamed look, like those of a child who simply cannot stop crying and eventually cries herself to sleep.

But Raquel was not asleep; she spoke, as Theo turned to me slowly with his finger to his lips.

"I went all the way down to the reservoir," she said. "It was quieter there than I could stand. I came back to hear the sound of your voice.

"But I will never know . . ." she said, and her own voice sounded as though it was coming from somewhere in her stomach. It was lower and somehow flatter. "All I know is that it hurts me to be near you. Like I am cooking on the inside.

"Because I say the things and they just slide off. It's like throwing snow at ice."

Theo's hand rested gently on her shoulder. "But you do want to be with me, don't you? All you have to do is want. You have always wanted to be with me." This was a prompt, as though he had coached her before in the answer. There was a note of trepidation there, too. He was afraid of what the real answer might be.

But Raquel was asleep after all, for her voice began to quaver suddenly, to slide, to half-sing syllables that I could not recognize, a kind of slippery flux of sonic essay. Then the syllables began to gather, to gel, and her mouth opened wider as she spoke louder, and more quickly, so that the words cohered out of their discrete parts. But just as I thought that I could begin to make out a series of words, a litany of declaration, a round of utterance (could it be that she said what I thought she said?), Raquel suddenly sat straight up, as though a wire at the top of her head had been pulled, and then crumpled forward into Theo's lap, where she lay quiet. I sat frozen as Theo stroked her hair; finally he looked around at me again, a sternness on his face that I hadn't seen before—like a parent, suddenly, protecting his only true priority—and motioned for me to go.

AT HOME I FOUND my own father stern and protective, waiting uncustomarily for me in the kitchen. It seemed Mr. Czabaj had lived up to his word and put in a call to let them know of my repeated absence from school. "What on earth, Ginger," my father asked, "is going on? What are you thinking? You girls have gotten a little bit out of hand lately. You and Cherry both need to think about the future—it's wonderful to have fun now, but you have to keep thinking about the future. Consider yourself on probation: I want to see you in your room every day after school doing your homework, or I'm going to say no more Mr. Nice Guy. No more fooling around. Now go on up and get started."

UPSTAIRS I LAY on my bed and thought of how Raquel had run just out of our sight, in the woods, and then disappeared. She had told me once of her suspicion that when she walked out of the sight and hearing of others she ceased to exist. Or, conversely—alternatively, but not exclusively—that whatever was out of her range of sensation ceased to exist. She knew the name for this. They call it solipsism, or sometimes, simply, self-interest, and they try to cure it, with psychology and medicine and politics, with philosophy when all else fails. I had to wonder if my virginity yet remained. Perhaps what Theo and I had done, not once but twice, had not been done at all, since Raquel had not seen it with her own eyes.

30.

All Hallows' Eve

Last October Cherry and I had costumed ourselves as punk rockers, in T-shirts our mothers artfully sliced holes in, T-shirts with safety pins stuck through, and jeans we found at the church thrift shop and decorated with slogans scavenged from televised and print media: "A" for Anarchy, Here Come the Warm Jets, God Save the Queen. *From what did a queen need saving?* I wasn't sure, but I had found an antique telephone cord in our garage, bright yellow, the spiraling kind, and worn it around my waist as a belt.

I didn't think I would bother with a costume this year. It had always been Cherry's job to spur me into make-believe. Without her I hadn't even been moved to visit the castle, not since my clash with Kip Brossard's motorcycle.

But I was surprised at how pleased I was to receive an invitation to an exclusive gathering in honor of All Hallows' Eve. A small card, tucked between the brake cables of my bicycle, in Raquel's hand, announced that we would feast and make merriment. Costumes required. This gave me one day to find my perfect disguise: What was I, really? More important, who did I wish to be, for this one night? I thought of dressing as a man. It would be easy—almost too easy. I could rummage through Jack's closet for his one tie—his clothes packed neatly away in cardboard boxes by my mother—and his navy blazer, and tuck my hair under a baseball cap, and draw a thin line with my mother's eyebrow pencil on my upper lip to make visible my latent masculinity. I imagined myself standing in the Motherwells' living room, a pillar among the swarm of other guests, a wineglass in my hand, wielding my temporary authority, my blithe unconcern, like a rapier. Raquel's laughing, convoluted appreciation. Theo's quick, mercenary appraisal. And who else would see me, in my harmless inversion? Who would the other guests be? Was this a gesture of goodwill toward the town, a long-overdue housewarming? Maybe Cherry would be there, with Randy, dressed as witch and ghost, or spider and fly, or bride and groom. The possibility of her presence provided me with a perfect lie and I told my parents that I would go home with her, would sleep at her house that night.

But when the day dawned, I could not prevent my mother from helping me with my costume. It was one of her earthly duties, and she would fulfill it; she came briskly into my room, her arms laden with cloth stuffs and a handful of sparkling items. "Honey," she exclaimed, when I showed her my sparse get-up, the slacks and button-down shirt I had culled from my own wardrobe, the jacket and tie and hat. I wasn't sure what to do for shoes. . . . "Don't you remember? Last year you said you wanted to be Ginger, from *Gilligan's Island*! Your namesake. It's such a great idea." It had been Cherry's idea; she wanted to be Mary Ann. "I've been scouting all year for a dress, and gloves, and costume jewelry. Look!" She dropped her armload on my bed and began sorting through the booty. A long, skinny, silvery dress with no sleeves, elbow-length white gloves, a pair of glittering, pointy pumps in white satin. Dangly earrings with crystals, a set of shiny, jingling bracelets. "I'll fluff up your hair, and I can draw a beauty mark on, and you'll look just beautiful." She had done all the work for me, and I had to hand it to her: she knew my size.

WRAPPED IN MY MOTHER'S plush evening cape, I sat in the passenger seat of the family car and surveyed the unnatural setting. But for the cars in the driveway, just their own two cars, one would have assumed that the house remained uninhabited. Bushes and beds in the yard had blossomed and dropped their blossoms and grown wildly unattended all summer, and now had returned to a state of untrained dormancy; the porch held the same dilapidated outdoor furniture. There was no sign of a homeowner's care, much less pride. "Well," my mother said, in the driver's seat, "I guess you're the first one here." I guessed so, too. "Are you sure they're home, sweetie? I don't see any lights." I could make out the faint glow of a candle in the front room, through the yellowed shade, but otherwise, she was right. The house was dark. It was Halloween, after all. . . . "Would you like me to come in with you? I don't want to cramp your style . . ." My mother offered this brightly, so as to skate over the obvious: she *wanted* to come in with me. We had passed loads of pleasure-seekers on our way to the Motherwells': toddling gangs of bumblebees and flowerpots, held tightly by the hand; bands of grade-school kids roving in prefab drugstore superhero and -heroine regalia; disdainful teenagers in a bare minimum of costume, hot for candy, pretending not to care whether they were tricked or treated. And all along I saw her carefully controlling her envy, her desire. She had been an actress, after all, and Halloween is what actors do every day. She missed it, and had poured the last ounces of her longing into the success of my costume this year, my starlet year, with my eyelashes laid on thick as caterpillars, my mouth a sticky, glossy mess, a beauty spot calibrated high on my left cheek, among freckles muted with powder.

But it was out of the question, and I heaved myself up from the low bucket seat in my handicapping dress and tottered toward the house on my high heels with the uncomfortable sensation of her bereft eyes glued to the back of my head. It's the kind of thing you have to shake off as soon as you can.

AND I DID, as I walked through the door, blinking in the gloom. Two figures were seated primly, almost punitively, side by side on the couch in the living room, a fat round candle on the coffee table before them, and no other light. I saw that it was my friends, but their costumes were so complete as to cast this certainty into doubt. They appeared to have slipped out of their own skins and into those of another young couple—one with an even closer relationship than theirs, it seemed, from the way they sat: erect; shoulders, hips, and thighs slammed together like the embattlement of a castle.

Raquel's thick hair was parted exactly in the center and combed tightly into a bun at the back of her neck. Her face was pale and plain, while her dark dress was wildly elaborate, with lace at the bodice, puffed and tapered sleeves, and many tiers sewn into its silk-beribboned skirt. The effect of these flourishes was merely to underscore the overwhelming mournfulness of the felted woolen gown. Theo's suit bore a corresponding set of grace notes signifying both wealth and grief: the tip of a black silk handkerchief peeked out of the breast pocket of his fine coat; his hat was round and plain like a Quaker's.

We all three gazed at one another for quite a while before Raquel spoke. "We don't often have the opportunity to reveal ourselves so clearly, do we," she said, and I blushed under my powder to feel the skeleton of my inner self, bones glowing unquenchably beneath the thin, silvery sheath. It made my skin hurt; I wished I could remove not just the thick makeup my mother had laid on, not just the dress into which she had zipped me, but also the casing of my flesh, to flay myself so that I could be free of the finality of the impression that I made. Short of that, I wished that I could wipe the mark I made off of the world, like a smudge off a snow globe.

"But didn't you tell me that you were coming as your poor brother?" Raquel's question seemed a sincere one, but I knew I had never said any such thing. What a horror that would have been, for my poor mother, so horrified already, on the anniversary of his death. It did occur to me then that my first feeble attempt at a costume, preempted by my mother, might have been read by the casual, yet savvy, observer as an unconscious attempt at a resurrection.

"I know you must miss him terribly," Raquel said, and I felt tears again prick up in my eyes like pins finding their way out of a pincushion. I did miss him, and never said so. After his death my parents did not often speak of him, but made offers of puppies, kittens, a rabbit, as though the Jack-shaped void ripped in the world could be patched by anything warm and soft. I, too, had made a habit of not speaking of Jack, and the more I thought about it the more certain I became that I had not spoken of Jack to Theo and Raquel. I had kept his death, indeed his life, his plain existence, "to myself," as they say; "close to my chest," as they say. It was a secret that gave me power inasmuch as it gave me unknowableness. It was my light, which I hid under a bushel. How could anyone pretend to know me when they did not know the biggest thing about me, which sometimes threatened to eclipse me?

"But I was looking forward to meeting him! A true friend, like your Cherry, will always give in to the temptation of sympathy. How sweet a fellow, how much you loved him, and how you alone have shouldered the weight of his death. Nothing can replace him," Raquel continued, as I reeled with the sudden spasm of my want—my brother, Cherry; my lost friends—"it is true, but this does not mean he must be forgotten. Tonight is a night for just such remembrances. And if we are lucky we may be visited, on such a night. Sit down, Ginger. We have work to do." She held her hand out to me, and the man beside her also reached toward me to close the circuit. A séance. My missing brother, a lonely ghost. He would like to come and meet these two, I thought, as he had in life liked anything that reminded him there was a world outside Wick, the outside world our mother had emerged from, after all, where people had names we'd never heard and excitement in the form of luck and trouble, speed and spirit, promised itself in the movies he watched and the music he played to himself through his headphones, the ones that still covered his ears in the back of the car when he was found, rocking out to nothing.

And I thought he would have been quite drawn to Theo, who cut a more dashing figure even than Randy; then I thought that things might have gone very differently for Theo if Jack were around, my big brother after all. Jack would have had to choose between the thrill of reckless endangerment and the innocence of his little sister. Maybe Jack could have had Raquel, I thought, an auspicious beginning to be sure.

A welter of dead interest, suppressed longing, purified terror churned in me and I turned toward the door, making faint noises about my shoes, how uncomfortable, how I needed to get my tennis shoes from the car. I could see its lights still against the living room wall, hear the engine idling. My mother waited.

"Ginger, don't go. You have suffered this bad dream enough. It's time to wake up." Raquel stood from the couch and I saw that in my heels, I had attained her great height.

"Don't run away, Ginger. My sister and I are so pleased, so honored, to have you here with us." Theo spoke coolly, evenly, and as he did he took Raquel's hand in his and pulled her back down next to him, then laid their clasped hands on his thigh. His gaze arrested me and I sank into a chair. "Jack will be pleased to be called forth, as we are pleased to be allowed to make our way freely in the world, to surface. We live submerged in the muck of our shameful past."

I thought they were right: Jack had been a sociable boy, with plenty of friends. He must be lonely. Unbearable, to think of his cold grave, in the plain new graveyard on the other end of town, where we never went. At first some kids, his gang, would visit the grave, and even set up a little shrine of sorts—he was that popular, that loved—but even love could not rescue him from real death. Maybe they had visited him tonight; would they notice if his spirit went missing and came to us here?

Then I heard the sound of my mother's car pulling away from the curb, making a U-turn, the little squeal of tires as she accelerated away from me. She had waited there until she was certain that someone was home.

"Do you know who we are," Raquel asked, and I nodded: I recognized them from the photograph. Or I recognized their bearing, their sheaths, their chrysalises. They turned to each other in mutual pleasure. "How gratifying," Raquel sang, a low song, and reached her hand around to Theo's cheek. She applied her lips, pale and dry, briefly to his. "Together in life, but too much so. It disturbed those around us. Together in death, until we were disturbed. Now we are together again in new life—bodies refreshed, faculties sharpened, love stronger than ever—and we will remain so as long as we are allowed. Will you allow us, Ginger?" Raquel extended her long fingers across the table to stroke the side of my face. I recoiled; I couldn't help myself. Their relationship was in every way so unnatural—their relationship to me.

I was not sure I could help them, much less myself. Then I did help myself. I stood up, as though to go, but did instead what any latent starlet would do under the circumstances. My head hit the corner of the table as I went down.

OUT OF AND INTO and out of consciousness I flew, a sparrow dazed by an encounter with a window, in a directed effort to retain the state of unknowing. My head jostled against Theo's solid shoulder in his cloth coat as he carried me upstairs and I dove down into it, pressing my face into the loose weave; Raquel's breath was warm on my cheek as she slid a pillow under my head and I melted into the pillow; I tossed into my life under a rough wool blanket, then tossed myself like a coin down a well back into the dark. Finally I simply slept, for long enough to dream of my mother and father wearing transparent masks that showed the blackness of their hearts against the whiteness of their skulls, my brother with a face like a bright golden coin at my window, *knock knock knock, let me in.* When I woke up it was because I was cold. It was morning. The window was open. It was the first of November and I lay on the pallet in Theo's study wearing his shorts, the third-world shorts he wore the first day I saw him, and a T-shirt that said "Oregon—We Love Dreamers." My head throbbed sharply, a spreading point of pain where it had made contact, and I drew the blanket over it and tried to forget that I was awake, but I could not. That recent unconsciousness, so benevolent, once lost was lost forever, and when I heard the sounds of dishes and forks and spoons downstairs, something cooking on the stove, the flutter of conversation, I realized that I was starving, and once I was starving, empty, I was filled up with a curiosity more potent than food, than knowledge, than any answering entity. It promised nothing but the provision of more, more. More. I rose and went to join them, whoever they would be in broad daylight.

31.

Late November

Raquel said she wanted to know the exact dimensions of Wick. This, sitting over coffee at the kitchen table. It was a deep, late fall day, and once more I had agreed not to go in for my shift at the Top Hat. I would stay right where I was. Theo was gone again to the city to see what he could find there.

It was Saturday and I knew the café would be busy, people stopping in for a milkshake or a grilled cheese or just for coffee and a chat with some of the other townsfolk. I felt sorry for Danielle, and for Billy, the little dishwasher, but at Raquel's behest I had called in to say that I had a very bad cold. A fall flu.

The streets, too, would be busy: men running in and out of the hardware store, children collecting in the doorway of the newsdealer, chewing gum and drinking sodas. Teenagers walking up and down the road aimlessly, in trios and pairs, grouping and regrouping. Women with small children in tow, maneuvering their bulky ways into the grocery store. All this activity in the commercial zone of Wick, in the slanting, deceptively mellow sunshine of mid-afternoon, late November.

Raquel was edgy at this hour. "I want to go among the people," she said, out of a protracted moment of consideration, "but not be of the people."

We tumbled out of the house into air that was sharper than it had looked and into Raquel's powder-blue Honda. It hadn't been driven in weeks, maybe months, and the engine turned over with the sound of dice shaken in a cup. "We'll have to let it warm up for a while," she said, and so we sat, and Raquel reached for the radio knob. She settled on a country-and-western station. "I could have been a country singer. I love the wordplay, the double entendres, the semantic reversals," she told me. "Another microcosmic reduction of our experience into palatable dialect and trope." I smiled and nodded, although I had no idea what she was talking about. Country music to me was just a sentimental outlet for people from the city.

We pulled out of the driveway and onto Route 7, heading south, toward town. I cracked my window a bit to cut the stale air in the car. Raquel began to make bright conversation. I didn't feel like talking. On such a beautiful day, it was enough for me—more than enough, actually—to just ride along and know that I was safe and warm, and that nothing would be demanded of me but that I be, and look, and breathe. The seat belt across my chest reminded me of this, and of being driven around by my mother, in the summertime, with Cherry in the backseat, and me playing with the radio dial until my mother would say "Stop! Enough already!" and we would giggle.

I wanted to tell Raquel of this dreamy, easy feeling. Each familiar sight of my town came quickly into view and just as quickly receded. The word "familiar" doesn't even apply, when describing something from which one has never been away. It would be like saying that the womb is familiar to the fetus.

RAQUEL DROVE SLOWLY, slowly past the little houses dotting the hill alongside Route 7. Perchik's dry cleaners on our left, the mill on our right, the riverbed running north to south behind it, perpendicular to the road. We crossed over the two-lane concrete bridge that signified our entry into the town proper.

"You know," Raquel said. "I can imagine feeling how you feel—I really can."

I just nodded. She needed no corroboration. We entered town and stopped at the one traffic light. Bank, shoe store, pharmacy, grocery. Four corners. She turned the car to the right, onto Main Street. We drove slowly past the parked cars and the shoppers, past the Top Hat and the insurance company with my father's shop above it. Squinting up, I thought for a second that I saw my mother's face in the window, and I thought I saw her see me, eyebrows raising. Then the sun was reflected off the window and we were past.

Where the shops end and houses begin, little ratty houses, Raquel turned the car around and we drove through the light again, taking a turn toward the village green. Some kids from school were hanging out at one end, tossing a Frisbee around. I thought I saw Cherry's black hair, her red corduroy jacket, as we drove by, but Raquel sped up and soon we were past the green, past the church and the graveyard and the Town Hall, and off on the Old Road, going up into the hills.

"You just don't know what it's like inside my brain," she said, and I could not help but grow a little irritated. Did she honestly think she knew what was inside mine? But she does, I thought then. She does.

"There is not one moment, waking or otherwise, that I am not being consumed by my own brain. And consuming it. My brain is eating itself, do you see? Am I here, with you, really, the way you are here with me, a captive audience? It doesn't matter what I say to you. Do you understand what I am saying?"

Her speech unfolded, as smooth and evenly modulated as ever—like a radio announcer's, it occurred to me—but her face was pale and her expression taut. She was nowhere near tears, but I somehow felt certain that she would weep soon, or had recently wept. The ghosts of tears.

"If you do understand what I'm saying to you," she continued, "it will be just another miserable joke at my expense. Oh, I am a monster, Ginger." Wryly, almost gently. "Do you understand, now? It would be a miracle, if you did." We wound up and up, in the little blue car, through the piney, hilly country, coming out into the open pastures of farmland. Little old houses, barns standing near in varying phases of dilapidation, strewn on either side of the road, at intervals, among the great fields.

Driving along. "Human lives are works of art. Complete with themes and leitmotif and clumsy symbolism. But we are not supposed to recognize this quality as we live them. That is what I call a curse. To make each second tick along. From the seat of the brain, pulling strings somewhere behind the eyeballs. Agonized."

The Wick town line bore down on us mercilessly. I noticed that she never placed her two hands on the wheel. She always left one lying in her lap. Now we had reached the summit of Wicker Hill. Raquel did a three-point turn, the car's rear end dangling far out over a ditch, and we headed back down toward town.

Raquel turned the car left on Route 7, back at the light, and we headed north again. We passed Mr. Motor's Auto-Body Shop, and had to swerve around a huge white truck parked along the roadside that said "Allied Technologies Automotive Appearance Specialists, since 1949," on its side. I pointed this out to Raquel, and she smiled a little disinterested smile that faded just as soon as it appeared.

We were past the Social Club, then the old barn on our right, coming around the hairpin turn, going uphill. We drove back through the center of town. Raquel turned the car toward the Old Road, heading, I guessed, toward the loop.

"I still believe that the difference humanity makes is incalculable, because it is a question of self-consciousness. In humans, self-consciousness varies only by degree, although it varies hugely. The day that a chipmunk sits up on a rock and tells me, or even just looks like it *wants* to tell me, that it's having trouble deciding what to eat, is the day that I will give up my title and join the ranks of those who see their place on the food chain. . . . You know, this all reminds me of one of my favorite stories, the allegory to end all allegories.

"I don't even remember where I first heard this. I can't tell stories. All I really recall is a servant, in some bushes beneath the window of the king, bearing a covered dish. Under the cover is a pure white snake, cooked, prepared simply for the king's consumption. It seems the king had overheard one day that in order to understand the language of the animals, the residents of that other kingdom just outside his window, one must eat of the rare white snake. At this point in the story, you, the listener, should be wondering just who it was he overheard say this. A sorcerer? A practical joker? Or was it a jackrabbit, speaking in human tongue.

"So he catches the fever of wanting. Now that he possesses this knowledge he must put it into action: he commands his servant to go out into the forest, return with the sublimely exoticized white snake, and bring it to him for his supper. This is where the story begins, in my memory, with that fabulous image of the weary, triumphant servant of the king, having spent all the long day in the forest entrapping the luminous, exquisite snake. Who knows what trials he underwent in its procurement? We can only imagine. See, this is the trouble I have with stories. It's the fleshing out part that bothers me.

"But ever onward with the engrossing narrative! The king, alone in his grandly appointed chamber, sits down and devours the white snake. It probably tastes a lot like frogs' legs, which supposedly taste like chicken. But a bit oilier, and stringier, I would bet. He cuts it up into little sections, small rings of snake, like calamari, and eats the whole thing. And then immediately goes out the window and into the forest, where, just as he had hoped, he converses freely with badgers and crows and wild boars and the occasional gazelle.

"He is gone for several months. The effects of the snake on the language centers are long lasting. And of course he is in a kind of ecstatic state of communion. The natural world! Opened up to him! He runs about in the forest and listens in on the unexpectedly fascinating dialogue of chipmunks, who chatter, their jaws stuffed with roughage. He understands wildcats when they address themselves to their god. He has interspecies communication skills! He serves as interpreter in the forest, settling disputes between hawks and voles, foxes and hounds. He is at one with what he believes to be the natural order, for the first time in his benighted, bejeweled, hierarchical life. In all his days of glory in the forest, however, he never sees another white snake.

"And this is because he has eaten the last one. An otter tells him so. And when the power of the previously ingested one begins to wear off, there is nothing for the devastated king to do but return home, to the castle, where he lives out the rest of his days in torpor and misery. It is the far greater ill, after all, to have a memory of a tongue stuck in your head with no capacity for speaking it, than to have had no tongue at all. The great king! The poor king. To remember the flavor but not the texture, to know that there was something so free, so wild, so necessary, that he could say, something being said all around him, but to have no recall of its content, its meat. Just like a dream. Not like riding a bicycle; that, they say, you never forget. But just like the way some people speak of the experience of having an emotion. Love, for instance. Or is love a metaphysical condition? Anyway, they say 'tis better to have loved and lost than never to have loved at all. But this was not so for the king. 'Twas misery to have understood so much! And then to fall back to not understanding.

"What fresh hell. What constantly fresh hell." Raquel sighed and leaned forward against the steering wheel.

We were stopped now at the end of the long access road, the road to nowhere, literally, or at least to nowhere that we could go and survive the going. In front of us was a footpath that led straight down to the edge of the water, to the submerged valley of lost ancestors, lost histories, lost names and truths and reasons.

I WONDERED, THEN, as Raquel turned the car toward home, and her multiplicity of stories faded from the air around us, if she and I were now best friends, as Cherry and I had been. But just as quickly as it entered my mind to wonder, I found the answer: if we were, I wouldn't have to ask myself the question in the first place. It's like magic that you don't ask it. About once a year, Cherry and I would pause for a moment in the middle of some day we were spending together, some formless, endless activity in which we participated, thoughtlessly, like two skinny monkeys, to survey our long, long history, and to conclude, inevitably, that it was good. We might laugh, then, that accomplished, and resume. Even the brevity of our exchange was a signature of our mutual perfection with relation to each other. We could be succinct together.

And now I found myself in the middle of a perfect fall day,

a day for exploring, for recounting, for dreaming, all on my own, with only this dismal, long-winded creature beside me as a reference point.

I don't think Raquel could have ever had one, a best friend, unless you count Theo, and I'm not sure that you can be best friends with someone who would kill you, given the chance, or who would fuck you and not kiss you. Someone who would eat you, or who would allow you to eat yourself. And watch you while you did eat yourself. But I'm confusing things: I was the one he fucks without a kiss. She was the one he watches while she eats.

As we drove past the Motherwells' driveway and then the high school, and then past the Qwik-Go, and then past the Lamplighter, and turned around at the Wick town line, it occurred to me that all of Raquel's talk was simply elaboration on one theme. She really was just killing silence, which could never be, for her, anything other than uncomfortable. Mr. Endicott had a phrase, about talking just to hear the sound of your own voice, which he used to use when Cherry and I had been on the phone for too long. Of course he was wrong: we talked just to hear the sound of each other's voice. But with Raquel it was more than that. For her, every silence, every break in conversation, was more than just a break, it was a breach. One was constantly called upon, in her presence, to literally *make* conversation, to pull it out of thin air, to conscientiously fill gaps which, with anyone else, might be stuffed by the accretion of a mutual history, of shared observation, of simple understanding. That's it, I suddenly realized, and almost felt moved to say *aha*, softly but aloud nevertheless, like a scientist too shy to shriek *Eureka*. With

Raquel there was no possibility of an understanding—not of coming to one, not of reaching one, certainly not the actuality of having one. It was as though time did not pass, in her company, as though each encounter with her was entirely new, as though there was no such thing as history, as continuity. One began with her afresh each time.

We pulled into the driveway but neither of us got out of the car. It suddenly felt to me just like that moment in movies when a couple is at the end of a date, when all that remains is for them to part ways, but a decision must be made about the tenor of that parting. Raquel made no motion to open the door, to get out. We turned slightly in our seats toward each other, repositioning knees and elbows.

"You do understand, now, what this is all about, don't you?" she asked me, not looking into my eyes but instead into the rearview mirror. I turned to look out the back: there was nothing behind us but the other side of the road. Then a car drove by, on its way out of town, probably, or to the Lamplighter for a quick flash of breasts, before dinner. I turned back and caught her eyes, which still held her question. I nodded my head yes, then no, then just as quickly yes again. I thought that I might literally nod my own head off.

I swiveled my torso to face her. "Love?" I croaked. Answering her, a large frog leapt out of my throat. She was startled—I suppose by the sound of my voice—and when her eyes darted into mine I saw something in them that made me look away, but not before she had done so first. Whatever it was was unbelievably difficult to observe, something like a hybrid of a dog who has just been hit by a truck but has not been killed, only had its rib cage crushed, its heart bleeding into its mouth, and a rock that has just been thrown through a plate-glass window. Or maybe the window itself.

Ten minutes had passed. I'm actually not sure at all how long we had been sitting there in the driveway, only that the sun had begun to set for real, and that it had grown chilly in the car. We reached simultaneously for our door handles, then stood for a moment looking at the sky, which was wreathed in long, striated clouds tinted morning-glory blue and rose, pale orange and violet. Faint stars showed through here and there.

"Now that's what I call 'firmament.' Nothing like a sunset to bring two people together, is there? Someone wrote about the fantastic properties of the setting sun, its position in the pantheon of natural phenomena. It does provide, really, the prime example of a sharable experience of aesthetic bliss, minus the critical distance, equaling 'beauty': the simulacra of objective reality.

"I am going to give birth to a child," she continued, never missing a beat. "In about six months. However long it takes. Will you help me around the house, then, when I've grown so huge I can't pick my own fork up off the floor where I've dropped it?"

I nodded, slowly, considering this scenario. Raquel at the table, big as a house, anemically pale from giving all her blood to Baby. The fork just out of her reach on the floor. Me, under the table to get it. I saw the fetus floating deep inside of her, in the dark, impossibly small for something so significant. The infant would be sickly, would require special care. Or maybe Raquel would not, as she had so often suggested, be able to sustain a life inside of her. An inner life.

But, in truth, I could only imagine that Raquel's pregnancy would be of the bloomingly healthy, regal sort.

"I only hope we can stay around that long," Raquel continued, after a long pause. "It may be that we'll be gone before you know it. One ought never to overstay one's welcome, Ginger—remember that."

32.

The holidays. It was Thanksgiving. Paper turkeys and burnished ears of Indian corn strung up all over town; my parents on stools at their Formica counter, making turkey sandwiches with jiggly cranberry jelly from a can, worrying about me. I wondered how the day would pass. My town made a big deal out of Thanksgiving. There was a parade down Main Street, with all the small children dressed up as Pilgrims. Many of the townspeople dressed up, too, just to watch, and later to sit in the stands at the football game at the high school. My parents were some of the few who didn't get the whole house trussed up like a turkey. I missed my parents terribly, suddenly. Raquel would have envied me, if she could have known what I was feeling. A tremulous concoction of pity and blood and vision: I saw them again in their sad, sturdy progress through the day, my mother rinsing dishes to put in the dishwasher, my father pausing behind her for a moment to give the tight muscles at the top of her shoulders a quick squeeze. They did not speak of me. They spoke of

Jack, in the only terms in which they spoke of him: his promise, his folly, his eternal glory. They wept. And here was I, getting older. I had promised to return home by three, for dinner at four.

We stretched out variously, like cats, on couches and in front of the fire Theo lit. The day was nippy and blue, very blue, with November's giant clouds moving slowly. I felt a strong desire to take a walk, to be outdoors in the day, to visit familiar sites, shops, to greet the people I knew. Or to turn a corner and see Cherry. Maybe instead I should walk away from town, down the Old Road to the reservoir. At this time of year the mosquitoes were all dead, and no one would be out hunting today, when the football games on TV had reached a frenzied peak.

It was such an unusual movement on my part that I felt I must explain myself. I stuttered, wool jacket in hand. Theo and Raquel exchanged a sly glance, and Raquel patted the couch next to where she sat.

"Here, come sit here," she said. I did not want to upset her, at any cost, and so I went and sat beside her although I felt an unprecedented urge to stay away, as far away as possible, to keep moving away.

"Don't leave now," she said, half-pleading. "Why, if you wait just a little while, we'll go with you. I haven't been down to the reservoir since that first time we went. Can you believe it?"

I looked sharply at her as she lied, or fabricated, or believed herself, but I could see not a trace of any more than the usual effort at speech on her face. I glanced at Theo and he was looking steadily at me. Oh, how I longed to be outside: to see the road, the streets, the town, the world; anything outside of the Motherwells' house, and their faces. I longed to see my parents, and I thought that Theo and Raquel would have laughed at me if they had known.

And I did not feel that I could leave them now, even though Raquel had just a day before implied that she, that they might leave me. Right now they both wanted me. Theo promised breakfast; as soon as he said the word I felt the emptiness of my gut. He went to the kitchen and came back in ten minutes with omelettes, infused with Swiss cheese, encrusted with chives.

As we ate, Raquel hatched an alternate plan for the day. "It's almost noon; let's take a little midday nap and then we'll go for a walk, the three of us, on the Old Road, down to the reservoir. I'll bring my camera. Then later I'll show you some of the family relics I have—the old photographs. Or we could even go up to that graveyard you told me about."

The thought of Raquel, with her intractable surface, her empty insides—now filling—strolling amongst the stones . . . I felt a stab of revulsion. A blast: my stomach turned, full of yellow eggs. I'd been feeling a bit nauseated lately, I'd noticed, and hadn't wanted anything much besides popcorn and big glasses of milk.

The fire was easily revived, and I lay stretched out on the sofa with a pink blanket Raquel draped over my legs even as I grouchily refused it. "You'll be glad you have it," she whispered, and then after pulling down the shades in the already dim living room she trailed up the stairs after Theo.

I DON'T KNOW what time it was when I awoke, but my urgent desire had not abated in my sleep. Daylight still shone through the drawn paper shades, yellowed and fly-spotted, and I guessed that there must be a couple of hours of it left at least. I rose and slipped into my tennis shoes, whose laces I had not unknotted since the first day Mr. Breslak sold them to my mother, and trod lightly on their flat soles as I went dutifully upstairs to wake Theo and Raquel, to invite them to come out and walk with me.

IT TOOK ME an awfully long time to reach the door to their room. I remember thinking that fear made time pass more slowly, quite measurably more slowly. But why was I afraid? I do not know. It could have been the dim hall, with the closed door at the end of it, around which I could not see any daylight coming through. They must have darkened the room. Would they be awake? Perhaps they were awake already, and murmuring softly to each other. Perhaps Raquel had chosen this moment of sleepy daytime to tell him of her pregnancy. Perhaps he was not fully awake when she told him, when she whispered into his ear, his ear with its secret chambers, its dark whorls and cabins of air and wind, with its acrid tang of which I had tasted with the tip of my tongue, my one caress, unreciprocated, and perhaps out of some dream he rose without thought, no conscious thought, but only with a subterranean desire to make her stop talking, to make her *just shut up*, and he took the pillow from under his head and rolled on top of her and placed the pillow over her face and smothered the life out of her. Would she resist? Why? And if she did, would he come awake more fully and realize his actions, or more accurately, their consequences?

But by this time I was to the door, and so terrified that I burst in without knocking, my breath coming in great gusts like wind in a sail. In the dark room Theo and Raquel lay lumped together indecipherably. I switched on the bedside lamp and stripped the covers back, disclosing a handsome, spooning nakedness: Raquel appeared quite pale surrounded by his dusky, dust-colored body; her sculptural whiteness inert in sleep, her dark hair lying over her face and in her mouth. I could detect no swelling in her belly.

READER, DO NOT ASK ME how I roused them. The gaps in my story are for everyone's sake. We left the house in single file and arrived at the Old Road moments later—again, do not ask me how we got there, all I remember now is the walk down the road that went, quite literally, nowhere. There was a flat kind of expectation on the walk. We were going to see a ruin, a desecration, a tomb, but one that looked just like a body of water.

"This is the most haunted road I've ever seen," Raquel whispered into the cadence of our footsteps. We had been walking for twenty minutes on the decrepit blacktop, through dying forest. Bare trees hung over our heads blankly. In summer they would form a canopy. There was no sign, no plaque to tell the traveler: "This Road Once Went Somewhere." I remembered that I had been told—by my father? Mr. Endicott?—that you could still see the remains of one of the drowned towns' village green, on a plateau above the rest of the town, an open space in the midst of trees. We began to search for it but found a confusing multiplicity of open spaces. After a while, we stopped speculating. Long-sleeping crickets woke up in the grass around us as the sun began to set.

"We may never reach this dead end," Raquel said, as we continued our otherwise silent march through the woods and the sun drooped ever lower in the sky. "What if we can't get home? What if we turn around now and walk back but we find that, though we walk, and walk, and walk, we never come back to the beginning of the road? And it gets darker and darker as we walk, and we feel that something is at our backs but when we look around it isn't there?"

"Or worse—" Theo said from somewhere behind me, but closer than it seemed possible for him to be, so that I jumped at the sensation of his warm breath on my neck, the turbulent smell of his breath, "worse . . ."

I looked around behind me—he was far too close, he was inside me—and saw a look on his face that I cannot describe here because it was in my dream, it was a dream, *I* was in the dream, and as I ran down the road, clutching what I thought was Raquel's hand but when I really looked at it, when I could bear to look at it what I held in my hand, it was some kind of formless rag of a hand, as though I'd pulled the meat right off her bones in a sudden exertion of the force I needed to get away, to get back to where the road began, and ended, to where Wick began and ended. I woke up, late-afternoon sun low in my face, dry-mouthed and dizzy with residual terror. I wanted water desperately, something to restore my arid tongue to its natural state. I needed to get home for dinner. I jerked myself up off my cramped side on the couch, swung my legs to the floor and sat up, only to feel a hand on my shoulder, a hot whisper in my ear: "Look outside, Ginger."

I turned around and followed Raquel's pleased gaze to the front windows, which were lit up not with daylight after all but with torchlight. It was dark out—I must have slept five hours or more—and from the front yard came the sound of crackling wood and of gathered voices. I started toward the window, but Raquel moved between me and it, her face lit and shaded alternately by the flickering of the fires outside. "Don't come any closer," she cautioned me. "If they see you who knows what they'll do. The last thing we need is an angry mob on our hands. Or perhaps that's the first thing we need."

"Who's out there?" Theo asked calmly as he came into the room with an armful of logs for the fireplace. But I had already slipped past him into the hallway and out the back door. I ran into the cold night, around to the front of the house, toward the sound of fire, toward the heat, and hid myself, crouching, behind a corner of the porch. I could watch through the railings.

ALTHOUGH THE SCENE was strangely familiar to me, there was no one I recognized among the crowd of villagers bearing torches. I guessed they had come from the Thanksgiving parade. My parents would not have been there. The women wore long dresses and shawls; their hair was pinned up at the backs of their heads. The men were in dark suits with stiff hats. They were a solemn bunch, but visibly agitated. I saw that a few women at the front of the group were sobbing, holding each other, while several men carried rifles. One of these broke free from the rest and advanced up the steps of the porch. He banged loudly on the door and shouted, "Send her out! Release her to us." From where I squatted I had a child's perspective: the man towered above me, his dark clothes blending with the dark around him, his rage causing him to shake slightly as he stood, arms straight at his sides, rifle pointing down, and waited. I wondered if he was waiting for me, if someone had finally come to claim me, the mechanism of my town with its cogs and wheels clicking spontaneously out of inaction like a child's toy brought to life in a child's movie. But I did not wonder for long.

The door opened, and I watched, craning my neck, as Raquel was handed out on to the porch, into the man's custody. He stood his rifle against the wall and reached into his pocket, whence he produced a rope. He turned her around to bind her hands behind her back, and now I could see that her belly was quite swollen, protruding tautly—not like Cherry's doughy thickening. Her head was held high, her long hair loose around her shoulders, her red wool sweater and blue jeans, slung low around her hips, incongruous. When her hands were bound the man turned her around again to face the crowd, who raised their torches and shouted a chorus of hateful promises: *She will be dead by morning, the life inside her, too. She will hang. She is already dead.*

I could not see Raquel's face as the man led her down the porch steps and into the crowd, but I could see that she did not protest, did not struggle, walked erect still as several men formed a phalanx around her and the whole mass turned away from the house and began to move off as one, down the road toward town, toward the village green, where a gallows had been erected.

BY THE LOGIC of dreams, as I knew them, I should have awakened then, at the acme of anxiety and horror and incapacity, with my heart beating wildly and sweat coursing down my sides.

But instead I went on dreaming, if that's what it was, past the point of maximum effect, and had thoughts inside my dream, lucid, if meandering thoughts. *What shall I do when I wake up*, I wondered. *If today is Thanksgiving, then I will be sixteen years old in just a few more days. Does that mean that I will have attained my majority? When can I vote? I know I can drive at sixteen. I cannot buy liquor legally till I'm twenty-one. At sixteen I believe I can legally have intercourse.* And then in my dream I thought I might go back inside the house and find Theo. The house would be empty but for the two of us and we could use their big bed. I could steady myself against the headboard if Theo would get behind me. My hands gripped the maplewood board and I felt his long, iron-stiff cock pressing against my ass, between the cheeks—could he get in? I wasn't sure it was physically possible, but then I felt his finger there, all slick with some kind of jelly—I saw the tube on the nightstand out of the corner of my eye—and he slipped his finger into my anus and worked the jelly around; then I felt the pressing, the pushing, and then more, filling me, and a feeling like I would be paralyzed from the waist down, or like I had an extra spine in me and would be held erect forever on the length of it. He reached around with one hand to use the headboard for leverage and with the other he squeezed my breasts, mashing them against the wall of my chest and then releasing, pinching my nipples and then releasing. All the while slowly in and out of my asshole. But now I wanted to feel him inside me, in the other place—I needed him to fuck me—and told him so.

AND WOKE AGAIN, the words dying on my lips, on the couch in the Motherwells' living room, and looked up into Raquel's face.

What I saw there was bemusement. Had I spoken aloud? Or had she simply seen my dream as I dreamt it, first her condemnation, the prelude to her execution, and then my ravishment, a scenario I had lifted wholesale from the useful pages of *The Beginner*. Would I always be a beginner? Did each encounter enact the loss of that innocence anew, and anew.

AGAIN, IT WAS JUST on the verge of darkness outside. This time I really had slept for hours. I could feel it in the stiffness of my shoulder where it had been wedged between the cushion and the back of the sofa. Saliva had dried on my cheek; the corners of my eyes were infiltrated with grit. I sat up and rubbed my face, blinking slowly into a dawning, draining vision of my parents sitting, waiting for me, at our holiday-laden dining room table. They were trying not to panic, not to be too protective, not to grasp as hard as they wished to at my life. Again Theo entered the room, carrying an armful of logs for the fireplace. Then the doorbell rang—that odd, creaky resonance in the still house. This might, after all, be them. We all turned to look toward the noise, and saw outside the window, on the porch, a flickering light, a flame.

Theo dropped the logs, strode to the hallway, and flung open the door. I could hear him exclaim, "You've got to be kidding!" and then he called to Raquel to bring a bucket of water from the kitchen. I went to stand behind him and saw on the doorstep one of Wick's favorite adolescent pranks: a paper bag, filled with human excrement—sometimes canine, if the prankster were lazy—and set on fire. The idea, of course, is that the recipient will instinctively move to stamp out the flames; in so doing, the shit in the bag is caused to spray and splatter all around, besmearing shoes and legs and porch and walls.

But Theo was not an alarmist, nor a reactionary. He waited calmly, like a storm cloud, while Raquel filled the bucket and brought it, then he simply poured water over the bag, dousing the flames. Now the sodden bag filled with shit sat on the porch, quieted. Theo pushed it to one side with his foot, and shut the door.

33.

It was a night for pranks, for vandalism, and I went along. I did not run along home; the impulse slept in me like a hostage, drugged. I had dreamed my way through Thanksgiving dinner, and I thought I might finally have broken some mechanism of shelter, of solace, of return. My parents would never guess where I was tonight.

"This is just the kind of dive in which a gang rape might occur." Raquel stood over by the lone pinball machine. As she spoke she turned her back to its blinking circuit of lights and made as if to lie back on the glass top. "I can just see Messrs. Grose, Warren, and Endicott lining up to take their turns with some hapless, stone-drunk Polish girl."

I must admit to being a bit shocked, standing stock-still by the door, not so much at the savagery she suggested, but at the fun she poked at our town's unspoken distinctions. She was dead-on; of course it would be one of the thick-legged, ruddy underclass that would receive such unkind treatment from our founding fathers. Just as it was those same girls, the stock from which I came, who traditionally became pregnant before their senior year and by the age of eighteen were minding the counter full-time at the doughnut shop, or the pharmacy, or collecting welfare to feed a burgeoning brood. None of that for me.

The Wick Social Club glowed enchantingly in the dark. Mirrored beer advertisements reflected the blink from the pinball machine and the serial chain of Christmas lights that was strung all around the rectangular bar. The stools were upside-down on the counter. Theo grabbed one, inverted it, straddled it.

"Anybody want a beer?" he asked, as casually as if he were the bartender, or the host at a poker game.

"Sure, I'll have one." Raquel matched the ease of his tone. "Just make sure it's not 'lite,' okay? Anything but that. And give Ginger something good, something to whet her whistle." She pronounced the "h"s in both words clearly, as though she were a flute.

"This is your first time inside here, isn't it, dearie?" I nodded as I crossed over to the bar to receive my drink from Theo, where he now stood behind the counter. He seemed to know his way around the liquor stock, just as, ten minutes earlier, he had known exactly how to go about breaking the back window with a minimum of noise, shimmying through and then releasing the bolt on the heavy safety door to let the two of us in politely, like a bouncer, or a proud proprietor.

But I was lying to Raquel, with neither purpose nor intentionality, and I liked the feeling of that small wedge. I had actually been inside the Social Club once before, when one Thursday night Cherry and I were sent by Mrs. Endicott to drag her husband home for dinner. I would have been about nine years old, and delighted to have the opportunity to intrude upon this mysterious all-adult, all-male arena. I remember watching Cherry flirt precociously with her father's friends, who chucked her chin and held her in embraces from which she laughingly struggled to be free.

I would guess that the men of Wick had found plenty of fodder for discussion since the arrival of the Motherwells. I must have said as much, sipping my drink (which was sweet but caused a shudder to run down my throat and then back up my spine, culminating in a sensation of there being more air between my ears than before), because Raquel and Theo looked at each other and laughed.

"I bet they have. I just bet they have," Theo intoned, and Raquel laughed even harder, fairly doubling over.

"How enigmatic we are!" she cried, through her gasping, through her amusement. "What could they possibly be making of us?"

"Whatever they want, would be my guess." Theo had pulled his stool up to the bar and he sat, facing the room, leaning back, elbows propped on the bar and beer in one hand. He looked unusually lean and tall tonight in the black clothing he had donned for our escapade. Raquel wore black as well, head to toe, and I, too, wore dark things borrowed from their drawers and closets. I felt lighthearted. The ice in my drink clicked against my teeth as I drained the glass. Raquel took it out of my hand and went behind the bar where she lifted bottles and tilted them, then shot a stream of something carbonated from what looked to me like a dentist's instrument, or a bike pump, or a magic wand.

"You know, you two. Our life here is just like an old horror movie. It's like the skeleton of the horror novel hanging in the closet with all the suits and dresses that we never wear. Young couple moves to small New England town. House drafty, locals suspicious. Strange rituals, omens of doom. Unreliable narrator. Cows lowing in the fields, arcane pagan religious festivals. The young wife is pregnant! What will be the outcome? Is her unborn the spawn of some bucolic, hood-wearing, agriculturally based, economically depressed demon? Or will light triumph over darkness and the couple escape out the other end of town, back onto the interstate, leaving behind dark clouds and other such symbols, remarkably unscathed? You know how those movies always end, though." Raquel tossed her hair in the half-light, gripping her drink. Her elbows on the bar shone whitely.

"Just when you think it's all over, everything back to normal, battles fought and won, there's some indication, some, I don't know, mark of the devil or glowing red eyes in the window or in the baby carriage, or new young couple, for that matter, to take the place of the old young couple, and to let you, the reader, know that in fact 'good' is perpetually at risk, and that the trials of Satan are everlasting, and that his minions walk the earth in human form untiringly, doing his work. Finding your weakness, entering your bloodstream, your workforce, your workplace, your interpersonal relationship, your bedroom, your sanctuary, your vision, your sleep, your rest, your dream; your death." Her low voice had such resonance in the dusty barroom, but still I was dubious. Through the increasingly glamorous haze of my first true buzz it didn't seem at all possible to me that there could ever come a new young couple who could take the place of the ones I had already found. And who had found me.

"You've thought this all through quite carefully, then." There was only a hint of sarcasm in Theo's voice.

"Is there anything I don't think through carefully, my darling. Have another?" She opened two beers and passed one to him. They drank deeply.

"I am no different from the good fictional people of Wick in this one respect: I make of everything what I want. I make of this town a reluctant haven; I make of you a recalcitrant soul mate; I make of this hellhole"—indicating the room with a sweep of her arm—"a playground for our antisocial tendencies. Get it?" She laughed. "Antisocial at the Social Club. If we can't be a part of it, then let's defame it and be the spoilers of it. . . . What do you say? At least in this way we will know, as will they, undoubtedly, that we were really here. Like Kilroy, whoever the hell that was." She picked up an empty bottle off the bar and, holding it by its neck, swung it at the unlit overhead light, whose stained-glass shade said Löwenbräu in big gothic German-style letters. The first blow sent glass flying in many directions. I instinctively took cover under my arm. I listened for a moment to the relative silence, then looked up just in time to see Theo pick up a bar stool and swing it at the disco ball that hung above the small dance floor. Tiny hexagons of mirror sprayed over the room. The ball still hung, less reflective now, and he took another swing at it, then moved on, picking up momentum, using the stool for a blunt instrument, smashing bottles and windows and glasses. Raquel stood, watching, unmoving, like the catalyst she was. When he headed for the pinball machine she said,

"Wait," and picking up a stool, walked over to where I stood, my drink clutched in my two hands like a chalice full of the blood of a sacrificed maiden. She offered me the stool with one hand while she removed the drink from me with the other, a fair trade.

"Don't you want to?" she asked me, as though she was urging me to try on an article of clothing at a shop, or to buy that same well-fitting article of clothing. My hands were listening to my brain and so they came up and grasped the metal stool by its vinyl-covered seat. I took a swing, grunting as I did. I had never used such force before against anything, living or inanimate. It felt like I had a different body, one thrashing, insisting, encountering resistance but with repeated efforts overcoming that opposition. The Plexiglas was thick but I broke through. The lights of the game eventually went out, amid a jangling of small bells.

"This is what it's like to do what you want," either Raquel or Theo, I couldn't tell which, whispered into my ear as they took the stool out of my hands and, acting as one, led me through the newly complete darkness, out the door, and to the parking lot. We got into Theo's car in silence, listening to the hum and banging of the Club's big generator in its shed at the edge of the parking lot, where it bordered abruptly on deep woods.

Someone was behind us on the dark road. It was hard to tell how far behind because the vehicle in question had its lights off, was driving through the dark with only our taillights to guide it. Craning around in the backseat, I could just make out our red and yellow reflections off their chrome. As we drove down a slight incline on the Old Road and turned off onto the loop road, I saw the silhouette of what looked like a two-humped camel—a helmeted rider?—flash against the side of the big old barn at the corner.

We parked in one of the makeshift spaces along the road and Theo killed the engine. "Let's go swimming," he said. "I bet the water's warmer than the air. Perfect for a midnight dip."

"That sounds grand. Just what I need. Last one in is a rotten egg. . . ." Raquel banged her door open and threw herself out of the car, disappearing fast into the darkness of the path to the water. The interior light remained on as her door remained open, and I wished she had closed it. It threw everything into too-sharp relief. Whoever had followed us—and reader, so help me, I thought I knew—could watch us in the car like turtles in a terrarium. A ghost rider. The ghost of a vandal. The ghost of a visitor. My true protector, steadfast and substantiated.

Theo watched Raquel go, then twisted around in his seat to give me a look. I imagined it, in the shadow-strewn interior of the car, to be one of fond amusement. Left over from his last look at her.

Then his warm hand found its way to mine where it rested on my knee. "You can take care of yourself, can't you, Ginger?" he said, and tilted his head at me as one would tilt a blade, to maximize the impact of its cutting edge. "You'll never do anything you don't want to do. I really appreciate that in you. It's a rare quality. Not everyone is as strong as you are, and the more you remember that, the more you can take care of yourself."

I was not at all certain that what he said was true, but he overrode any tentative stabs at self-knowledge I might have made, my dull-edged rapier. I could feel myself believing him regardless, absorbing his conviction, granting his words a kind of amnesty. This was not the first time, nor would it be the last, that I would be exposed in this way. To have someone tell you something about yourself—something they've noticed, notated, interpreted, concluded—whether it is true or not, whether you agree with it or not, whether you understand it or not, is like being fucked. An entry into your person—an opportunity seized, sometimes by force—a rolling over on top. It presses, it commands. It, in certain extreme circumstances, violates. I remember Mr. Penrose telling me, when I was a little girl sitting at his counter, sipping my shake through a straw that bent cleverly to meet my lips, that I was a smart girl, and that a smart girl like me wouldn't need to work too hard to make it in life. That good things would come to me. "Just you wait and see. And when they do, I want you to come on into the café and say 'Hey, Mr. Penrose, you were right!' And I'll still be here, serving you a milkshake." I remember very well the sense of involution that accompanied me out of the café that day: What did it mean that he could just look at me and see these things about me? See my future? I was not hiding myself well enough—I was not protecting myself from the clouds of vision, the collections of impressions that might form around me. They would know me! I needed to deflect them, I concluded, and to do so I would require some kind of spell. A cloak of invisibility. I would see if Cherry and I couldn't find one in the green book at the library.

But our spell had failed. I remember Mr. Endicott barging into the bathroom at their house one bright morning, just as I was rising off the toilet seat to pull up my underwear and pants. I was twelve. I had forgotten to lock the door. "Oh Ginger, I'm sorry," he said, and then laughed heartily as he backed out of the room: "I guess you're a true redhead, aren't you!" I could hear him laughing his way down the hall. And then, although we were often seated across from each other at the dining room table, over plates of meat and potatoes and salad, he never looked at me again.

THEO PATTED MY HAND, there in the car, then paused a moment to stroke it, then a moment longer to take it up in his own and bring it toward his lips. I let my hand travel in his, hardly able to feel it. All the months I had waited and watched him, so closely, wanting a delicate, intentional touch like this one, something to answer the sympathy I felt with him, came back to me as I froze—and watched him slide his tongue between my index and middle fingers. This was something closer to a kiss but falling still far short. He dropped my hand and looked up at me; my expression was, I hoped, one of tremulous appreciation, though it felt more like embarrassment, or worry, and I held it while he opened his door and slid out of the car. "Aren't you coming?" he asked.

This informal invitation—I must rise to meet it, as I had been rising and rising, all summer long. Down the dark path, and onto the beach. A half-moon had risen also, and hung above the reservoir, throwing its light uselessly onto the nonreflective mist that was draped like a shroud over the surface of the water. Fifty feet out from the shore I saw Raquel's head like a mountaintop poking up through low clouds—"Hey, it's really nice," she called; "you should come in!"—and then Theo had stripped off his clothes and run the first few paces, and dove. The drops that splashed up and hit me where I stood, my back to the dark trees, shoulders hunched in the frosty air, did indeed feel warmer by comparison.

Theo did not surface for a long while. I saw Raquel spin in the water, looking around her in every direction for him. Then she screamed, and vanished, her hands flying up above her head, last to disappear. Now Theo popped up in her stead, a seal's head, sleek and dark. I guessed that he was standing on her shoulders in the water, weighting her, drowning her. I wondered where my ghostly rider was right now. A phantasm of the motorcycle he'd coveted parked in a bush alongside the road, he lurked somewhere in the dark trees, on the path, maybe right behind me. Reader, you will understand me in the most literal of ways when I tell you that I had an idea—it had crossed my mind like a stone dropped from a great height. I had allowed an idea to cross my mind and then stay there, to be dwelt upon, worried, fleshed out. I thought, or believed—or hoped, and in hoping, believed—that it was my brother, Jack, who had followed us, and who was watching now. His lonely ghost, summoned on Halloween while I lapsed into fugue, inserting itself into our schemes with growing insistence. He did not like what he saw, did not like that which I had entered into, or contracted myself to. Something smelled foul to my brother—something I could not name to myself. Something was awry, and he would intervene.

In the worst way, I wanted to welcome him, and not be afraid, as I would naturally be of any other ghost.

I unlocked my body and forced myself to turn, a low moan escaping me at the effort, but there was no one on the beach with me. Or no one I could see. My eyes had adjusted fully and now I scanned the ground for tall grasses, small piles of dead leaves, the remains of a little campfire nearby. If I looked at it all very carefully maybe I could keep it from morphing into dead bodies, into rotting corpses, into grotesque leavings, phenomena I am always prepared to encounter at water's edge, where such things wash up, where decay is a given.

Theo gave a yelp and a laugh. I turned back to the water just as Raquel's head popped up next to his and she laughed, too, slapping at him with her open palms. "You bastard!"

"What, you don't like water? I thought witches loved water!" He made a great arc with his arm across the surface, sending a wave into her face, propelling himself backward. She spluttered.

"No, idiot, witches hate water! Remember: 'I'm melting, I'm melting!'" Raquel did a convincing impersonation of the famous green prototype from one of my mother's favorite old movies. "I'm getting away from you," she teased. "You're obviously out of your mind. . . ." Raquel launched herself languidly and began swimming farther out, with smooth backstrokes. Theo swam after her, and soon they were both out beyond where I could see.

I STOOD AND COUNTED STARS. I imagined Jack, breathing and solicitous, watching from the trees. Something human did not frighten me. In fact I thought that if I turned once more, and saw my brother there in the darkness, in whatever form he would take, that I would speak to him calmly, and tell him that I wanted him to take me home.

That I could, if I wanted to, go home—and there crumple like a child on the floor of my room—occurred to me as authoritatively as a lucid moment in a dream. I could go home. I could wake up. Right now.

THEO SWAM toward the shore, toward me, alone.

He emerged from the water glittering, shivering, and made toward the small pile of his clothes. He wiped his T-shirt over his face and pulled it on, then his sweater. Then he approached me, where I kept my watch on the shore, inviolate in the darkness, and held out his jeans: "Dry me off," he said. Like a servant, I took the jeans, and though they were rough and stiff, I began to rub them across his buttocks and thighs, not hard enough to abrade but with enough force to bring some warmth to his skin. I rubbed his inner thighs. I knelt at his feet and rubbed his calves. I saw that he was rubbing himself, his cock, with his sweater. I was down at his feet; it rose above my head. He stopped his motions and took my face in his hands, brought it close to his crotch, then maneuvered himself into my mouth, his hand guiding himself like a microphone, or a metal detector. I tasted the cold water on his skin. For only a moment did I forget the darkness all around us, and what might come out of it—only long enough to remember to keep my lips soft, and cover my teeth with them as best I could, and allow my own slobber to lubricate his passage. He did the rest, using my mouth as a sort of socket, a vault, a hearth. It was a poor collaboration. It was repetitive and convulsive. He was fucking my face. It went on for a while, until eventually I began to feel as though I might cry. Something might come out of my face. The imminence of that release made it impossible for me to accept anything more. I pulled away, kneeling back on my haunches, closing my mouth, wiping it dry and trying to freeze my face, my organs, my ducts, so that the prodigious tears could not emerge. I froze in a crouch with my eyes open wide like a gryphon suspended forever in the lonely air high on the side of a cathedral, high up for my God.

And then my ghost came running out of the trees.

"WHAT THE FUCK?" he yelled, prosaically, a kind of battle cry, as he reached us. I could feel the cold coming off him, off his toughened skin. It felt like he had a thicker skin, like some kind of reptile. He was cold, and thick-skinned—shorter and boxier than in life. He wrenched my shoulders and tossed me onto my back in the sand. Now he turned and wrestled Theo to the ground; several blows were delivered.

And then a second figure came flying out behind him from the trees, a large round head, a motorcycle helmet. I rolled and tucked myself into a ball, covering my face, a beetle with a hard shell.

I HEARD THE SOUND of weeping before I knew that Cherry was beside me. Or the familiar sound of her weeping alerted me to her presence. I will always remember the strange cacophony on the quiet shore that night: the connection of flesh and fist was awkward, a thick, nonproductive *thump*, without any of the elegance or inevitability one is trained to expect by years of televised brutality; her weeping was pitiful, despairing, agonized. She cried *for* me. As though she represented me.

THEY FOUGHT FOR SOME MINUTES, and Cherry took my hand in hers as we watched. Her weeping quieted and I heard the sharp intake of her breath when a particularly nasty blow landed. It was only when Theo managed to evade the grasp of his attacker for long enough to snatch his jeans and shoes off the beach, and to barrel into the bushes, and crash down the path to the car—I heard a door slam and the engine start up, then the sound of his tires on the sandy road—that I thought again of Raquel, who had, I believe, been left behind. The form lay on his side in the sand, rubbing his neck. I saw his pointed face in the moonlight. A human form in the sand, materialized. The simplest explanation for everything. It was Randy. "Dude was going to strangle me," he said, in my direction.

I told him.

"Holy shit," he said. "You mean she's still out there somewhere? Ah, fuck. Maybe she . . . she could have swum back to shore and just not come back here. Maybe she got confused and couldn't find her way. We should call for her. . . ?" I reminded him of her name. He roamed the little beach, projecting the dead name in all directions.

There was no reply.

"Shit," he said breathlessly. "She can't just have disappeared. Listen, are you okay? That asshole—I'm sorry. I should have busted in sooner but I . . ." I imagined Randy crouched in the woods, so corporeal, waiting for a perfect juncture of incriminating activity but reluctant to break up the moonlit tableau, so poignant. Perhaps he had learned something.

I thanked him.

"Listen," he said, letting his head drop down between his shoulders so that his gaze was on the sand beneath our feet. He passed his hand across his brow, his eyes, as though to wipe them clean of unsavory visions, then breathed in deeply, abruptly, almost a snort, a return to action. "Here's what we have to do. We've got to go get the cops. I can tell them the whole story. What he . . ."

"What he did to you!" Cherry finished his sentence, to save me any further embarrassment, but in her doing so I *was* further embarrassed—powerless. In this version the passive and active roles had been reversed: Theo had, in a sense, given *me* a blow job. I saw myself darkly on my knees in the sand, hooded and shackled.

"You girls go wait by the road. I'll be back as soon as I can." I nodded. Randy took off his leather jacket and threw it around my shoulders. It was unexpectedly heavy, a borrowed skin. He turned and started up the path, and did not look back at us. Cherry moved to follow him, to lead me by the hand, and I saw her, pivoting half away as I used to see her in the dark corridors of the castle, where we wound our way from one small silent room to another, Cherry the elder in the cool dark, a torch flickering in the hand that did not hold mine. But now I did not immediately follow. My hand dropped from hers, and without that warmth and the light of her human face, I was alone in the dark, by the edge of the reservoir. Alone without a ghost.

And in a strange combination, an irreducible mixture of ultimate vulnerability and ultimate power, I felt the jacket like a layer of chain mail against the plain, unnameable horror at my back. The night, the thick woods, the impossibly deep, shrouded water, the drowned girls and their long lives. The impending fear. Fear itself.

Epilogue

Jack would have found a way out, if he had lived, I'm sure of it.

And in being alive I had always assumed that I, too, would leave Wick, but I had never gone so far as to imagine how, or when. College, the most obvious means of transport, still seemed far off to me at sixteen, though my mother never failed to put in a good word for her alma mater when the subject came up. The truth was I knew of very few who had ventured beyond a semester or two at the community college, almost an hour away, and I found it hard to grasp what it would mean to truly *go off to college*. Would I live in a dormitory, like the ones I had read about, with dozens of girls I had never met before? I imagined something more like young Jane Eyre's stay at the school for poor girls than a modern institution, built with money from the state. We would sleep in narrow beds in rows. The innumerability of it brought to mind Raquel's projections of the workers at the mill: they could not be counted.

So perhaps what I experienced was relief, when I realized that I *would* stay in Wick. The finality of it dawned on me the day I rode my bicycle out to the Ramapack cemetery, on Route 7, an unseasonably mild March day, and strolled around looking for the Goode family gravestones. My nose ran, and I wiped it on the sleeve of my jacket. The symptoms had so far been few and easy to conceal: an aversion to certain foods, attributable to my recent ordeal; a bit of fatigue, also easy to lump in with "what I had gone through"; the aforementioned runny nose. My breasts had grown large, and hard as rocks, hot and tender to the touch, but the first symptom would appear to the casual observer to be appropriate to my developing form, and the second was known only to me.

It did not take me long to find them, a whole family plot's worth, crudely but feelingly carved stones featuring willow trees and urns, and hands clasped in prayer, strewn carelessly in among like stones as though in a bid for anonymity. Emily and her brother Jacob were born, and died, within twelve months of each other. They did not have any use for a life apart. Emily died at the hands of the unforgiving town. Jacob died at sea.

I felt the baby move inside me, as I sat in the graveyard with my back against a tree, a bare tree whose base was dotted with crocuses. It felt like a minnow in a bowl. In an earlier time, of course, such a pregnancy would have been all the force that was needed to eject a young girl out of her community and into an even more striking anonymity, that of a city amongst whose inhabitants she might sink out of sight with her shame.

But I was not ashamed. More *curious:* more alive. This was something I had not foreseen. As I sat under the tree I imagined that the baby would be born in the heat of the summer, into the bosom of my family. He or she would grow up alongside Cherry's daughter, who had arrived prematurely, in February. Cherry had told me that Randy's bad dreams woke her in the middle of the night more often, more reliably, than the baby's weak cries.

I am not ashamed, then, and now. I am only terrified for a minute or two—one moment, in all—to imagine Raquel coming upon me in the graveyard, weaving, flickering, blinking for a moment behind the tree I lean on, emerging from behind it and behind me wearing one of several possible costumes: dripping wet and dark against the broad daylight, and stinking of abandonment, and vengeful.

Now I am a young girl, *now* a teenager, someday I will be full-grown. I'm sure I must have been a baby once; I feel the warm weight of myself even as I move off, relieved of any burden, even of my solitude. My mother knew where to go. She took me away from Wick, more than a three-hour drive, and in a small city, on a white table, with solicitous practitioners around, I felt a prick, and then a tug. Not pain, but an ungainly vector against which I must brace myself, an eternity shoving away from my body. She held me and murmured to me, as the doctor patted my bent leg and redraped my gown. From here, my mother said, unexpectedly, she would help me go anywhere I wanted—I need not return to Wick;

she had been researching and learned of several residential schools where I might earn my diploma, and then, she continued, move on to a fine college, then later on to some dreamy city, far or near, in which I would stride down long blocks with my long legs. Her arms as she held me and related such visions were warm.

SUPERNATURAL is when you wake up in the middle of the night, as I occasionally do, and did just last night, with your hands crossed peacefully at the wrist over your chest, like a corpse lying in a coffin in a grave. Unconsciously prefiguring. You have to put these things right out of your mind in order to go back to sleep. Or what would you do, for that matter, if you finally really saw something in the dark at the back of your closet, when you opened the door quickly, as if to surprise it out of being there? I don't know how many times a day I've taken a moment to predict what profane materialization might await me around that corner, or in my room when I get home. It's this old trick of outwitting one's own creation: if I imagine it fully first, then it can't be so. *I'll take the life right out of it.* Every night, in my childhood, before I went to sleep, I'd gaze at the shadow on the wall next to my bed and turn it into the silhouette of a witch, a crone on a broomstick, warts and all. That accomplished, I could rest assured that the shadow would not do anything like this of its own accord, while I slept on in the dark.

But *here*, in Wick, is the future, in which I am not to be left alone—I am to be accompanied, and supported, even cradled by my friends and my relations. *Now*, and *now*, and now again. There is no end to this story, in my version or any other. An X marks the spot where I rest, remain, and you can't tell from where you sit, or stand, if I am an X on a diagram—a place, a situation, a process—or a timeline. If this is a map, or a history, or a beginning.

Acknowledgments

Excerpts from *The Beginners* appeared in *Open City* and *trnsfr*; many thanks to Joanna Yas, Tom Beller, and Alban Fischer. And thanks to Joydeep Roy-Battacharya, Janet Steen, and most of all Ira Sher, for astute readings and friendship and love. And a million thanks to Bill Clegg for years and years.